Kathy Ryan's work as an occult investigator often leads her to the outskirts of society, law, and even reality...

Knowing that other dimensions exist is one thing. Venturing into them is quite another. In the course of its experiments, Paragon Corp—a government-sourced theoretical physics research institute—has discovered a supposedly empty alternate world. There is strange, alien flora but seemingly no sentient beings...just a huge, abandoned city that a team of scientists is sent to explore.

Then the scientists disappear. Kathy Ryan is hired to make her first foray into an alternate dimension in order to locate the team, bring them back, and close the gate for good. Instead, she discovers that this supposedly dead city may be nothing of the kind. Her rescue mission has become a terrifying race to prevent the potential destruction of the boundary between two worlds—before mayhem reigns over both...

Visit us at www.kensingtonbooks.com

Also by Mary SanGiovanni

Savage Woods

The Kathy Ryan Series by Mary SanGiovanni
Behind the Door
Inside the Asylum
Beyond the Gate

Also Featuring Kathy Ryan
Chills

Beyond the Gate

A Kathy Ryan Novel

Mary SanGiovanni

LYRICAL UNDERGROUND
Kensington Publishing Corp.
www.kensingtonbooks.com

LYRICAL UNDERGROUND BOOKS are published by

Kensington Publishing Corp.
119 West 40th Street
New York, NY 10018

All Kensington titles, imprints, and distributed lines are available at special quantity discounts for bulk purchases for sales promotion, premiums, fundraising, educational, or institutional use.

Special book excerpts or customized printings can also be created to fit specific needs. For details, write or phone the office of the Kensington Sales Manager: Kensington Publishing Corp., 119 West 40th Street, New York, NY 10018. Attn. Sales Department. Phone: 1-800-221-2647.

Lyrical Underground and Lyrical Underground logo Reg. US Pat. & TM Off.

First Electronic Edition: November 2019
ISBN-13: 978-1-5161-0684-4 (ebook)
ISBN-10: 1-5161-0684-9 (ebook)

First Print Edition: November 2019
ISBN-13: 978-1-5161-0687-5
ISBN-10: 1-5161-0687-3

Printed in the United States of America

Prologue

On the video debriefing, one can see a stocky man with a surprisingly cherubic face, given his profession, sitting uncomfortably on a metal folding chair. Before him is a card table as utilitarian as the chair is, on which the video camera is ostensibly placed. Whoever is conducting the interview is off-camera; his voice is low, humorless, and suggests a vague air of education. The voice states for official record that the date is 3 March 2019, and that the following interview of Officer Carl Hornsby is being conducted at Paragon Corp, Quarantine Facility 18.

"Can you, in your own words," the serious voice begins, "tell us the events of this morning's incident as you perceived them? Please be as specific and detailed as possible."

The stocky man, presumably Carl Hornsby, clears his throat, shifts his bulk awkwardly in his seat, and says, "Okay. Sure. This is the official record?" He gestures at the camera while looking over it, presumably at the owner of the serious voice.

"Yes, Officer Hornsby. Any incident involving Paragon Corporation or its employees is taken extremely seriously, and we endeavor to collect as much information as possible in order to rectify, modify, and solidify good business practices."

Carl's reaction to this is a subtle ripple of features that only the most astute observer might take for suspicion. He says, "Okay, well, Lefine and I—"

The serious voice breaks in here, "For the record, that is Lieutenant Darryl Lefine, forty-seven, of Haversham, New Jersey."

"Right," Carl says. "My partner. So anyway, we arrived at the residence at 1806 Forge Road, Haversham, at approximately 7:43 a.m. We were responding to a wellness check call put in to our dispatcher by a neighbor,

Kurt Kriswell, who lived across the street and, as I understand it, was an acquaintance of Dr. Van Houten's." On the tape, Carl pauses, glances directly into the camera and then looks back up and over its field of vision again. "I hesitate to use the word 'friend.' The man was described as highly intelligent, neat, and organized, but was socially awkward and—".

The serious voice breaks in again to say, "Reference neighbor Kurt Kriswell, Interview 3 in Appendix 2, and wife Alaina, Interview 4 in Appendix 2."

Carl, whose features again ripple with something that might be annoyance at being interrupted or discomfort from the chair, continues. "—a loner. He was a bit of a loner. Upon interviewing the Kriswells, we learned that Dr. Van Houten, who they described as a stickler for routine, had not been seen coming or going in days. He lived and died by schedules, they said, and his clearly breaking his morning and evening routine was cause for alarm." As Carl talks, that cherubic expression morphs subtly, and one can see the cop beneath. It might strike someone watching the video that the minute shifts in expression indicate he is more comfortable wearing that face, the cop face, than the pleasant and almost childlike aspect used to relate to others.

"The Kriswells told us they had tried to get in. Dr. Van Houten kept a spare key in a secret section of loose siding, near the front door, but they were unable to locate that key. The Kriswells then pointed out the first-floor windows toward the rear and the eastern side of the residence. Our first indication of something truly outside the norm was Kriswell's description of an object on the floor at the rear of the house."

"Could you please relate that conversation as close to verbatim as you can recall?" the serious voice asks.

Carl clears his throat again and says, "Uh, well, I asked Mr. Kriswell if it was possible that Dr. Van Houten had gone on a vacation and just not told anybody. Mr. Kriswell got this weird look on his face and told me no. He said, 'John doesn't take vacations. I think he's in there. Hurt.' Then his wife said, 'Tell them, Kurt. Tell them what you saw. Tell them what you told me.'"

Carl glances at the camera again. Each time he does so, there's a flicker in his eyes of mistrust, like he somehow thinks the camera is going to betray him by twisting his words. "Kurt let out this long sigh and then said, 'There's a huddled mass in the back room there. John's spare bedroom. It's covered in shadows and it's shivering violently. The windows are closed. It can't be the wind moving it around like that. It's big, too. The size of a man. Even ...even kind of the shape of a man. But I don't think it's made of anything a man is made of.' When I asked him what he meant by that, he just shook his head and told me to go see for myself."

"What did you think then about what the Kriswells told you?" the serious voice asks.

Carl shrugs. "Nothing much, at first. When you've been patrolling Haversham as long as Lefine and I have, you hear it all: psychotic creatures parading around as nurses over at the hospital, doorways to Hell in the woods, UFOs, cryptids, even giants. You get all kinds of crazy reports, and you go out to each one and reassure the frantic local, most times someone who's been drinking all night or smoking weed or can only see out of one eye and even then not so good nowadays. Some of it, yeah, it's legitimately strange. We have a file for those incidents. But mostly, human beings make terrible witnesses, because they see what they want to, or worse, what they really don't want to, and not what's there. And people in this town, they talk about it. They even talk about what you folks are doing up here on the hill."

This time, the uncomfortable cough comes from off-camera, and the serious voice says, "Okay. Please continue."

"Can I get a glass of water? I'm parched."

"Certainly. Julian, will you get Officer Hornsby a glass of water?"

There are some shuffling sounds off-camera as, one can assume, Julian gets up to fetch a glass of water for Carl. The police officer seems to confirm this by watching someone move away from him. Then he fixes his gaze on the owner of the serious voice again.

"So Lefine and I thank the Kriswells and move around back. From our vantage point through the rear window, it's hard to see much of anything. I'm guessing it was Mr. Kriswell's familiarity with the home which made him more quickly and easily able to recognize something out of place. At first, we didn't see anything like what had been described. Then Lefine said, 'Carl, look.' I did. And I saw it."

On the video, a male forearm and hand descend on the image and deliver Carl a bottle of Poland Spring water, which Carl takes and cracks open with a smile and an appreciative nod to the arm's owner. After taking a healthy gulp from the bottle, he replaces the cap and says, "Lefine's flashlight was trained on what we perceived as a gray blanket over a huddled body crouching on the floor. He handed the flashlight over to me and told me he'd see to it that the Kriswells returned to their residence and then meet me inside to see if we needed an ambulance or the CSU.

"Kriswell had told me that the front door had a deadbolt, since Dr. Van Houten was apparently as much a stickler for security as schedules.

The back door, though, was a chain and I was able to force the lock pretty easily, having probable cause to enter. That was around …hold on, I'll tell you." Carl shifts in his chair with a tiny grunt, reaches into a back pocket of his pants, and pulls out a little black notebook. "That was around 7:55 a.m. My preliminary observations set off some red flags. That the house was in darkness wasn't all that strange, but I tried the light switches in that back mudroom, the kitchen, and in the dining room, but no juice. I noted that there was an apparent circuit breaker failure. I found the spare bedroom off from the dining room. The door was closed but unlocked. When I went in, I detected a faint unpleasant smell—a mix of them, really. A light smell beneath a heavier kind of stink. The former reminded me of rubbing alcohol. It was some sort of chemical like that, and at first I thought I ought to get out of there because that chemical smell seemed to fill the inside of my head and make me a little dizzy." Before the serious voice can put the question to him, Carl elaborates. "My vision blurred just a little, just so that all the corners of things looked stretched or squished. Furniture sat at odd slants, that sort of thing. And I could see laughing faces in the curtains or the grain of wood in doors. Then that cleared up and went away, so I kept going.

"Anyway, the other smell—I knew that one. I don't think you can be a cop as long as I have and never smell human decay. Something was dead or dying in that house." He takes another gulp of water and sighs before continuing. He's sweating a little now, although he doesn't seem nervous. Rather, it seems like he's tensing, trying subconsciously to pull away from what he's remembering.

"I cleared the rest of the house first. There was no one else there. That's one of those parts of the job that never gets easier. You never know what to expect. You shouldn't expect anything anyway, because then you get sloppy and start missing things. Forget to check behind a door or something and get shot. I guess I didn't really think I'd find another person. Didn't really think I'd find Dr. Van Houten, to be honest. What I did find in the first floor bathroom was assorted first aid supplies in the sink and strewn about the bathroom." He checks his notebook again. "Gauze, bandages and bandage tape, iodine, hydrogen peroxide, and aloe gel. There was also a kind of burgundy-colored film over everything. I don't think it was blood, but it had that kind of consistency, if blood were just a little fuzzy. It's hard to explain. I didn't touch the stuff, but it was splattered all over the sink basin and on several crumpled up tissues in the wastebasket.

"I met Lt. Lefine in the kitchen and we proceeded to the rear spare bedroom. Lefine discovered a fetal form approximately three feet from the foot of the bed."

Here the serious voice cuts in again to reference Appendix A-1, labeled Marked Floor Plan of Van Houten Residence. During this brief interlude, Carl takes another long sip of water. He isn't looking at the owner of the serious voice now; he's fidgeting with the cap to the water bottle. It would be hard to tell from his expression exactly what he's thinking (or perhaps what he feels about the memory he's relating), but it's seeping through in little downturned lines around his eyes and eyebrows.

When he starts talking again, his voice is a little softer, a little more gruff. "It was where the smell of rubbing alcohol and rot was strongest. It wasn't a gray blanket we found, but I think you know that." He looks up finally from his fidgeting and targets the owner of the serious voice with a level gaze. "Initial observation showed it to be a kind of growth reminiscent of fluffy dust which had completely overtaken the form beneath. There was a form beneath, and it was moving. Kriswell had been right. And it was nearly the size of a man. Nearly.

"Lefine had a box of rubber gloves in our patrol car's glove compartment, so he ran out and got us each a pair. We knelt by the form and inspected it more closely. I couldn't speak officially on record as to what it was, but it appeared to be millions of tiny mushrooms that smeared into a kind of oil when touched. We tried to pull some of it free and it disintegrated on our fingers." Carl does his best to repress a small shudder, but the video picks it up. "We found that whatever it was, it had rooted itself into semi-liquefied layers of human skin. Our tugging at it only pulled loose the skin beneath, and more of that burgundy gel oozed up from between the hairlike stalks. And the stuff vibrated. Different spots at different times, big patches of it, creating the appearance of shivering. It was the stuff shivering, although whether it was due to our voices or our poking at it or because of the form beneath, well, that I don't know." Carl arches an eyebrow at them, maybe hoping they would explain, but several seconds pass in silence, so he continues.

"The body—by this point, we had come to think of it as a body, although we couldn't confirm that it was dead or even human at all. Anyway the body twitched then and seemed to uncurl, and suddenly we're looking down on a face. Well, part of a face." Carl shakes his head. When he speaks again, his voice is as low and serious as that of his interviewer. "We saw one blue eye, the right, lidless and staring up at us. We also made out a partial left hand with a man's ring which I imagine will be identified as

Mary SanGiovanni

belonging to Dr. Van Houten. Lefine noted part of a right knee, shin and foot. Those had exposed bone, although that stuff was working hard to cover it up again. Like moss on an old tree trunk.

"Then I caught a whiff of something stale and dusty and Lefine mentioned something about spores, so we backed way off. Lefine called in the CSU, and we sat and waited. I remember mentioning to Lefine that prints lifted from the house would probably match prints from that partial left hand." Carl gestures with his own. "I suppose you'll be adding the coroner's findings to one of your Appendices, there."

"We would be most appreciative, although we conduct such tests here at our labs as well." The serious voice spaces each word just enough to indicate this is generous information on his part, and neither to be questioned or elaborated upon.

Carl nods. "Yeah, so Lefine went outside to call CSU and notify Hazmat and CDC per protocol, I don't know what happened out there, other than Lefine grumbling in passing that you guys were already on the lawn, waiting for us, and took his phone."

"And you, Officer Hornsby—you stayed inside to secure the scene?"

The police officer looks down at his bottle of water again. His body language and the expression on his face suggest that he wishes he could dive into it and swim away from the whole sordid affair.

"I did."

"And did you see anything else? Anything of note?"

Carl looks up again, over the field of view of the camera. His expression is not kind. It is hard, not very much like a cherub at all. "Like what?"

"You tell us. Please. If there was any other observation you made—"

This time Carl cuts off the serious voice. "There was. I observed that calling the CSU might have been premature."

"In what way, Officer Hornsby?"

Carl finishes off the last of his water and lets the weight of his hand thump the empty bottle loudly on the table. He glares at the owner of the serious voice.

"The man—what was left of him that was still a man—was alive. Fuck. We didn't ...we couldn't ...It tried to talk. I think it was trying to ask for help, and that—that's what I still hear in my head, the sound it made."

"Thank you, Officer Hornsby. This interview has concluded. The time is now—"

"I hope to God," Carl says, still glaring, "that when you killed him, you did it quick. Did him at least that one small favor."

"Officer—"

"Don't," Carl says, looking into the camera for the last time. "Don't. I told you all I know. Now let me go the fuck home already."

* * * *

Kathy Ryan had been back a few days from her most recent consulting job when she received several electronic files regarding the Paragon Corporation. She had to admit both to herself and to her boyfriend, Reece Teagan, that she was surprised the request for help had come from Paragon itself. The materials described their most recent government-subsidized project, MK-Ostium, which involved the first successful human endeavor in opening an inter-dimensional portal and the discovery of a world on the other side. Paragon had admitted to all of it with surprising candor, and had provided both semi-public and private information outlining the problem at hand. Kathy had been given police reports and news articles, in-house email correspondence, schematics, memoranda, articles, and a number of notes and journal entries from a key player in the discovery and exploration of the newly discovered world.

The Network had, amazingly, been able to provide little else that Paragon hadn't turned over already, and that suggested to her that Paragon's problem was significant enough that even they recognized the need to outsource for a solution. It was Kathy's experience that people who messed around with such things usually didn't have the foresight or common sense to do anything other than try to cover it up. Their asking Kathy for help suggested a mere cover-up wouldn't be enough, and while she could appreciate Paragon's forthrightness, it meant the problem was bigger than company resources could handle.

In Kathy's line of work, that was invariably a very bad sign.

* * * *

Paragon Corporation email transcripts:

From: **j.rodriguez@paragoncorp.com**
To: **c.banks@paragoncorp.com**
CC: **r.gordon@paragoncorp.com; t.vogel@paragoncorp.com**
Date: 1 March 2019
Subject: Team meeting

Claire –
John's missing. I was over at the safe house two days ago with the Paragon and MJ-12 sweepers—thought maybe I could get to him before they did. No luck. He and his notes have disappeared. I think he might have gone back home.

We all need to be on the same page. I've cc'ed Rick and Terry on this—they should be aware. We need a team meeting on Monday.

I think John's in trouble.

Jose

Dr. Jose Rodriguez, Cryptocultural Anthropology
Paragon Corporation
Dept. of Exploration
Facility 18
973-555-8062

* * * *

Paragon Corporation company email transcripts:

From: c.banks@paragoncorp.com
To: Greenteamgroup
Date: 4 March 2019
Subject: Clean Up Code 5

Team—we have a contagion issue. Department Chief George R. Sherman of AtX-904736/MK-Ostium has requested immediate containment of the property at 1806 Forge Road, Haversham, New Jersey. I regret to report that Dr. John Van Houten has been terminated. The public statement regarding John's death will be "short illness" and followed by a closed coffin service for friends and colleagues to pay their respects. John has no immediate family—his body already has been sent through to the other side.

Company memorial brunch is tomorrow at 9 a.m. in the Parasol Cafe section of the cafeteria on subfloor 30.

Dr. Claire Banks, Cryptobiological Sciences
Paragon Corporation
Dept. of Exploration
Facility 18
973-555-8064

* * * *

Excerpt from the Bloomwood Ledger, March 5, 2019

HAVERSHAM, NJ—The body of 58-year-old theoretical physicist Dr. John Van Houten was discovered at 8 p.m. on Sunday, March 3, in his home. While police would not give details, they did issue a statement that the cause of Van Houten's death was "undetermined, pending medical examination."

Van Houten had been employed for the last thirty years at Paragon Corporation's Facility 18 in Haversham in their anthropology research department, according to sources. Paragon officials issued a statement yesterday that Van Houten's death was unrelated to his research work at Facility 18.

Surrounding residents say that Van Houten was a model neighbor. He maintained a fastidiously neat yard, kept to himself but was polite when spoken to, didn't make noise, had no children or other family, pets, or visitors, and was, according to neighbors, very much a creature of habit. He left for work at the Paragon Corporation at 8 a.m. every morning and returned home by 7 p.m. every evening. When the newspapers began to pile up on his front stoop, a nearby resident, Alaina Kriswell, as stated to the Ledger, thought it likely something was wrong and pressed her husband to go across the street and knock on the door. Kurt Kriswell did, but no one answered. The door was locked but through a window, he saw what he described as "a huddled mass covered in shadows, shivering violently." He and his wife called the police.

Neither Officer Carl Hornsby, first on the scene, nor his partner, Lt. Darryl Lefine, was available for comment on the cause of death or condition of the body. For reasons unclear at the time of this writing, representatives of the Paragon Corporation were on the scene...

* * * *

From the journal of Claire Banks, Tuesday, April 2, 2019

It will be hours still before the sun goes down. The sky, now hazy blue, has twin orbs of silvery-white making slow rotations across its dome; we are fairly certain they are moons. Tonight, we believe it may be overcast, with a soft batting of grayish clouds to keep the sharp steel peaks of the mountains beyond from letting strange stars and illimitable black pour through.

Other than John's exploratory robots, which Paragon has been sending through for the last two months, we're the first from this world to touch the soil of a world in an alternate universe. It's so exciting! We have been here now six times. John had to be convinced to join us; he was content to tinker with those robots, but we managed to convince him in the end by agreeing to bring only limited but efficient equipment with small, smart teams so as to minimize the Observer Effect. We have been following blue team's protocols for safety, reducing risk of contamination with our presence, and avoiding the alteration of our surroundings as much as we can.

I wish John were still here to see it all.

Six times, and still, this place fascinates me. I'd like to describe it here in as much detail as I can, and for future reference. This journal entry will serve as a basis for a supplemental report.

Beyond the forest about three miles to, I assume, the east (if the direction of the faint sun's and twin moons' movement is any true indication), there is an immense ocean of very dark indigo. Its shoreline runs as far north as the mountains, which it seems to skirt around, and as far south as we can see. Its waves crash haphazardly in teapot tempests along the rocky and shell-less shoreline. We have seen no signs of aquatic animal life so far, but we suspect the ocean is incredibly vast, perhaps even dominating the surface area of this world, and we hope to tackle its whole ecosystem and its potential uncovered mysteries in future visits.

Miles to the distant north stand dark, silver-tipped mountains, and at their foothills, fields of what we discovered to be wildflowers, gorgeous and vibrantly colored, which peter out as the grassy plains meet the thinning edges of the forest. On our fourth and fifth trips to this world, we sent small scouting parties as far as the foothills to bring back samples of the wildflowers and rocks. Given the sheer size of the mountains themselves,

I suspect we'll have to bring better rock-scaling equipment or perhaps John's reconfigured drones to explore the mountain elevations. It looks like the peaks are covered in either snow or ash, and I'd love to get a sample.

Our primary focus so far, though, has been the forest, which we suspect covers miles to the west and south. It may take up a significant portion of this particular landmass, in fact. Lush fern-like vegetation, green with red tips—which remind me, I admit, of the long plumes of Musketeer hats—as well as ivy with spider webbing of reds and golds amid the green leaves grows rich and abundant along the forest floors and in between the tree trunks. The trees themselves hold no leaves—perhaps it is a late autumn or even a winter season here—but they bear odd bulbous fruit reminiscent of apricots. The stark white trunks reach like arabesque arms of bone toward the burning orange-and-plum-colored sky, offering the fruit.

As I reread this, I'm smiling at the descriptions I've offered. They may seem overly romanticized or cornily poetic, but something about being here seems to be bringing out of me a true aesthetic appreciation of the place. My words, I think, do justice to what I described, both in accurate sensory depiction and in capturing our sense of wonder here. We've really found something incredible. I can imagine how this alien life, this very first glimpse into a living, multi-cellular vibrancy from the first and so far only accessible world in the only alternate universe of those we have newly discovered, might excite and thrill the media, artists, the hearts of poets and dreamers. I know *we* have been thrilled and excited. It is too soon, though, to share the discovery with the world, of course. There are so many things to consider—the potential for population expansion, the untapped resources, the strategic military possibilities—and while Paragon is a multinational corporation, dominion is a delicate subject to be broached with the utmost political diplomacy. Right now, this world is a delicious secret, the taste of which is constantly on our tongues, but our teams understand the need for absolute discretion. We've all signed non-disclosure agreements as lengthy as *War and Peace*. It's worth it, though, to be part of something so revolutionary.

Anyway, back to this world. We found seeds in those tree fruits, at least two or three samples of which will eventually be preserved with all possible precaution in Paragon's International Institute of Theoretical Sciences, Facility 4, in Albany, NY. Seeds from an alternate universe, seeds containing the blueprints of life from another world—this is the common man's link to the stuff of dreams! It has crossed my mind that successful extraction might very well lead to a senior managerial position at the Institute, as well as a number of lucrative research opportunities for members of the Green Team, as we are currently most intimately familiar with the biological aspects of this new world. I can only hope that in the future, we will also become as intimately acquainted with the cultural, anthropological, and archaeological aspects as well.

At present, our focus is to learn all we can about this place, and our secondary (although I hesitate to rank it as any less important) objective is to obtain sustainable proof of life. This latter goal has been a little hard to accomplish. So far, all the flora in the growing catalog (no fauna has yet been discovered) has been documented in extensive notes, intricately rendered drawings, digital photographs, and even videos. However, no living (or even inanimate) sample has survived the transport back through, except the aforementioned handful of fruit seeds, somehow miraculously undamaged amid the withered dust of all the other samples. We discovered this immediate desiccation process when a dangling curl of ivy touched the mouth of the opening between the two worlds, and the contact caused a blight which leeched all color and all moisture from the plant before it exploded in a fine gray mist of powder. This is primarily what happens to any plant matter, soil, and even stones we carry back through to Earth.

The effect of transport on the new world's flora initially did raise at least a few eyebrows regarding human health risks, especially after what happened to John back in March; these, however, have been quickly and more than happily resolved by my team here and Blue Team back at the lab, whose exhaustive research preceding and following our cross-over leads them to believe we have no causes for alarm. What seems to be affected are the native organic materials coming from the new world to Earth (fruit seeds being the exception), but so far as both teams can tell, not the other way around. Subsequent visits with live human explorers, myself included, have supported this. While we still can't say for sure what infected John, we have (luckily!) been unable to reproduce that problem. Medics confirmed the presence of a kind of spore in John's lungs, and his notes reference a patch of mushrooms which our team has been unable to locate, and so the current theory regarding his illness and death holds that he inhaled spores from the fungus he found. Strangely, these spores, it turns out, implode when exposed to the open air of our world, and seem unable to germinate in human lungs, so perhaps John had some genetic code or predisposition that made him vulnerable. Tests are still being run.

Regarding the atmosphere and soil of this new world, our tests confirm it is compatible with Earth's, although there are differing levels of nitrogen and argon, and trace amounts of silicon as well as a minute amount of xenon. I have been reliably informed that the xenon is not affecting the oxygen levels and is at a level innocuous to humans. Field tests have concluded there are no tactile poisons in the saps or oils of the plants, no detectable airborne toxins or germs of any note, nothing alarming in the soil or the rock, and, as I mentioned, no evident predatory or dangerous animal life (although we still quarantine and check for hitch-hiking insects and the like upon each return). At present, I feel mentally alert, physically healthy, and energetic—I can vouch for my own clean bills of health from the military exams as well as those of the Paragon Corporation.

Even in the wildest dreams of my childhood, even as an imaginative young girl envisioning life on other planets, fantasy worlds, magic and monsters and aliens—even I never dreamed we'd see a discovery like this in my lifetime, let alone a discovery made by my team. Here is the human introduction to a new world, not light years away, not millions of years and billions of dollars' worth of technology and research beyond human grasp, but here, in bright color, in warm air and mild fragrant breezes, in the crashing waves, soft sand, and the spongy, mossy ground beneath our feet, and yet beyond all known or even suggested limits of space and time.

Speaking of space and time, the latter seems to move irregularly here—not faster, exactly, just…different. It's a little hard to keep track of days. And for some reason, I always feel like my ears just popped.

I bet a lot of scientists will wonder how we found this place. I am aware of the possible ramifications of explaining in detail, even in this personal journal, the steps of our discovery. I'll forgo that, for national and personal security reasons. Let it suffice to say that PC was contracted by a weapons development and research lab in New Jersey working on a U.S. Department of Energy-subsidized project known as MK-Ostium, where my team and I were asked to assist in particular with a branch of study based on Everett's theory on parallel universes and Oxford's mathematical discoveries to support it, combined with string theory and certain work done at the University of Wisconsin-Madison in theoretical physics. The extent of our results was unexpected but very pleasing.

We found a means of opening a kind of door or portal to another world.

Oh! I can't believe I forgot to mention its name! Officially, Paragon has dubbed this place G-01-01-409763. The designation is classified, and it would be a violation of the classification to disclose that, even in this journal. The Green Team and I, though, affectionately call it Hesychia after the goddess of silence—John's idea—because this place is as quiet as a tomb.

From the journal of Claire Banks, Wednesday, April 3, 2019

My team has, during each trip, tried to map out what few stars make it through the canopy of clouds, and thus determine if the constellations above are familiar in any way or not. Of course, we discovered they are not; we were quite sure early on that we're looking on stars not from a distant part of the known universe, but quite likely from another universe altogether. Subsequent to our first visit, our mathematical calculations of the geometry of this world, its physical laws and other significant deviations of known universe-wide science, have all led the team to conclude that this place is not from any fathomable part of our universe, but from an entirely alien alternate dimension, which makes each discovery here thrilling... and a little eerie.

We're sitting now in a clearing in the immense forest where we cross through. I mentioned in my last entry the gateway we discovered. It took about a month and a half to stabilize, as it kept flickering in and out of existence, but we came upon a solution to keep it open for as long as we need it to be—a door stopper, if you will, which the blue team on the Earth side, we're told, can pull out in an emergency. It's about the size and measurements of a normal door...or of a grave, as Jose joked. We can't determine its thickness, though. Test results vary or come back inconclusive. It's strange, really, like a one-way mirror of sorts. To look through it from our side, you'd think to see the clearing, but you don't, and from this side of the new world, we see nothing of the lab. The substance of the portal itself is a viscous black fluid that constantly swirls, catching twinkling lights and clouds of colors and moving them around and through each other like tiny galaxies and nebulae. If night were a liquid thing, I think it would be like this. It feels wet to pass through, slick like baby oil, but the feeling is temporary and unique to the passing; none of it stays on your skin or in your hair. To try to catch it in a cup or pull it out into one or the other side only causes it to thin to the point of evaporation.

It's the stuff of the other dimension, the substance of an alternate universe, I think. No...it's the stuff beyond the universe. At the end of it. The stuff between the universe we know and...others.

From the journal of Claire Banks, Thursday, April 4, 2019

Couldn't wait to update the journal today. We've discovered a city! In moving west along the forest's northernmost edge, following the mountains and the wildflower fields, we found an immense collection of stones hewn and shaped in a deliberate way, carved with specific and repeating shapes in bas-relief. It was an outer wall! We kept following its length right to a front gate! As previously mentioned, we've found no animal tracks or droppings, no evidence of grazing or nesting, no indication of any animal life at all, but here, right here, is evidence of design, of architecture, of sentient intelligence! It's taking all our willpower not to rush in and look around, but scientific protocol requires patience, attention to minute details, and careful, precise action. Observation first, exploration after.

But oh my God, I'm so excited!

From the journal of Claire Banks, Tuesday, April 9th, 2019

Tonight, I think, we're going to enter the city.

We've been down to the front gate during the day, but for the last five nights, we have observed the city itself from camp. We've made our way to a foothill a mile or so from the forest edge and set up camp there because it offers a good view down into the city. We've observed the strange stone buildings, dark gray and tinged with veins of glowing blues and greens. As the sky above darkens, we've watched the soft glow of blue lights come on, shining through glass-like globes or keystone-shaped fixtures in crisscrossing gold holders at the bases of staircases, adorning archways, and flanking doorways all throughout the city. As with the rest of this world, we've found no evidence of *living* sentient life in our preliminary observations, and so we've come to think of it as "the dead city." A little creepy, I know, but Jose coined the phrase and it's just sort of stuck. We don't know if the inhabitants abandoned the city or simply died out in some long-ago past, but we feel fairly certain that the lights are an automatic mechanism which simply hasn't wound down yet. How many nights those hearth and home fires have needlessly kept burning, waiting for their travelers, their engineers and architects to come home, we can't possibly know. It's sad, in a way—like how fingernails and hair keep growing after a body dies.

We probably could have moved to enter the city itself yesterday, but… we didn't. The lights are something of a comfort; they give our minds something to hold on to in this strange, alien space. Darkness at home can be unsettling, but strange darkness in an entirely different world, the shifting, moving darkness of wild terrain beneath an alien sky somehow mostly untouched by the glow of twin moons, can at times be absolutely terrifying, even if you're pretty scientifically sure it contains nothing more frightening than vines and fruit trees. It's the fear of the unknown, I guess, that fear of strange noises you can't identify or even liken to something familiar. So we've waited beneath the cold non-glow of the moons and the feeble spray of starlight and watched the lights come on, a promise of night life gearing toward wakefulness. So far, no night life has ever come.

Terry offered the possibility that the city-dwellers may have gone underground. We can't imagine why, though, unless the conditions which make the plant life so abundant and which allow us to breathe and move comfortably in this world are somehow new and inhospitable to those who came before.

Jose believes we're looking on the remnants of a dead civilization, and without any real concrete proof of that, the team has sort of adopted that theory as a working model. It...I don't know, it *feels* right somehow. Maybe part of us wants it to be true because we're not ready to come face to face with sentient beings from another dimension. It's almost too much to wrap our brains around. Maybe we feel safer or somehow less invasive if we believe we're exploring a monument to something long gone rather than the home of something living. I don't really know.

All I can say is that the team is getting anxious to explore. I am, too. There's a feeling in the air that something is about to happen, some magnificent find, some amazing discovery.

After this evening's delivery of the daily journal notes through the doorway, we'll be on our way.

* * * *

UNITED STATES DEPARTMENT OF THE AIR FORCE
MJ-12 OPNAC/MK-OSTIUM
April 15, 2018
To: EDWIN BILSBY, CEO
From: DC GEORGE R. SHERMAN, PARAGON CORPORATION
CC: DR. CARTER GREENWOOD

Subject: DEAD CITY

Paragon Green Team still missing. No correspondence since 9 April, 2019. Surviving member of recon team unconscious and quarantined. Intel reports outline potential dangers to continued exploration and colonization

(See Appendix I, Sections 9-14). Projection reports detail potential for biological weaponization (See Appendix II, paragraphs A-C).

Recommendation: Recovery of biological agents immune to desiccation process (See Appendix I, Section 2) for weaponization a priority. SOM-112 guidelines should be followed to the letter (please refer to Chapter 5, Sections I and II). Subsequent relocation or cancellation of non-essential personnel is recommended. Portal should be sealed upon recovery of biological agents. Discreet consultant to assist in recovery and closure vetted and contacted.

Chapter 1

Kathy Ryan had to sew up a gaping hole into another dimension—and if possible, find a team of missing people before they were lost forever. And she had not one single clue as to how to accomplish either.

There had been a lead as to the whereabouts of the missing Paragon Corporation employees. A single member of the recon team, who had been sent to the other side of the portal to recover Claire Banks and her people, had managed to stumble back through the gateway. He'd been alone and in pretty bad shape, but he was alive. A lot of the debriefing statement he'd made was jumbled. He'd been in shock, badly hurt on both physical and psychological levels by what he only seemed able to refer to as the "Wraiths from the trapezoids." He hadn't been able to tell them much; he claimed he couldn't remember most of his experience beyond crossing through the gateway, and what he could remember were snippets so horrible that even his nightmares tried to eject them from his mind. Kathy suspected he knew somewhere deep down that, despite the genuine and significant gaps in his memory and his ability to relate any useful information, he'd seen too much, knew too much. Even if he couldn't remember, it was still all back there in his brain somewhere. He was a carrier of that most feared and dangerous virus, knowledge, and that made him something of a ticking time bomb, set to go off and recall everything. That made him a threat, either to himself or the corporation or both, and he was scared.

Despite the fugue surrounding most of the broken man's experience, there had been some useful tidbits. Kathy had found that a lot of times the trick to reading government and corporate documentation, especially that of groups working in under such clandestine conditions as Paragon, was to read what was *not* stated in that documentation. The surviving recon member's debriefing report had been the one piece of information she'd had to request, based on a passing reference to it from a memo. Paragon hadn't handed it over with the initial materials, and there was usually a reason for that beyond mere oversight. She suspected the omission was because of a short section near the end where the man, a Lieutenant Jeremy Briggs, goes off in the weeds with the interviewing scientist, a Dr. Greenwood:

Greenwood: And you can't remember anything else?

Briggs: No, sir.

Greenwood: How about your escape? How did you find the portal?

Briggs: It was in the forest, where we'd come in. I, uh, don't really remember how I got back there, though.

Greenwood: Were you alone?

Briggs: Sir?

Greenwood: Were any team members with you at this time?

Briggs: No, sir, not that I recall. I don't remember when I lost them. It was somewhere back by the statues, though. I remember that. Back where the statues were.

Greenwood: And you don't remember anything spurring you to run? Anything chasing you?

Briggs: The Wraiths from the Trapezoids. They brought light...and then blood. And the voices were awful.

Greenwood: I'm not sure I understand, Lieutenant. Can you explain?

Briggs: The whispers told me awful things. They took the Green Team. Did you know that? Ask Rodriguez. And then they tried to follow me from the city, and—

[A pause in the recording]

Greenwood: Is there something wrong, Lt. Briggs?

Briggs: Can you—can you get rid of that curtain there?

[the shuffling sound of someone moving in a folding chair]

Greenwood: That one there?

Briggs: There's too much of it. It has too much space to do things.

Greenwood: I suppose we could open it, if you prefer...

Briggs: You oughta take it down and burn it. That would be better.

Greenwood: What's wrong with the curtain?

[A pause in the recording]

Briggs: It's making faces at me. Fucked up faces.

Kathy had listened to that recording three times. The third time, she thought she'd heard whispering in the background once Briggs had mentioned the curtains, but it went without remark or acknowledgment from anyone else on the recording. Regardless, there were a few possible reasons why Paragon had overlooked sending it. The most likely was that the corporation thought what Kathy did—that whatever Briggs was seeing, or possibly hearing, was not a result of pre-existing mental illness or even trauma.

It was something else, something which contradicted the belief Claire Banks had stated in her journal that nothing from the far side of the gate could be brought back.

Kathy hadn't been able to reach Lt. Briggs by phone or email, so she'd driven three and a half hours to Picatinny Arsenal Army Base in Morris County, New Jersey, where he was stationed post-quarantine, to talk to him.

Lt. Jeremy Briggs had gotten into a fatal car crash three days before her arrival. Despite a consistently clean bill of health throughout his army career, the coroner's report cited enough cocaine and uppers in his system to have exploded his heart long before he'd ever gotten behind the wheel of his car. He'd left behind a bewildered sister and mother who proved, understandably in their grief and utter confusion, to be of little help, insisting their Jeremy had never done drugs in his life.

What it meant materially to Kathy's new case was that nothing the man had said could be followed up with an interview. The only possible lead to what might have happened to the Green Team had literally gone up in flames.

She would have to cast a wider net.

Through the Network, she had access to a part of the Internet where the most powerful and secret occult knowledge was exchanged regularly, and cultists congregated and shared information without fear of exposure, accidental or otherwise. Like the Dark Web, the sites had their own special addresses and a specific browser through which they could be accessed. Some sites required ISPs from a carefully curated and restricted list. Others provided a convoluted breadcrumb trail to find any actual information. The users called it the Indigo Web or the Starless Web, and it had bred a culture complete with its own language and memes, its own limited commerce, and its own cloaked social media platforms. Kathy didn't expect to find anyone who had physically been to this new world, but she thought she might be able to find reference to someone's magickal practices accessing information on it.

She switched browsers and searched under both "G-01-01-409763" and "Hesychia" but found nothing. Frowning, she tried the phrase "Wraiths from the trapezoids" and was surprised when the search engine pulled up three results. Two were simply links to the third, which was a message board post on an occult forum about psychic dreams involving a dead city. The original post was dated 2014, and the responses were mostly vapid offers of sympathy, questionable advice, or useless responses to other posters. Kathy was about to give up when a more recent reply to the thread caught her eye. Posted on May 1st, 2019—two days ago—it was only a few lines, but enough to pique her interest:

militman84:You're talking about a real place, and it's dangerous. I've been there, but I can't say any more about that. I'm risking my life just posting this. Don't dream there anymore, and for God's sake, don't open any gateways. The Wraiths will find you and the trapezoids will bring them here. If you believe nothing else I'm posting, at least, for the sake of the world on this side of the gate, believe that.

Kathy reread the entry with a grim satisfaction, then printed it out. It was the use of "Wraiths" and "trapezoids" that gave the post credibility in Kathy's mind. According to Paragon Corporation documentation, the only people who had been in the room to hear Jeremy Briggs stutter through terrified whispers about the "Wraiths from the trapezoids" were DC George R. Sherman, Dr. Carter Greenwood, Dr. Robert Northwright, and Colonel Jacob P. Anderson. None of his fellow team members were believed to have survived. However, the lieutenant's words suggested that possibly the only other people who would have known about these Wraiths from the trapezoids—the only people who might refer to them as such in this world—were Claire Banks's Green Team itself.

"Ask Rodriguez," Briggs had said, as if it were a fact that Rodriguez was alive and accounted for and available to be asked anything at all. Was it a credible conclusion? She couldn't ask Briggs, but maybe...maybe she could ask "militman84," whoever that might be.

It was clear to her that the last part of the conversation between Briggs and Greenwood was a significant lead—not just for her, but for Paragon as well. And yet, there was absolutely no follow-up on any of it. There was no further information in any of the correspondences, nothing in notes or emails, not even margin scribbles. It was, Kathy thought, one of the conspicuously sparse points in an otherwise detailed disclosure, and she suspected that meant the many things they had disclosed to her were not nearly as numerous as those they were still keeping from her.

It was possible that "militman84" might well be the only key to a number of those particular locked doors.

Kathy had never had the technological know-how or patience for the more complicated arts of computer hacking, but she did know Network members who did. They had given her some software and a few simple commands to trace identities, even on the Indigo web. The ISP of the computer used by "militman84" belonged to a Warner Müller of 35 Orchard Street in Haversham, New Jersey. The name didn't ring a bell from any of the Paragon information, but that wasn't necessarily a problem. If not an alias, then Müller might be a family member or trusted friend giving asylum to a Paragon employee off the grid, or maybe even to a Green Team member who had been recovered or somehow escaped.

Kathy didn't think Paragon was aware of either the poster or Warner Müller, or there would not have been a post for her to find. Neither Paragon nor any of their government affiliations would want "militman84" posting information about a top secret project. If Kathy had found this post, it would have been naïve to think it would be her secret for very long, especially if "militman84" was indeed someone who had escaped Hesychia. It was a point she kept coming back to in her mind. If Briggs was somehow not the only person to have ever been to Hesychia and return, *but* he was the only one Paragon had recorded proof of having returned, then this other person had found a way back that was *not* through the Paragon gateway. That meant another way in and out of Hesychia. In Kathy's experience, one doorway between dimensions was bad. Two might well be disastrous.

She shut down the browser, that grim excitement tingling in her chest and limbs. It was time to get going. If "militman84" wasn't dead already, it was possible Kathy was on borrowed time to find him. Paragon and especially the government's various security groups made it a point to tie up loose ends, or make them disappear entirely. If she couldn't find "militman84" before one of them did, he might just end up like Briggs.

Kathy stood and went to the kitchen. She needed to stretch and think. Warner Müller's contact information had come from an encrypted source which, so far as she could tell, had only ever been decrypted once—by her. That meant those people looking to silence "militman84" one way or another hadn't quite found him yet. Her gut told her this person was the lead she needed, but she was running out of time.

She took the vodka out of the freezer, stared at it a moment, then unscrewed the cap and took a swig. It occurred to her as she rubbed her aching neck with her free hand and stretched the tense muscles in her back and legs that she had been doing this kind of work a long time. She had learned some terrifying truths she could never unlearn, and in the face of those truths, in trying to take in their scope and power, she was exhausted. She often wondered if anything she did made a difference. All these other dimensions were like tides from multiple oceans, crashing on one little shore from all different directions. Although sometimes they ebbed, pulling back into their own dark vastness, they inevitably flowed forward again, washing toward Earth and eroding the security of its isolation. And it was happening more and more often now. Network data going back almost three thousand years had shown a negligible increase, as well as the occasional and manageable spike during historic cataclysmic events or eras of great upheaval. The spikes were extremely few and far between, though, and that nearly imperceptible rise had never been any reason for alarm.

Over the last 250 years, though, the incidents of other-dimensional interference had taken a sharp upturn. Further, she'd never had so much field work in the entirety of her career as she'd had in the last ten years. It meant something. It was hard to say just what, but the correlation of the data was pointing to something big on the way.

So many years, she thought as she took another swig of vodka. *So many years of—what? Chipping icicles off an iceberg?*

Was she really stopping any cataclysmic catastrophes, or just putting off the inevitable?

Like an echo in her mind, her brother's words returned to her: *"You're not as different from me as you think...I wanted you to think I helped save the world to keep you safe from evil. Evil like...me. But I think...I dunno, I think maybe I did it so there would be other chances for those stressors to break you. As long as you have a world to keep saving, there's a chance one day those stressors will make you just like me. Then—"*

She took a final swig of vodka and replaced the cap. Her brother, Toby, was a monster. He'd been a monster for longer than she'd been someone who fought them. And he'd only helped her save the world because he wanted it to go on to someday be attacked again. Maybe he knew more about inter-dimensional endgames than she'd thought. Maybe he just hoped for worlds to keep colliding, over and over and over, until the stress of trying to fix it finally broke Kathy. He seemed to think that there was just one switch to flip, just one crack in the facade to widen, and Kathy would abandon all sense of human empathy or compassion and become a killer like him.

Maybe he was right. She had always believed there was a chasm, an illimitable gulf of difference between them, but...maybe he was right, and all it would take was one collision too many.

She opened the fridge and replaced the vodka on the shelf, then picked up her purse off the counter. Reece was working a night shift on a murder case—a teenaged girl who'd been found with her throat slit. They both kept odd schedules and that was okay, but she wished just then that she could see him before she left, just to hug him quickly and give him a kiss and tell him she loved him, for all that the love of someone like her might mean.

Instead, she sent him a quick text to let him know she was off to New Jersey for a new case, and that she'd call him when she could. She followed it up with a heart emoji. Then she swept up her car keys from the small table by the front door, and with her thoughts trailing behind her like smoke, she was on her way to New Jersey.

* * * *

On the thirty-first subfloor beneath the Paragon Corporation building complex, the gateway between this world and the other rippled and swirled. Had there been anyone in the containment lab just then, he or she might have found it hypnotizing to watch, with its twinkling lights and colors that emerged and sank within the black. One might almost have imagined living things swimming beneath the surface, silhouettes darker than the fluid of the gate. One might have been tempted to put a hand through the fluid, to feel its cold wet-not-wetness on the skin and the shiver that moved through one's body from making contact. If there had been someone in the containment lab, that someone might have seen the odd distortion at its center, as if it were being spilled sideways, or perhaps being pulled at by something sticky.

There was no one in the lab, though. The cameras whirred on from the observation control room, capturing video of the gate, and while the distortion showed up in the recordings, the muscled claw that reached through it when the distortion snapped back did not.

The claw fingers stretched and the palm flexed as if it had been cramped for a long time. As the fluid of the gate receded, the rough ashen skin, reminiscent of birch bark, began to smoke and curl, but the owner of the claw took no notice. The filmy eye at the center of the palm blinked, adjusting to the harsh light, and the long, hard talons, so dark a blue as to be almost black, glinted.

The claw trembled a moment, and then stopped smoking. The charred marks healed until they were little more than smudges of soot. The fingers spread wide, then hooked as if grasping at the foreign air, before the claw receded back through the gate.

There was no one in the lab to notice, and so there was no one in the lab to worry.

* * * *

When the curtains began to make faces at Warner Müller and whisper terrible things into the oppressive atmosphere of the living room, he decided he needed some air.

It had been three weeks since he'd promised his sister-in-law he'd give her brother a place to lie low for a while. Three weeks of feeding and sheltering a madman, was what Müller had thought at first. The things that man said in his sleep as he tossed and turned on Müller's couch were strange, to say the least, but it was the look in his eyes that was really unsettling. It was as if he'd seen something so horribly bright that it had left an imprint behind his eyes and a pulsing corona on his field of vision. Everywhere he looked, he was still seeing that terrible, bright thing, and no matter how many times he blinked, it wouldn't go away or even fade. He hadn't spoken much during the time he'd been in Müller's home, but he didn't need to. The haunted expression on his face and the hesitant way in which he moved said more than words could, even in his night-time ramblings.

Then came the man's confession three days prior. Müller thought of it as a confession, but as such things went, it wasn't much. The man had been dreaming on the couch, and had awoken with a shout. Müller, who had been passing through the living room with a sandwich, had paused uneasily to check on his house guest, who'd been sweating and sucking in lungfuls of air. The man had looked up at him and muttered, "I escaped. It was horrible. Horrible." He'd put his head in his hands, but then bolted upright suddenly as if shocked. He'd uttered a little cry, cast a wounded, suspicious glance at the back of the couch behind him, and said, "Did you feel that? *Can* you feel that? It's all around us. I didn't really escape. You can't escape them. They infect you, and…and that infection comes through." He started laughing to himself then muttered, "I didn't know. How could I? Nothing that came back through from there survived. But *not* nothing, I guess. Not nothing…and it makes you crazy, gets into your dreams and the floor and the air and the walls and makes *them* crazy." He gestured all around him. "It gets into the fabric of the world. I just…I didn't know. I didn't know."

"Are you okay?" Müller had felt silly even asking the question—clearly, the man on the couch hadn't been okay—but he hadn't been sure what else to say to such a litany of crazy statements. "Can I get you some water or something?"

"No, thank you." After a moment, he'd risen shakily, muttering something under his breath that Müller thought might have been "just didn't know," and retreated to his room. Müller had found himself relieved to be rid of the man's presence, but had felt guilty for feeling that way. He'd stood for a moment in the center of the living room, staring at the couch as if the nightmare his houseguest had left behind could come up from the cushions and envelop him if he sat there.

A silly thought…but he'd chosen the nearby easy chair anyway.

It was as he'd chewed thoughtfully on a bite of sandwich that a section of the curtains about eight inches down from the top had scrunched together and pulled themselves into the features of an angry face.

Müller had blinked, swallowed the bit of food in his mouth, and, moving the small rimmed glasses perched on the bridge of his nose, rubbed his eyes. He'd been tired. Work had been piling up at the office, bills had been piling up at home, and his head had been aching a lot lately right behind the eyes. He'd glanced back up at the curtains, which had hung smooth and not at all face-like, as he'd known they would. He had just exhaled in relief when another spot in the curtains, lower and off to the right, had pulled together into a face, more distorted and angrier-looking than the first.

"What the bloody hell?" he'd said to himself. He usually wasn't one to use harsh language of any kind and never in mixed company, but the surrealism of the face in the curtains had drawn it out of him. He'd stood and made his way past the couch of nightmares and over to the curtains, stopping about three feet from the face. His proximity had distorted the features once more, morphing them into mere wrinkles and thread pulls in the fabric. Nothing sinister there.

What was it that he'd been told before? *"…gets into your dreams and the floor and the air and the walls and makes* them *crazy. It gets into the fabric of the world."* The words were clearly playing on his tired brain. The notion of faces in the curtains was ridiculous. And yet…

He'd yanked the curtains open, bunching and binding the fabric by the hooks to either side of the window. The faces may have been tricks of the eyes, but the effect had been disturbing nonetheless. He didn't want to see it.

That had been three days ago. In the time since, he'd seen the curtain-faces again, as well as faces in the wood paneling of the finished basement, one of the potted plants Dehlia kept in the kitchen, and in the plaster cracks in the den wall. The nightmares had indeed seeped from the couch cushions toward Müller's bed, getting into the fabric of his pillow and then into his head. For three nights in a row he'd had horrible dreams about a huge altar of rough-hewn rock in a great stone city, and of the unspeakably brutal acts of violence committed on that altar to appease monstrosities so horrible that even his dream-self couldn't look directly at them. The dreams were always filled with whispering descriptions of the violence, and of the pain and suffering caused by it, whispering that told him it would never end, that bodies could be made to be pulled and stretched and shredded and remolded on and on and on for the lifetimes of galaxies, and that madness would be no escape...

He often woke from these dreams as his house guest had, shaking and sweating and gasping for air. Dehlia, who would have slept like stone through apocalyptic explosions and rending of the earth, barely noticed, even when he shouted himself awake. She'd mumble non-words in her sleep that her dream self probably thought were soothing, then turn over and return to her light snoring.

The living room had become almost unbearable, though Müller wasn't sure why. Nothing had changed physically—the furniture stood where it always had, the tables dust-free and the chair and couch cushions free of lint, the carpet neatly vacuumed and the afternoon sunset stretching its warm, golden fingers through the window. It was something in the air though, something palpable enough for Müller to taste in the back of his throat, something he felt like a weight on his shoulders, sagging them. When he was in the living room, especially alone—and he was often alone, since Dahlia worked and then had yoga or painting or book club or whatever, and their house guest hadn't left his room except to go to the bathroom in those last three days—he felt the weight of whatever had been brought into his house, whatever his brother-in-law was running from. Standing too long in the center of the room made his head hurt and his stomach turn a little.

When, on the third day, he went out to get the mail from the box at the curb and, turning back toward the house, found one of the living room couch cushions inexplicably on the front porch, a part of him immediately suspected it was a trap.

A trap, the rational part of his mind countered sarcastically. *Really? And just who, exactly, is trying to trap you? And for what purpose?*

The thing in the curtains, the instinct-part of Müller thought. *It wants to lead me back into the living room.*

He made his way with uneasy steps back to the porch and picked up the cushion. The fabric felt damp and somehow slippery, igniting an instant revulsion in him. He wanted to toss it toward the curb, to get it as far away from him as possible, but the rational part of his mind chided him for being stupid. It was a damned couch cushion, and that was all.

Still, he thought he could feel the wet-but-not-wet wrongness of the fabric, could almost smell it.

He carried it back into the house, breathing shallowly to keep whatever it was from getting into his lungs. When he reached the living room couch, he did toss the cushion onto it, then quickly fitted it back into place and stepped away from it.

He turned to go, and that was when he saw the new face in the curtains. It had taken on the features of a countenance from one of those awful dreams, and before he could catch the sound in his throat, he cried out loud. The noise was vulnerably resounding in the empty, heavy room, and Müller couldn't shake the feeling that it had somehow woken something up that he would have done better to tiptoe past.

His eyes on the curtain-face, he backed toward the doorway. The face turned to him and began whispering.

Müller knew the words weren't English, but he understood them. He didn't know how—the syllables were long and ugly, like trying to navigate chunks of glass in his mouth—but the language was familiar on a primal level, like something he knew through his skin, his cells, his very animal instincts.

That he did understand them was not nearly as mystifying to him as what the words were saying. Right now, the curtain-face was whispering about the torture and death of his wife and grown daughters, about a horrific series of monstrous acts inflicted on them that would ultimately reduce their softest tissue to a bloody, bubbling mess and their minds to empty shells trapping a ceaseless echo of horror whose reverberations would stir the last liquefying nerves in their bodies with agony. It made him queasy to listen; those ghastly things wouldn't stay in his ears, but instead traveled to his brain to explode into images he could feel all over as well as see behind his eyes. His vision grew fuzzy and white. He could feel washes of unpleasant heat drawing a prickly sweat out of his skin. It was getting hard to breathe, painful even just to draw in air. He thought his body might have been slowly sinking toward the floor or possibly even that damned couch, and he panicked. If he felt the cool hard surface of the wood planks, he might be okay. If he sank into those cushions, though, that were soft in that terribly wrong way, they would suffocate him, overpower him with fabric germs he couldn't see, choke him with faint odors of rot and death that had soaked into the fibers long ago and hibernated there, those cushions drenched with nightmares...

When his cheek brushed against and then settled on a too-warm cushion of the couch, he screamed, or at least thought he did, but whether any actual sound came out, he couldn't be sure. He wanted his hands to prop him up and away from that cushion, his arms to shove him back, but his cheek still felt the couch and his skin still crawled at the sensation. He couldn't see; he thought his eyes might be closed but everything was white instead of black. That his eyes might still be open struck him as even worse, and he tried to close them, to blot out the white with the familiar darkness behind his lids. Pain engulfed the eye closest to the couch cushion, and then his vision finally did change, first to gray, and then to black. He felt a brief sensation of falling, and then conscious thought sank into the couch and made way for something else to seep up and take its place.

* * * *

Müller awoke to rough hands shaking his arm and a voice far off that was vaguely familiar, but not enough to conjure a name in his groggy mind.

"Warner! Warner, come on, man! Jesus, this is bad. Look, I can't call 911—I need you to wake up. Warner!"

Müller opened his eyes and for a moment, his chest hitched. He was looking at a white expanse again...although, he noticed with relief after a second, it was only the ceiling. He was on his back.

On the couch.

He jerked so suddenly and so hard that he fell off onto the rug. Above him, his brother-in-law looked down at him, concerned. He offered a hand to Müller to pull him to his feet. Müller was surprised to find the young man was as strong as he was.

"Stay off the couch," he told Müller, who glanced back uneasily at the faint impression his body had made in the cushions. *Dead weight*, he thought.

"How long was I out?" Müller asked. A steady throbbing pain had begun just behind his right eye, the one that he remembered had been close to the couch cushion.

The other man shook his head. "I don't know, man. I don't know. All I know is, when I came in here, you were breathing funny, like these short, panting breaths, and you were very pale. And then...that started." He gestured at Müller's right eye.

"What started?" Müller's hand moved to touch the cheekbone just beneath the eye. He flinched. The skin there was swollen and tight, and he could feel heat radiating off of it. The mere touch of his fingertips had sent a bolt of pain through his head.

"I hope it isn't some kind of blood poisoning," the young man said. "Here, let me show you." He took Müller's arm and led him gently toward the first-floor bathroom, flicked on the light, and then stepped out of the way so Müller could see.

"Oh my God in Heaven." The face in the mirror was as white as Müller's vision had been, but the orb of his right eye was entirely a shiny black. It was as if a dark supernova had exploded in his pupil and expanded across the entire eye. Or, Müller thought grimly, like something had gone out entirely there, a dark part of space where stars and planets alike had died.

The skin of his eye socket had turned a crumbly-looking black as well, and tendrils like tiny veins of ink had branched out beneath the skin across the whole top of his cheek, reaching down toward his jaw. The skin beneath the thin, red-lined threads of black was as swollen and waxy as it felt. The infection that had reduced his eye to an ebony orb was spreading quickly.

"Oh my God," he repeated again. "What the hell is that? What's happening to me?"

"I don't know," the man beside him said, trying to sound calm. Both his eyes were fine, but they looked scared as they traced the tiny pathways across his cheek. "But we'll figure it out, okay? We'll get you to a doctor and, uh, get you fixed up in no time."

"It was the couch," Müller muttered. "First the curtains, but then the couch…it was the couch that got me."

The fear in the other man's eyes flickered for just a second to understanding, then back to fear.

"You know," Müller said, and what little anger he could muster made the infection pulse beneath his skin. "You know what this is, don't you? Tell me what's happening to me."

"I don't know. I swear. I only—"

"Yes, you do!"

"You wouldn't believe me if I told you. You need a doc—"

"For God's sake, Jose—just tell me!"

Jose Rodriguez glanced from Müller's face to his reflection and back again. He sighed. "Okay, I'll try. I'll explain in the car, huh? Let me drive you to the Urgent Care clinic on Beaumont."

"No…no, not yet. Tell me first." As crazy as it felt to say it, Müller knew he couldn't go to a doctor. Something inside him insisted on stalling, for his own safety.

"Okay, fine, fine. Let's at least go somewhere far away from the living room, huh? I'll try to explain."

Chapter 2

Ever since the disintegrating man, Carl Hornsby had been having strange dreams.

His wife Alison was a light sleeper, so he'd taken to the couch the last week or so, despite her protests to the contrary. The couch was hard on his back, but Alison was a nurse, and sleep was more precious to her than sex and chocolate. Carl hadn't slept more than a few hours a night anyway since joining the police force nineteen years prior, so the back aches were a bearable and hopefully temporary trade-off to make sure that his wife got the sleep she needed.

Unfortunately, those few hours of sleep he *did* get, he really needed, and the dreams were starting to wear into him. No matter what he did, just before dawn, his sleeping self was pulled into nightmares that in some ways were so real they might have been memories. Their realism, though, only made the surreal things that happened that much more awful.

In one dream, he wandered from room to room in a house that was, by dream-logic, supposed to be his but looked nothing like it. As he did so, he took great pains to avoid touching the layers of fluffy gray dust that had accumulated on all the furniture. Within some rooms, it had begun to collect like a five o'clock shadow on the walls and even gather in the corners of the ceiling. His dream-self was revolted by it, nauseated by it, but he couldn't seem to get away from it.

In another, he was on a small island with an indigo ocean stretching as far as the horizon in every direction. The island was rocky and constantly buffeted by storms, and he could hear the screams of drowning men and women, drowning children, but he couldn't see them and he couldn't save them. Eventually their bloated and chewed-on bodies would wash ashore, stinking of dead fish and leaving inky trails of fluids and pulverized viscera in the violent surf.

In another dream, Carl's skin would dissolve, starting with his fingertips, crossing the backs of his hands and up his arms, then spreading across his chest. By the time the rot had climbed up his neck and begun to sink into and eat away at the flesh on his cheeks, he'd manage to shake himself awake.

The worst were the ones where he was trapped in what seemed like an endless labyrinth of city streets made of some kind of faintly glowing blue stone. The buildings lurched and staggered, their surfaces not quite matching their frames. Their slopes and angles refused to match up as they grasped dizzyingly toward a bruise-colored sky overhead. In those, the shadows gave way to movement, and the movement shrank and swelled into shapes that weren't quite people. In those dreams, there were faces in curtained windows that whispered the most horrific things. In fact, there were faces everywhere he looked—in the stony surfaces of the buildings, in the architectural details, even in the street itself. Many looked like they were laughing—or screaming. Few of them looked entirely human.

In the dreams about the city, he felt loss. It blew it across his back like a chilly breeze, giving him goosebumps. He felt desperation each time his feet pounded the stones of the street. He felt a kind of drunk aggression that the whispers of the myriad faces seemed to pour into, and the more lost in the maze of streets he got, the angrier he felt, and the less shocking the things that the faces were whispering about seemed to be. He wanted the bloodshed, the violence, the depravity they spoke of. And when he woke, he couldn't shake the feeling that in the blackout time between the dream and waking, that he had done terrible, terrible things.

He'd been quarantined after that call on the Van Houten house, he and Lefine both. They'd been put into a large white van with PARAGON CORPORATION painted neatly on the side in red and blue. He supposed the subtle suggestion of patriotism in the coloring was meant to counteract the nefarious and sinister reputation such privately funded and federally affiliated weapons research corporations always seemed to have. Carl, who spent stakeouts listening to Clyde Lewis's Ground Zero podcast and Coast to Coast AM, had all of David Icke's books on aliens and other consciousnesses, and never missed a Steven M. Greer lecture if it was even remotely local, was not reassured. He felt instinctively nettled by Paragon's presence at the scene and almost threatened by the corporation's insistence that he and Lefine enjoy a free medical checkup with the finest professionals Paragon Corporation money could buy.

The staff both in the van and at Facility 18 itself, a stucco building as white as the van with the same neat, no-nonsense lettering in red and blue across the top, had been exceedingly respectful and polite. They'd done their best to be soothing and pleasant while pointedly dodging questions that Carl and Lefine had peppered them with throughout the experience. Carl had been told, for example, that he and his partner were being quarantined for their safety as first responders, since it was believed Van Houten had contracted a kind of superflu in the lab where he worked.

Carl didn't believe it, of course, although his own general practitioner confirmed a few days later what the government doctors had told him— he was free and clear of disease. That all his tests were negative, he supposed, was the only true thing the Paragon personnel had told him. He suspected they already knew he would be fine, and had, instead, intercepted Carl and his partner to learn what they knew about Van Houten and his metamorphosis. The police officers didn't know much, except that John Van Houten didn't have any kind of superflu. No strain, no matter how bad, did...*that* to a body.

That man had been reduced to a quivering mass of gray dust that looked as if it might somehow be greasy or smeary if touched. Whatever had formerly been actual human being had been mostly eaten through by the stuff, so that other than the basic shape, which had itself been losing form, there would have been nothing to suggest it had ever been a person.

Except...except that it had still been alive. It had reached out with some appendage, something that had once been an arm, maybe, as if it were pleading for help, and Carl would have sworn it had tried to talk. God help the thing, it had tried to *talk*. What had come out wasn't words, more of a syllabic gurgle, but it had purpose. There was meaning behind it, although that meaning was lost with the dissolution of John Van Houten's vocal cords.

Carl was pretty sure that the Paragon and government folks had rushed him out of Van Houten's house so that he wouldn't see them put the gray mass out of its misery. What they had loaded into the back of a truck in a dark green thick vinyl bag had stopped quivering entirely.

Upon Carl's release from quarantine, he'd had to sign a non-disclosure agreement. Carl had, in fact, been made to feel like his release from quarantine was in large part contingent upon his signing of the document. He'd been assured it would not conflict with his professional duties, since federal officials were now taking over the death investigation, and that it was the wish of the Van Houten family that the entire matter be kept quiet. He supposed that had been another reason for detaining him—to assure his silence. As if to underscore the point, he had been compensated with a sizeable check from Paragon and a warm reception from his commanding officer the morning he'd returned to work. His boss had strongly advised him to just enjoy being a "hero" for saving the town of Haversham from a possible outbreak of superflu, and to forget about answers to any other questions he might have. Paragon was a wealthy and powerful company with a literal arsenal of government support, and they liked tidy conclusions. It wasn't in Carl's best interest to be untidy in that regard.

Still, Carl had become a cop precisely because he wasn't the kind of guy who just let questions lie unanswered. He didn't just let things go. He generally saw that as a character strength, and not a flaw. For Alison's sake, though, he'd tried to just put the whole thing out of his mind, to be glad he hadn't contracted their so-called superflu, and deposit his check.

However, swallowing it all, he was sure, was the reason he was having bad dreams. It had to stop.

On his off hours when Alison was sleeping and he couldn't, he looked into the Paragon Corporation and was amazed to find that there was very, very little to find. Their web presence was, if anything, understated—no social media platforms and a website that was subtly reticent in supplying information for those who didn't already land there with knowledge and a purpose. There was a sparse "About the Company" page, declaring that Paragon Corporation had been founded in 1942 by Henry Garvin Wallinger, a business entrepreneur with old family money. The company was primarily known for developing conventional, chemical, biological, and nuclear munitions for the government, but there were branches that extensively researched medical and pharmaceutical advancements and technologies, environmental protection strategies, and even non-aeronautic terraforming and interplanetary colonization methods, dipping occasionally into robotics engineering.

For such a busy company theoretically looking to better humanity, the planet, and beyond, they were an awfully tight-lipped group. No crowing about their great works, no media outlets reporting for good or ill on their doings, no interviews with big-wigs, nothing.

It didn't surprise Carl, he supposed, but there was no contact page or any reference to emails or phone numbers on the Paragon website, either. There were only two names anywhere on the site at all, both buried way down in the footer of the Home page in tiny type—a George R. Sherman, listed as a Department Chief, and an Edwin Bilsby, CEO. The former name was hyperlinked to a very generic email, queries@paragoncorp.com.

Despite four emails requesting information, Carl had received no response from Sherman or Bilsby, and hadn't really expected to. He did receive a generic answer from some nameless intern who thanked him for his interest in the company, and for his understanding that his inquiries could be met only with limited responses. National security and all, Carl was told. *Sorry, you're not tall enough for this ride*, was more like it.

He decided to look into individual employees at Faculty 18 instead. Through channels at work, he had learned little that he didn't already know or surmise from his own experience. For the last sixteen years, John Van Houten had worked at Paragon in their research division on projects related to theoretical physics, a topic Carl knew nothing about. The man's memorial service was closed to the public, which made sense, but contrary to what Carl had been told in quarantine, there was no surviving Van Houten family to care about discretion. A brief retrospective of Van Houten's life noted his multiple doctorates from Yale in astrophysics and robotics, his visiting scholarships at various prestigious universities, his revolutionary contributions to string theory, and his research regarding dark matter and alternate universes and dimensions. There was little on the man's personal life or the specifics of his job at Paragon other than an obituary in the local paper, which pretty much regurgitated what other sources said.

The rumors about town regarding the corporation and its employees were not much help, either. There was a reason a conspiracy nut like Carl thrived in a place like Haversham, and that was because the place had always been a magnet for tragedy of the strangest sort, the kinds of things that proved the adage that truth was stranger than fiction. In Haversham, that kind of strange ran beneath the town like ley lines or the pipework of some terrible supernatural machine. Carl knew this; all the cops knew it. People were skittish with that hospital for the criminally insane on the hill, and that Giants' Table dolmen out in the woods where all those hikers went missing. People were isolated by choice and socially quirky in Haversham, and always had been. A lot of towns out that way—Thrall, Zarephath, Blight's Corners—they were all like that. For places where weird was natural, anything unexplainable was eventually given to the rumor mill to sort out. So it was hard to take seriously rumors like the Paragon Corporation's Haversham office experimenting with a super-secret CERN-like device powered by the minds of the broken, the shattered, and the insane. Even in Haversham, with a police force generally inclined to cite conspiracy theories even in their reports, police work still had to be firmly rooted in facts. Regarding the work at Paragon, there were no facts to work with.

Overall, the hunt for answers regarding the disintegrating man had been intensely frustrating. He had hit so many dead-ends regarding John

Van Houten that even he had nearly reached the point of cold-casing the whole thing and resigning himself to the nightmares. They were getting worse, though. Much worse...

On the same day that Warner Müller was attacked by his couch, Carl Hornsby woke up on his covered in sweat, with echoes of guilt pulsing through him like a heartbeat. He'd had a terrible time of things in that labyrinth city, and although he couldn't remember all the particulars, he could still feel the animal lust that had driven him to do barbaric things to terrified, half-naked echoes of people —things that no god in any universe could forgive.

He also felt the pressure of needing to take a piss, and that quickly took precedence. Moaning, he hoisted himself off the couch and made his way toward the first-floor bathroom. He barely glanced at the haggard face in the mirror, at the beginnings of waxy gray that were replacing the light brown of his hair, at the lines around his eyes like tiny fissures in rock, or the way his eyes themselves always seemed to be looking somewhere else. Nowadays, everything ached—the joints of his fingers and knees when it was going to rain, his back, his neck, his chest when he got too stressed. And when he woke up from bad dreams, the aches and the faraway look of glazed discomfort that accompanied them was just a little more than he needed to see when starting a new day.

His morning routine was uneventful, unless one counted his lingering in the shower a little longer to let the hot water pelt his aching muscles for a while. It wasn't until he happened to glance with casual disinterest at the new memo on his desk that the first inklings of a light at the end of the broken-sleep tunnel twinkled before him:

Haversham Police Department
Operations Division
Municipal Building, 404 East Prospect Avenue, Suite 140, Haversham NJ 07873

Interoffice Memorandum

To: Patrol Divisions Personnel
Date: May 3rd, 2019
From: Captain Joseph Kowalski
Subject: Consultant Protocol re: Kathy Ryan

On May 5, 2019, legal and corporate occult security consultant Katherine M. Ryan will be arriving in town to discuss some matters of utmost sensitivity regarding the Paragon Corporation, specifically the Haversham office, Facility 18, located at 551 West Caldera Street. Should Ms. Ryan choose to interview you, please note that the nature of your conversation is to be held in the strictest of confidence per corporation request, barring anything your sworn oath as a law enforcement officer would compel you to disclose. Please provide Ms. Ryan with readily forthcoming answers and whatever else she may ask you to assist in, again provided that it does not violate your ethical code and legal responsibility as an officer.

I know that as representatives of this police department, you'll do your brothers and sisters in blue proud and your exemplary conduct and assistance will reflect positively on the department in particular and the town as a whole.

Thank you for your cooperation in this manner.

The usual grumbling commenced, including complaints of condescension from Kowalski, wastes of police time and the unlikelihood of overtime pay, having to hold the hand of government people, and, half-whispered and half-jokingly, the old familiar rumors about Paragon Corporation. Carl wasn't complaining, though. He intended to make himself indispensable to this Kathy Ryan person and, one way or another, get the answers he needed. If anyone knew why Paragon let one of their best and brightest turn into some kind of giant, possibly contagious dust bunny that they then put down like a rabid dog, or how it was even possible for John Van Houten to have become a giant dust bunny in the first place, this woman would. It was all there in the subtext of the memo: this woman knew things, wanted to talk about things.

Let her talk, Carl thought. *I want to listen.*

* * * *

If "militman84" was running from the Paragon Corporation, he hadn't run very far. Kathy passed the Paragon facility on the hill and less than half an hour later turned onto Orchard Avenue in Haversham, around five o'clock in the afternoon. The house on the property was a white colonial with navy trim, clearly old but well-maintained. The mailbox at the curb confirmed house number 35 and the name Müller. She parked and got out of her car, making her way up the stone path to the front porch. She noticed that the curtains in one of the downstairs windows were torn to shreds, as if someone had slashed at them repeatedly with something sharp. Frowning, she noted to herself that there might be a problem in a room on the front left side of the house. She had a gun in the bag slung over her shoulder; she hoped she wouldn't need it, but its presence reassured her.

It didn't bode well for Mr. Militman, though.

She knocked on the door and then waited. After a few minutes, she knocked again.

When there was still no answer, Kathy tried the knob, justifying to herself that since she wasn't police, she didn't need a warrant. She was simply a concerned citizen, alerted to possible trouble by the slashed curtains in the window.

"Hello? Mr. Müller? Are you home?"

The front hall was dark; light from the open door caught tiny dust motes twisting in the still air.

"Mr. Warner Müller?" she called again, stepping over the threshold.

A moan came from the room on the left, a living room—the one with the slashed curtains, she noticed. She moved to the doorway and peered in.

The room was empty as far as Kathy could tell. A chair stood on one side, while a couch took up a good portion of the back wall. Like the house, neither piece of furniture was new, but they looked serviceable, comfortable enough, and clean…well, except for that odd brown stain on one of the couch cushions. From where Kathy stood, it looked sort of like the impression of a face.

She was about to turn away when she heard the whispering. It seemed to be coming from several voices in different sections of the wall, and although she couldn't make out all the words, she got the gist of the things the whispering suggested. They were awful—things about Reece, things about her brother, things it suggested she do to both, and things it swore they wanted to do to her. The thing was, the longer she stood there listening to it, the harder it was to pull away. She could see faces in the light and shadow playing off the wall through the torn curtains, and those faces made terrible promises. She began to feel lightheaded and tried to brace herself against the door frame to pull herself free of the room, but she could only manage to sway back and forth where she stood. The whispering got louder and louder inside her head until it filled up her skull, and she thought she might be falling…

A hand clamped down on her shoulder and the world came back into focus. The whispering cut off as if someone had shut off a static station on a radio, and faces, if they had ever been there to begin with, were no more than slips of light and dark cast onto a white wall. Even the stain on the couch cushion had grown shapeless.

She whirled around to find a barefoot man in blue jeans and a white sleeveless undershirt, his black hair rumpled from sleep, or maybe sleeplessness. She was surprised to find his face looked familiar to her. She recognized him from his Paragon personnel file—Jose Rodriguez.

"Mr. Rodriguez," she said, a little out of breath, though she wasn't sure why. She was sure something unnatural had happened, but in reeling from it, she couldn't quite wrap her brain around it just then.

He looked surprised, and drew his hand away. "Do I know you?"

"I'm Kathy Ryan," she said. "And first of all, thank you. Whatever just happened—"

"The room's infected," he muttered. "You need to get away from it."

"Infected? Well, I appreciate your help just now."

He shrugged, and then, as if it had just occurred to him, asked, "How did you get in here?"

"The door was unlocked," she replied, nonplussed. "I knocked a few times, but no one answered. And I saw the state of the curtains, so I came in."

"Are you a cop?"

"No," she answered, and left it at that for the time being.

"You looking for Warner?" Rodriguez asked.

She shook her head, offering a small smile. "Not really. I was actually looking for you."

He frowned, genuinely confused. "But no one knows I'm here. No one knows I'm out. I—" He stopped, glancing around slowly. "I got out and…" His voice trailed off.

"You've survived something traumatic; I understand that," she replied in her best attempt at a soothing voice. "I know about your employment under Ms. Claire Banks at Paragon, and your participation in MK-Ostium. I know about the other world you found—Hesychia, you call it—and about the disappearance of your team. Paragon has hired me to find out what happened and bring them back, if I can." Seeing the question on his face, she added, "I found you through your post on a conspiracy website. I'm assuming you thought it safe, given the forum and its evident disregard for anything like true facts, logic, or sane and cogent debate."

Rodriguez eyed her with weary suspicion. "Are you…here to eliminate me for talking about it?"

Kathy offered what she hoped was a warm smile. "No, of course not, Mr. Rodriguez. I saw to it that both your post and your ISP footprint were removed from the site, so I can't imagine the government would see any reason to remove you at present. If anything, I think they would find your debriefing them on your experience incredibly helpful. Right now, you are the only link left to your field team. I was hoping you could fill me in on what happened to them."

The shift in Rodriguez's facial expression to one of genuine fear might have moved Kathy to sympathy if she didn't need the information she was sure he had.

"I'm not going back there," he said in a shaky voice. "I'm not. I'd rather you just shot me right here."

Kathy shook her head. "You don't have to. But I am going to need you to tell me why. What happened in that other world?"

Rodriguez looked at her blankly for a moment, then turned away. "I should check on Warner."

"Then I'll come with you."

He paused, turning suddenly to her. "You're not a reporter?"

"No."

"Or a cop? A sweeper, then?"

"No, Mr. Rodriguez. I'm just a consultant, hired to find your team," she said.

He searched her face and, seeming to find something there to satisfy him, he nodded and gestured for her to follow him. Kathy never much cared for people scrutinizing her face so closely, but she noticed Rodriguez neither glanced at the scar across her eye socket and cheek, nor made obvious attempts *not* to. It was as if he truly didn't notice it, or frankly didn't care, and whether that was intentional or not, Kathy liked him for it.

She followed him through a few rooms of the house to a back guest room off from the kitchen. It was sparsely decorated, with a simple twin bed, a few sepia portraits of dour-faced people, and a needlepoint of a beach scene. On the bed, a thin, balding man in his fifties lay on his back beneath a thin blanket, his hands trembling. One side of his face was red and splotchy, and beneath it, a spider web working of black veins snaked beneath the skin.

"What happened to him?" Kathy asked.

"He's not contagious," Rodriguez informed her. The tattoos on his upper arms rippled over lean muscles as he fussed at the man's blankets. "At least, not by contact. Prolonged exposure to the living room did it, and anything from that place, you only catch it if you're exposed to the source, not other infected people."

"Is that what happened with John Van Houten?"

Rodriguez looked up at her. He had brown eyes nestled in a face with tanned, lightly lined skin. Those eyes were kind enough, but they had seen a lot, and the exhaustion in them was a bone-deep thing, an exhaustion of the soul as well as the body.

"It killed John," he told her. "The mushroom things he found had spores, and they latched onto…something in him. Something they only found in him. This," he gestured at the man on the bed, "is from the faces."

Kathy didn't answer, and Rodriguez seemed to take her silence as disbelief.

"I know it sounds crazy," he said. "But you said you knew—about Hesychia, I mean. We thought nothing from there could come back through here. Not counting seeds, not one single organic sample we collected survived, not one. Except whatever came back in John's body. And…and the faces. Maybe they came back in me."

Kathy sat down at the foot of the bed. "Let's start at the beginning," she said. "Or at the end, and work our way back. Whichever's easier. It's my job—my particular skill set, if you will—to stop these kinds of things from happening, and put inter-dimensional and multi-universal things back where they belong. But I need information. I need to know what you know, okay?"

Rodriguez nodded. "Okay. Okay. Here's what I know."

Chapter 3

Jose Rodriguez had been excited at first to be a part of the Green Team. As a boy growing up in New Jersey, he'd dreamed of being an astronaut, of seeing the moon or maybe other planets. He fantasized about being the first person to discover multicellular alien life. In school, he had studied biology, linguistics, archeology, anthropology, calculus, and astronomy, all with an eye toward developing skills that might prove useful when interacting with alien civilizations. When Paragon recruited him out of college, it hadn't been an astronautics gig, but the pay was good, the benefits package was amazing, and it was a job researching all the things that backed right up to interplanetary travel and colonization.

What really sold him, though, was the nondisclosure agreement he signed regarding work on alien linguistic and anthropological materials soon to be collected through their new MK-Ostium project. When they informed him he would be part of the actual field team crossing an inter-dimensional gateway to an alien world in an alien universe, he'd kept his professional face just long enough for his bosses to leave the lab, and then he'd tap-danced with glee and excitement like a crazy fool for a good five minutes.

Then he'd had an anxiety attack, and then, after a good night's sleep, he'd seen the opportunity for what it was—a chance to live that childhood dream of other worlds and alien life. He might be famous some day for his work on the project, as would all the members of the Green Team. Hell, they might even be historical figures, pioneers ushering in a new era of limitless possibilities. Whatever happened, the corporation would be watching, the government would be watching, and in time, maybe the world would be watching. The work he did had to be his absolute best.

At first, every day brought new discoveries of plant life, rocks, soil samples, even strange constellations in the sky. They'd cataloged everything in as much detail as possible, and brought back pages of notes, sketches, and video. There'd been no animal life and certainly no sign of sentient life, not at first, but that was okay. Hesychia was beautiful, peaceful, eerie, and kind of magical, and so far as Rodriguez and the rest of the team could tell, perfectly safe. The thing with John had been tragic, but the scientists on both sides of the gateway had quickly determined that the rot he was suffering from was attacking something specific to his DNA. Like Warner—Rodriguez gestured to the man in the bed as he talked to Kathy— the spores already inside were not a threat to anyone else but John Van Houten. Paragon's top scientists had confirmed it.

However, there was always the possibility of mutation, of the adaptation of the infecting agent. Rodriguez had put forth the theory early on, but he hadn't been sure, hadn't had proof really. He'd been assured multiple times that no conditions in the lab could produce mutations or adaptation or anything other than the wasting and desiccation of the organic samples. Even the seeds they had brought back were starting to rot a little. He'd been inclined to trust their conclusions until he'd escaped and seen what was becoming of Warner's living room. Whatever haunted that world, it hitched rides with some kinds of hosts and attached to others, adapting to ones that seemed to suit what looked to him like arbitrary criteria. It could influence the mind as well as the body, and tailor specific degradation of both, unique to the host. It would have been fascinating—an entire book in it, he'd thought—if it weren't so terrifying.

The first few times, the Green Team had returned to the lab after every session, sometimes after putting in fourteen-hour shifts, staggering arrivals and departures to be able to observe the new world at different times of day and night. It was exhausting, exciting work. Once they had convinced themselves of safety and had grown somewhat accustomed to the new world, they'd stayed for extended sessions—a few days, a couple of nights.

Then they'd found the city.

At this point, Kathy retrieved an iPad from her bag. "What you've told me so far matches up with the materials I received from Paragon, but if you don't mind, I'd like to take notes on this part."

He waved his assent and continued. "I'd never seen anything like it. Hell, I'm not sure I can even explain it. The streets, the great protective wall around the city, and even some of the buildings are made from this dark gray stone with glowing blue and green veins in it. The surface—it's not entirely flat, but it's smooth—clearly someone had worked on it, you know? The city wall's gate and a lot of the architectural scroll work and arabesques are made of a kind of iridescent blue metal. We took samples, and back in the lab they said that 85-90% of both the stone and metal are composites we don't have in this world, namely because the elements and compounds either don't exist at all here, or because their versions in this world are too volatile and unstable. So again, we're thinking we've got evidence of something intelligent, something capable of architecture, stonemasonry, and probably even chemistry.

"And the proportions—these people must have been huge. The city wall we estimated to be about three hundred and forty feet high, the gate maybe three-fifty or three-sixty. The buildings seem to rival the cliff behind the city, although it was hard to tell how tall they actually were, because of the way they slant and zigzag. The doorways and archways, though—they were about a hundred and fifty feet, easy."

He shook his head. "There were signs of occupancy, but…not in the ways you'd expect. There was…I dunno, a *sense* of something present, but no bodies—no people. Not even cemeteries for the bones of whoever used to be there. Just…all the set dressings of a civilization. And…the faces. I don't know if it is part of their architecture or the ghosts of their dead or what, but those faces are everywhere. There's a word for it, when you can see faces in wood grain and tree leaves and stuff."

"Pareidolia," Kathy said.

Rodriguez snapped his fingers. "That's it. It's a psychological thing. That's what we thought was going on at first, that maybe because we were in such a strange and empty and *inhuman* place that we were seeing faces to, I don't know, bring a kind of human normalcy to it all. But it was more than that. It was more than just needing to humanize the inhuman.

"See, the faces…they'd whisper to you when you were trying to sleep. They'd tell you things to confuse you, get you lost. We wandered for hours before realizing that even when we tried to backtrack and cover the same ground, we only saw new streets, new side alleys, and new abandoned buildings. The city was impossibly large. The faces…maybe they changed the layout every night. Or maybe layouts don't…*lay* right, there. All I know is, we got lost—for days, maybe weeks. In the city, the lengths of nights and days began to vary, sometimes by a few hours and sometimes by a lot longer."

He almost smiled then, and looked up from the pattern of Warner Müller's blankets to meet her gaze. "We found a library. Can you believe that? At least, we thought it was a library. Shelves and shelves of stone three or four feet thick, and books—there were actual books! When we managed to get a few open, the surface would ripple and shift and project these holographic, three-dimensional runes. I tell ya, I couldn't wait to get one back to the lab and try to translate it, but..."

He shook his head again. The weariness in and around his eyes magnified. "I still see those runes sometimes when I close my eyes. If I had even the slightest talent in sculpting, I'd try to make one, just to have a physical version to study, to translate. Of course, God only knows what I'd be putting out there into the world, what I'd be *saying*, just bringing it into existence." He glanced at Kathy. "Anything that comes from that other world causes death. It's all cursed. It's all poison."

"So," Kathy saved the notes on her iPad and scrolled down to a new page. "Is the library where you escaped from?"

"Uh, no," Jose said, scratching his head. "No. We, uh...we holed up there that night, ate some, slept some. Then we tried to go back the way we came. Of course, that didn't work. We just ended up moving further into the city. It has a center, we discovered. Once we found that, it seemed like all roads kept leading us right back to it. And that...that was where we ran into real trouble.

"See, there was this town square. Well, it wasn't really a square. It was more of a hexagon, and at each point, there was a pedestal topped with a statue. Those statues...they are the only things in town that don't have a face. Big winged things, they are, almost like angels but not quite. Nothing holy about them at all. Nothing comforting. Maybe...maybe they're more like demons. Anyway, they hold up the trapezoids like they're some kind of offering."

"What exactly are the trapezoids?" Kathy asked. "I've heard mention of them, and of the Wraiths."

"The Wraiths," Jose repeated in a voice barely above a whisper. "Yeah. The city, see, it only *looks* dead. It isn't, though. The architects may be gone, but the Wraiths are still there. They...recede sometimes into the trapezoids, but they're always there. The trapezoids are enormous, made of some kind of crystal, and at night, they glow and then the Wraiths come out. They were the ones who took the others. Claire, Rick, Terry. I don't know where."

"Why..." Kathy's question trailed off.

"Why did they take the others and leave me? Heh. I wish I knew. Truly."

"So then what did you do?"

"Well, I'd be a liar if I said I stuck around and tried to figure out where they all went. The corporation didn't hire me for my bravery. Hell no. So anyway, one minute the crystal trapezoids were glowing, and the next, there was this blue light, and then *poof*! I was alone, and the trapezoids were dark again. I was scared. I ran. It was...it was seeing all their stuff on the ground that did it, I think. Everything of theirs had been left behind—their backpacks, their clothes, their watches, their dental fillings. The screws and plate in Rick's leg and Terry's stent. Claire's IUD.

"So I ran, and I probably kept moving for a while—maybe a day or so. I stopped only to doze for a few minutes or eat something from my bag... but then I had to go back. See, I ran out of food, and I knew the others' bags would still have some. So I went back. And I stayed. A few nights, I guess it was. I climbed up on this awning, kind of, and I watched those damned trapezoids and I saw them glow, night after night, and I waited for them to bring me my team back or for me to disappear, too, in the blue light, but it never happened.

"And the Wraiths were there every night, too, though I didn't see them at the time. They showed up, I guess, when the trapezoids began to glow. That's when the air changed, and I could feel them. You know that feeling when you think someone's behind you...like, you can almost feel a heartbeat or a breath, or sense movement, but there's no sound...and you turn around and no one's there?"

Kathy nodded.

"It was like that. I'd feel something, but never see anyone. When I got tired of waiting, of watching for the Wraiths, I guess, I climbed down off the awning and stood in the center of the trapezoids, willing whoever was in them to come take me, too. When I saw the blue glow, I was just as relieved as I was scared, because I didn't...I just didn't want to be alone anymore, so far from home. Maybe that's hard to understand, but—"

"It isn't that hard. I can imagine," Kathy said softly.

Rodriguez considered her answer for a moment as if he might ask her what she meant, but then seemed to decide against it. He continued with his story, although Kathy could see he was getting tired. "Well, that's where my head was at. I wanted them to take me, too. For a few seconds, all I could see was the blue glow, and I thought about my third grade girlfriend. Yeah, you can smile. It's okay. It's kind of funny. I mean, before I even knew enough to appreciate women for all the right reasons, I remember thinking Abbie Reynolds was pretty and she gave me candy at snack time and she liked the same video games that I did, she let me hold her hand. I don't know why she popped into my head just then, except maybe it was the last truly innocent memory of someone I cared about that I can remember having. That was just before my mom's death and my dad leaving my brother and me with our aunt, and everything else just sort of falling apart. Before the dream of other worlds and other life forms became the best escape plan I could come up with.

"Anyway, I didn't know what to expect. I didn't realize I'd closed my eyes until the blue began to fade and for a moment, there was absolutely nothing. And when I opened them…"

Rodriguez's eyes teared up a little then. "Excuse me," he said as he wiped at them with the back of his hand. "Ahh…When I opened them, I was on a mountain path. It wound in and out along the cliffside, and of all the time I'd spent not knowing where I was, I'd never felt so sure that I'd be lost forever as I did on that path."

"Did you run into anyone on the path?"

"Anyone human, you mean? Yeah, I did, actually. How did you…"

"He mentioned you. He told us to ask you about the Wraiths, like he thought you were back on this side of the gate again. He was part of the recon team, the only one who made it out, and we weren't sure if his mentioning you was a credible lead or the beginnings of madness."

"I—I honestly didn't believe he was real. I thought, maybe…that I'd imagined him, that I'd needed to see another human being, not just a whispering face. I didn't really believe they'd send anyone for us. I—I don't know. I wasn't thinking straight by then. He was on a cliff across from me, but far—too far to reach, and I think he told me he'd come get me. I couldn't catch everything he was saying, and honestly, by that point, I wouldn't have trusted the Virgin Mary. I think I may have said something about the Wraiths and the trapezoids and told him to go back the way he came. After that, I don't know what happened to him."

"He came back through the gateway."

"He couldn't have looked very hard for us, then."

"But you didn't come back that way. You found another gate, right?"

Rodriguez's brow furrowed and he frowned. "I…guess I must have. I don't recall much, to be honest. I just remember walking on that mountain path in the heat and the dust, right after seeing that guy, in fact, and then I was waking up on a paved street. I *thought* I was back, but I couldn't be sure, not until I saw several people—real people, people I *knew* were real. But even now, it seems impossible that I could have found my way out. I get these flickers of doubt where I can't help wondering if this isn't just another hallucination, if maybe I never really made it back at all…"

"I can only imagine how traumatic and exhausting your experience was," Kathy said.

Rodriguez sank a little against the bed, his gaze fixed on Warner Müller. The older man's face hadn't changed during the course of Rodriguez's story, but his breathing had smoothed out some. He said something Kathy didn't quite catch.

"I'm sorry, what was that?"

"I said, I believe it now. Seeing his face like this, I believe I'm back because that place let me come back. It wanted me to. This," he gestured at Müller, "is probably the only reason I was allowed to come back. It's ironic, really."

Kathy tilted her head, studying the man in the bed.

"This is going to kill Warner," Jose continued, "and I don't know how to stop it. I tried to make him go to a hospital, but he wouldn't go. Not that it would have done any good, I guess."

"Does he have family?"

"A wife," Rodriguez replied. "Two grown daughters."

"And calling an ambulance…"

"Paragon monitors police lines, EMT radio, firefighters, all of it. He'd never make it to a hospital, and neither would any of the people who tried to help him. The sweepers would see to that. Besides, there's no treatment for what he has—not in this world. Not yet."

"Does his wife know?"

Rodriguez shook his head. "She won't be home for hours. I suspect he'll be dead long before then. He…"

As Rodriguez's voice trailed off, Müller's skin began to crackle. It sounded to Kathy like wood burning in a fireplace, complete with the popping of knots. In fact, it began to take on a crisping, burnt quality like grilled meat, blackening and splitting open, then quickly turning gray and powdery and blowing away.

"Oh shit! Shit!" Rodriguez hopped up and backed away.

"We need to get out of this room," Kathy said. "Come on."

Before either could react further, large greenish stains began to seep up through the blanket, turning the pale blue fibers black. Nearly all of the exposed skin of Müller's body was a soft, fluffy gray now, like dust gathered onto an old skeleton. Whether Müller could feel it, or if, indeed, he was still alive at all, Kathy couldn't tell. She hoped he couldn't.

When the skeleton collapsed into itself, Rodriguez let loose a little cry.

"We'll need to find a safe way to dispose of the remains, the blanket. Probably the sheets," Kathy said. It occurred to her a moment after that some sensitivity might be in order, so she patted Rodriguez on the shoulder. "I'm sorry, Jose."

Rodriguez didn't say anything. His horrified gaze was fixed on the sopping blanket which, even now, was drying, the blackish stains crusting and flaking. The impression of Müller's head still left a cupped indent in the pillow, dusted with the remnant gray fluff. It was eerie, like a negative impression of Müller was still there, the inverse of Müller, an empty Müller turned inside out.

"We'll take care of that."

Startled, Kathy and Rodriguez turned toward the new voice behind them. A large man with granite features and sharp lines in his face regarded them coolly. His massive muscles bulged beneath Army fatigues. He cut an imposing figure, something the man was evidently both aware of and used to his advantage. In his bulky arms, he held a gun as long as Kathy herself.

"Sergeant First Class John Markham," the man said in the same loud, crisp voice. "On retainer with Paragon Corporation." In a marginally softer tone, he said, "My condolences on the passing of Mr. Müller. I can assure you we will handle his remains with the respect and care he was due. But for safety and health reasons, I need you both to accompany me off the premises. Mr. Rodriguez, Ms. Ryan, your assistance is needed at Facility 18. The two of you will have to come with me."

* * * *

The consultant didn't show up at the precinct that afternoon. Although Carl was disappointed, he wasn't surprised. There was something very strange going on with the whole situation. Carl had been in law enforcement long enough to know the shuffling of truths when he saw it. He believed that every socio-political machine in the world ran on unpleasant decisions and deep secrets, and the maintenance of both by the powerful people who made those decisions and kept those secrets. He wasn't sure how Ms. Kathy Ryan factored into either, but he suspected her role fell somewhere in between.

He'd tried to do some investigative work regarding Kathy Ryan and to figure out just what an occult security specialist did. There was less about her online than there was of the Paragon Corporation. A few news articles mentioned cases where she had assisted police—a serial murder during a freak snowstorm in Colby, Connecticut, some undefined trouble across the PA border in Zarephath, and a series of murders in Newlyn, Connecticut at their own hospital for the criminally insane. None of the articles defined her role in those cases, or shed any light about the occult aspects, other than to say her involvement was in a consulting role, and that she occasionally offered training for law enforcement on cases that included cult activity or elements of zealous practitioners of ancient religions. One news article quoted her as saying, "The world is strange—stranger than people think. I just do my part to keep it together and sane."

One link a few pages into the search results listed Kathy as the number one contract consultant working today who "evaluates and assists with crimes of a scope outside normal parameters, defining that to mean anything involving cults, black magick, serial murder, the paranormal, cryptids, inter-dimensional or multiversal infringement, and related oppressions."

One other article, buried at the bottom of page 7 on the Google search results, offered a preview of the link with relevant keywords highlighted: "Like, real monsters. Seriously fucked up shit. And **Kathy Ryan** saved our lives. No one would believe what..." However, when Carl tried to click on the link, it was broken, and he landed on a page that gave him a 404 error.

Further searches brought up a Murderpedia entry on Toby Ryan, a cult member and serial killer responsible for a number of women's deaths thirty years prior. The entry indicated that Toby Ryan was incarcerated in Connecticut-Newlyn Hospital, and that while both his parents were dead and he had never married and had no children, he did have a sibling living in Connecticut. The information made him frown. He had begun to develop a profile of Kathy Ryan as One of Them, driven by promises of power and money and maybe gifts from the almighty Satan himself. It seemed, although he didn't understand everything the sites were suggesting about her line of work, like she might very well be One of Us instead, fighting the good fight against those who want to play gods with money, medicine, technology, and the future of the world. Those who liked tidy conclusions and tying up loose ends.

As for Carl himself, it was not lost on him that he and Lefine might be considered said loose ends. They had, evidently, seen something they weren't supposed to. It might have been coincidence that Lefine had called in sick that morning, but Carl didn't think so. Lefine never called in sick; the man could have broken bones and would still find a stick on the side of the road to prop himself up if he had to in order to hobble to work. Lefine's tenacity was one of the things Carl admired about his partner.

He decided to stop by Lefine's house on the way home from the precinct.

Lt. Darryl Lefine was a man of fascinating contrasts and complements. He was thin enough to blend into the background to just listen and observe, but tall enough to discourage trouble from veering his way. The man knew a little something about everything, too, which Carl believed stemmed from a storied background he never spoke of. A man of few if any words, he was logical and serious—perhaps contemplative was a better word—and yet under the right circumstances, he could hold his own in any conversation and genuinely charm the people he was speaking to. He could also silence a particularly unruly prisoner or even a room full of people with a single look; Carl had seen him do it. People who assumed Darryl Lefine was a pushover assumed wrong. He chalked up the commanding and charming qualities both to a kind of social deftness learned from his grandmama. There wasn't a single person Carl could think of that didn't like Lefine, including several of those unruly prisoners, and yet he had few friends and had been alone since his divorce from Emma Lefine Caldwell fifteen years prior.

Perhaps the most unusual quirk Lefine possessed was the utter indifference with which he regarded his residence on Armitage Road, just before Ardmoor Hill and Haversham Hospital for the Criminally Insane. Most of the folks in Haversham wanted no part of that whole area and in fact went to great lengths to avoid it, as if the ground itself was toxic somehow. This included other cops, who tried to give Lefine a hard time about living "downwind of the crazies." Lefine never responded, although he did confide in Carl once that he had a family member up at the hospital. Of course, he didn't elaborate—on personal matters, Lefine never did—but Carl supposed that he had more sympathy for the crazies than fear.

The little house on Armitage Road was a neat white Craftsman-style house with dark gray trim, a curbside mailbox with LEFINE in white lettering, and a tidily mowed lawn. There were few houses left on the street, and Lefine liked it that way. He had peace and quiet and privacy now that he'd chased off the white folks, he'd tell Carl with a small smile, and that suited him just fine.

Carl parked in front of the house and cut the ignition. The sun had nearly sunk beyond Ardmoor Hill by then, casting long shadows that gathered between and beneath the detritus of suburban life, but there were no lights on in the house. Carl frowned and got out of the car.

Before he had even made it to the front door, he'd drawn his gun, though the realization, the weight of the weapon in his hand, surprised him. He wasn't sure consciously why he even needed his gun out, but decided it was something in the air—a kind of electric impatience in the wind for something to happen, an aggression in the way the darkness draped across the front porch. Whatever had triggered Carl's instinct wasn't as obvious as the instinct itself, but Carl trusted the latter implicitly.

He knocked on the front door and waited. Several seconds ticked by in the growing darkness, and Carl was about to knock again when he heard the shuffling of feet. A moment later, the door opened and Darryl Lefine, shivering in a bathrobe, gave him a silent nod and let him in.

"You look like shit," Carl said, and gave his partner half of a grin he couldn't quite manage to keep on his face.

"You flatter me," Lefine replied without smiling. He looked awful. His eyes were red, half sunken in puffy bags, and his lips were dry. He smelled vaguely of dust; Carl caught a whiff as his partner shuffled by, gesturing weakly for Carl to follow. He looked grayer, leaner, more lined than before.

"Seriously, man," Carl said as Lefine gestured toward the living room couch. "You look like a truck hit you. You okay?"

"Want a beer?"

Carl nodded and Lefine tossed him one from a six-pack on a side table near his big, blue-velvet easy chair. "Hey, are you supposed to be mixing beer and cold medicine?" He cracked open the can.

"Not on cold medicine," Lefine said, sinking into the easy chair across from Carl.

"No problem, then," Carl said, taking a sip. "So what's wrong with you?"

Lefine looked into his own beer. It occurred to Carl that he seldom saw the man drink the stuff. Lefine was usually a wine or Scotch man, and he twirled his can a little like he so often twirled the ice in his Scotch. Finally, Lefine said, "According to doctors, it's all in my head."

Carl frowned. "What the hell does that mean?"

Lefine peered up at him over the thin wire frames of his glasses. He seemed to be considering something. With some reluctance, Carl noted, he put his beer down on the side table and then pulled the arms of the robe up to his elbows.

"Jesus," Carl said, studying Lefine's arms in horror. "Does it hurt?"

The skin on Carl's forearms, once a healthy brown, was now a nearly translucent scar-pink and swollen. Beneath the uppermost layers, blackish roots had taken hold of flesh and muscle, and tiny sprouts of gray had pushed up in tender-looking, flaking spots. The sprouts looked to Carl like thin, tiny wire brush branches. They had snagged some fuzz from the inside of Lefine's robe, and that somehow made them look more painful. Carl couldn't be sure, but it seemed like the branches were vibrating slightly.

"Hurts like hell. And it's not just on my arms. Got it on my chest, too, and there's a patch on my outer left thigh that seems to be spreading toward my knee. But don't worry—I'm told it's not contagious."

"Well, what the fuck is it?"

Lefine shrugged. "My GP said he'd never seen anything like it. Said it was some kind of fungal growth and gave me an antifungal cream. But I thought it might be related to that Van Houten case, so I went back and had one of those doctors from the quarantine facility check me over. They took samples, did tests. Had three different doctors there confirm it was unrelated. Said it was a kind of mutated Morgellons disease."

"I think they might have, uh..." Carl wasn't sure how to finish the sentence tactfully.

"Lied?"

"I was going to say, 'made a mistake,'" Carl replied.

"They lied." Lefine pulled his sleeves down gingerly. "At least about what it *was*, although I believe they told me the truth about what it *wasn't*."

"So, what are you supposed to do now?"

"Wait." Lefine shrugged. "Wait until the pills they gave me kick in. They said it should clear up in two weeks."

Carl frowned. There was an undercurrent of unease in Lefine's tone that Carl had never heard before. "You don't believe that, though."

"I don't know what I believe. They're telling me I have a chronic disease that mostly only strikes white women, and that's if it's even a disease at all. And they're telling me they have pills that clear up this chronic imaginary disease in two weeks. That sound funny to you? 'Cause it sure as hell sounds funny to me."

"Sounds funny to me, too, buddy," Carl agreed. "You look into what's in those pills?"

"Was just about to when you—" Lefine stopped, his head cocked as if listening to something in the distance. He scratched absently at one forearm over the robe, but was otherwise perfectly still. "Did you hear that?"

"Hear what?"

Lefine held up a finger to pause Carl. "That," he said. "That whispering."

Carl listened for several seconds but heard nothing beyond the hum of the fridge in the next room and the light ticking of the old clock on the wall above the TV. "I don't hear anything, Lefine," he said.

"You don't hear that?" Lefine sounded genuinely perplexed.

"Nope."

"That whispering? It sounds like...like *'welcome home, welcome home'* over and over."

"I told you, I don't hear anything. Sure you didn't leave a TV on somewhere upstairs? Or a radio maybe?"

Lefine looked at him as if he were stupid. "I'm sick, Horns, not senile."

"I'm sorry. I just don't—"

"Shhh!" Lefine's finger flew to his lips. "There! There it is again."

To humor his partner, Carl listened. He was getting ready to grumpily reply that he *still* didn't hear anything and that maybe Lefine should go back to the doctor and get his ears checked when he thought he caught a low hissing sound. Craning his neck in that direction, he listened as the hissing melted into whispered syllables, though try as he might, he couldn't make out what the words were.

"Are you fucking with me?" Carl asked.

Lefine, ever serious, replied. "Have I ever struck you as the joking type?"

"You have not."

"Well then, there you go."

"What is that sound, then? Where is it coming from?"

Lefine shrugged. "Been hearing it on and off the last two days. Can't make heads nor tails of it. I'll be honest, Horns—I'm just glad you can hear it, too."

The two lapsed into silence for a while, listening. Carl was pretty sure he could still hear the whispering, but it had sunk in volume to more of a suggestion of sound than anything identifiable in his ears. Still, he thought it was repeating a message over and over, like Lefine had said. It wasn't *'come home,'* though. Carl was pretty sure of that. And the longer he listened to it, the more uneasy he became.

"Lefine, I think we should go."

Lefine cocked an eyebrow at him.

"I'm serious," he said, getting to his feet. "I'll explain in the car. Let's go."

They had been partners long enough that Lefine trusted Carl's instinct almost as much as Carl himself. Lefine got to his feet as well and without a word, led Carl back down the hall and out the front door.

It wasn't until they were in Carl's car and he'd started the engine that Lefine finally asked, "So what's going on?"

"The whispering," Carl said. "I could hear it, like I said."

"Okay. And?"

"And it wasn't saying, 'Welcome home.' It was saying, 'The ill come home.'"

Lefine shook his head. "That doesn't—"

"There was more. Maybe you only heard part of it, but there was more. Different voices, all over each other. 'The ill come home. The ill come home to die.'"

Chapter 4

Sergeant Markham led Kathy and Rodriguez to a nondescript black sedan with tinted windows. A large man in mirrored sunglasses and a suit stood at the front passenger door, his posture distinctly military in its learned rigidity. Another man, similarly sized and dressed, stood on the street side of the car by the driver's side door. Rodriguez looked worried, his gaze darting wildly around the otherwise empty street, and Kathy got the impression that the two men watching them approach would pounce on Rodriguez like wolves if his anxiety sent him running. Rodriguez must have gotten the same notion from the men, since he let them usher him to an open back door and politely stuff him inside the car.

Kathy met the mirrored gaze of the driver's side man, although she had to look up to do it. He reached out to assist her, seemed to gauge from her expression that it would be better not to, and simply opened the door for her. She nodded at him and got in the car. Markham got in after her.

For a long time, no one spoke—the Paragon men through nature or training, Rodriguez likely out of nerves, and Kathy because it was an opportunity to observe. She wasn't worried the men would hurt her; their bosses, after all, had hired her to do exactly what she'd done, and even if they were displeased for some reason, they needed her. Besides, Kathy had been in far worse situations.

Rodriguez, however…Kathy wasn't sure what would happen there. Nevertheless, she offered him a reassuring smile. He tried to return it, but it faltered on his face.

Finally, as if waiting for the right minute to finally tick off, Markham turned to her and Rodriguez and said, "My apologies, Ms. Ryan, Mr. Rodriguez, for any unpleasantness or confusion back at Mr. Müller's house. We've found that these clean-up situations are often best dealt with quickly and quietly, and of course, in the best interest of your health and well-being, with you both a safe distance from the premises." Despite his commanding voice, there was a refinement to his speech which was probably meant to foster trust—a gentle giant with the muscles to protect and the shoulders one could cry on. Whether such an impression was warranted, Kathy couldn't say.

"Where are you taking us?" Kathy asked. Nothing about her, so far as she believed, projected that same warmth. Sincerity, maybe, and frankness, surely, but Kathy was neither gentle nor cuddly.

"Back to the Paragon headquarters. We would like both of you to debrief us on the data you have thus far collected."

"Data?" Rodriguez asked.

"Your experiences in particular, Mr. Rodriguez, as well as any other discoveries, impressions, notes—everything pertaining to your connection with the project."

Kathy noted that Markham seemed to be carefully skirting the mention of specific details and names, even within the ostensibly safe confines of the Paragon company car.

"So…you're not going to kill us?"

Markham's mouth flickered in a brief smile. "Of course not, Mr. Rodriguez. You are considered right now to be a very valuable asset to the company. My mission and number one priority is to get you back to Facility 18 safely to talk to Dr. Greenwood. He is overseeing the recovery efforts and working on a task force to develop the next steps in the project. I have been informed that he wishes to check in with Ms. Ryan on what she advises is the best course of action going forward. Further, Dr. Greenwood believes your report will assist in the recovery of Green Team members, and…" He hesitated.

"And?" Kathy prompted.

"And possibly answer questions about what happened to my men. I was in charge of the recon team. I lost them all and I want to know why."

"I'm sorry," Kathy said, and genuinely meant it.

Markham didn't seem to know what to say, so he just nodded a thanks.

The car lapsed into silence again until finally it slowed at a security gate. The driver conferred with the guard on duty, although Kathy couldn't hear what, exactly, was being said. A moment later, the gate opened, and the car continued up a winding road toward a large, nondescript, pale gray building at the top of a hill.

"Home again," Rodriguez said with a faint whiff of sarcasm. "That Claire and Terry and Rick should be so lucky."

"We want to bring them home as well," Markham said, and he sounded sincere enough.

Rodriguez cast him a look that betrayed doubt, but he said nothing further.

The car pulled in front of the building, and Markham gestured for Kathy and Rodriguez to get out. Kathy opened the door, and Rodriguez reluctantly followed her out of the car. Markham led them to the glass double doors, and offered his thumb to a small gray box for identification. The box beeped its acceptance, and the glass doors slid open.

Before them, a white tiled lobby stretched before them, with an equally white counter to either side. Metal detectors stood next to the counters and imposing-looking uniformed men stood next to the detectors. Markham gestured toward one of the metal detectors and they were ushered through without incident. They were led down a long, deliberately nondescript hallway and ushered into an elevator. Kathy noticed there were two panels of buttons, one labeled "Floors" and a much larger one labeled "Subfloors." Markham ran a key card over a small panel above both, then chose number 24 from the "Subfloor" panel and stood back.

Markham had said very little since the car, other than to clarify a direction through the building. On the elevator, though, his silence grew deeper, more intense, and his whole person seemed to tense up, as if the further into the belly of the Paragon beast they went, the more uneasy he felt. To Kathy, that did not bode well.

After several long minutes of silence, Rodriguez finally said, "Subfloor 24? That's where we're going?"

"Yes, sir," Markham said.

"There's nothing there."

"Pardon?"

"Subfloor 24—there's nothing there. It's a dead floor. Empty. Decommissioned. The card keys aren't even supposed to work for that floor. What are you going to do with us there?"

Markham glanced at him briefly, then replied, "It's not empty anymore."

A moment later, the elevator dinged, the doors opened, and Markham shepherded them out.

Kathy's first impression of subfloor 24 was that Rodriguez was right; it was a dead floor. Construction sheeting hung by industrial staples from wooden beams and lay in crumpled heaps on the floor. The electrical wiring on the outer walls and ceiling was exposed. There were no inner walls built yet, and no drop ceiling panels, but in some areas, a framework-in-progress had been started. In the center of the floor was what looked like a large Plexiglas room, maybe fifteen by fifteen feet, in Kathy's estimation. There were four folding chairs and a wooden table inside the enclosure, a soft spotlight overhead just to illuminate the enclosure's contents, and a single Plexiglas door, facing the trio. Kathy would have felt more uneasy, but it occurred to her then that Markham had never taken her bag away from her, and she still had the gun in it. A shoot-out on a subfloor of some secret weapons facility was certainly not ideal, but, as she kept coming back to with an internal grimace, she had often been in worse situations.

"So, what, this is like, the torture floor or something?" Rodriguez asked. There was a hint of tension in his voice, although he did an admirable job of sounding casually sarcastic.

"Mr. Rodriguez, as I mentioned, we have no intention of hurting you. My mission was to retrieve you and Ms. Ryan and bring you here for debriefing. My understanding of the events of the evening is that upon the completion of the debriefing, you will be fed and provided accommodations for the night."

"And after that?"

Something flickered across Markham's features, albeit briefly. Kathy thought it was uncertainty, but it might have been unease.

"Beyond that is outside the parameters of my mission and my involvement," Markham said.

"Why here," Kathy asked, "on an unfinished floor? Of all the floors in this building and all the subfloors, why this one?"

"Because this one," a cultured male voice from behind them said, "contains a very special kind of quarantine room."

The three turned to see an old man, more wrinkle than skin and possibly more bone than flesh. White hair encircled his head like a laurel. He wore a tan sweater and pants, and over that, a lab coat. He emerged further from the shadows, although from a quick glance, Kathy couldn't tell where he had come from before that. She'd done a cursory glance of the floor and had supposed them to be alone. There didn't appear to be any other doors than the elevator, and they were standing too close to it not to have heard it open behind them.

"Forgive my startling you," the man said as he approached them, extending his hand. Kathy shook it, followed by Rodriguez, who was eyeing the old man as if he were a mumbling lunatic on a street corner. "I'm Dr. Greenwood, Carter Greenwood. I'm lead researcher on the MK-Ostium Project."

"How come Claire's never mentioned you?" Rodriguez said. "I thought we knew everyone working on Ostium."

Greenwood chuckled. "I'm afraid no one ever knows everyone involved in a project like this. I know of you, though, and the rest of the Green Team. Directly, my research was centered more on the processing of data retrieved by your team, particularly in the area of biological contamination. Basically, we developed the protocols to minimize cross-contamination between worlds. It was we—the blue team, that is—who assessed health risk pre- and post-quarantine, as well as fully examining Dr. Van Houten's remains for potential spread of infection there. And we determined the likelihood of your introducing foreign contaminants in the other world, as well. All of which I'd like to discuss in some further detail with the three of you. Please, this way."

He led them toward the enclosure, punched in a code on a band around his wrist, and the door swung open. He walked in first, ostensibly to show them they were not prisoners but guests, and gestured for them to sit. They did, with Markham somewhat hesitantly taking the furthest seat from Greenwood.

The scientist continued. "When your team disappeared, we were, of course, very worried. That we have you alive and well is an immeasurable relief, Mr. Rodriguez."

"Uh, thanks," Rodriguez said.

"Of course, if there is any way we can recover the rest of your team, it is of the utmost priority," Greenwood said. "And to that end, anything you can tell us would be incredibly helpful. I have invited Sgt. Markham as well, in case you can offer any closure regarding his poor men. As you may know by now, we hired Ms. Ryan here to evaluate the available information regarding Ostium, assess the risks, and offer advice about the recovery of your team and conclusion of the project. My understanding is that she is the best in the business regarding this kind of thing."

"That's kind of you to say," Kathy said. She couldn't help but feel guarded around the man, although he came across as polite, even warm. He was, perhaps, too polite, too cultured in his mannerisms and speech, as if he'd practiced this moment often to avoid raising suspicion about the motives beneath it.

"I have been advised that you are aware of an unfortunate and unforeseen situation."

"You mean people literally turning to dust? Faces growing out of inanimate objects? Nightmares and whispering? All the mutations I told you people could happen, that you assured me couldn't and wouldn't? That situation?"

Greenwood's practiced smile faltered just slightly. "Yes, Mr. Rodriguez. The graying disease is statistically an incredibly rare side-effect of visiting G-01-01-409763, one we felt and still feel confident presents only under the most unique and infrequent conditions. Dr. Van Houten's untimely passing is a sincerely regrettable tragedy, but multiple attempts to reproduce the same conditions in the lab returned negative results, each and every time. None of the data we worked with indicated anything like this could or would happen once, let alone again."

Seeing their expressions, Greenwood said, "What I mean to say is, nothing in our research indicated the presence of any kind of pathogen, contaminant, or entity returning with team members from the other side— not in the quarantine chamber surrounding the gate, and certainly not outside the quarantine chamber. And yet, as you have indicated, something...organic but not corporeal seems to have attached itself to your team. Something undetectable when attached to carriers, and only observable once it has chosen a host to act upon." He steepled his fingers. "At first we couldn't detect its presence in carriers. We could only observe it in later stages of progression of its infection, and the problem there was that the infection seems to affect different people in different ways at different rates, *if* it even affects them at all. Repeated and prolonged exposure seem to make little difference in terms of initial infection, but the symptoms are cumulative. So you see, it's been extremely difficult to test for. But then we developed this room." He gestured to the Plexiglas box around him.

"What does it do?" Kathy asked.

"It serves a few purposes, which I will try to explain in simple terms, if I can. We believe the entities I mentioned above have discovered something about humans, possibly something in the DNA code, that allows them to attach to physical bodies and survive the crossover from their world into this one. During the attachment, they are either unable or unwilling to attack the carrier, and we have some evidence to support that the act of attaching introduces an immunity to that carrier which prevents later infection. This room, firstly, determines if that immunity exists by scanning those within it. We can also determine from scans whether or not the attaching entity remains attached, or if it has moved on to inhabit—to infest, really—non-organic objects in the environment. We believe this is important in isolating and corralling the entities which have already successfully detached on this side of the gate.

"Secondly, we have discovered that while there are three progressive stages of infection from these entities, not all who are exposed develop them. The first stage is not unlike the attachment process—like you mentioned, the seeing of faces, temporary disorientation, bad dreams, whispering, that sort of thing. The second stage involves mental manipulation, hallucinations, physical deformities and ailments. The third stage...well, I assume you are all aware of the condition in which Dr. Van Houten was found."

No one replied, but Dr. Greenwood went on. "We have not yet determined what causes some to develop infection after exposure and others not to. We don't know why some progress with the disease to the point of graying and others do not. All we can determine is that the infection is spread from exposure to the entities, not to other infected individuals. So we have built this room to neutralize entities that may still be attached to carriers so that they don't unwittingly release the entities elsewhere. We are currently reconfiguring the quarantine chamber surrounding the gateway to do the same thing, so that in the future, we can avoid propagating the infecting entities on this side of the gate.

"On the other side of the gate, Sergeant Markham has lost an entire recon squad, and you, Mr. Rodriguez, have lost your colleagues. On this side, we have lost people for whom exposure to these entities results in a catastrophic illness. While the progression seems to happen rarely, and thank God for that, when it does, it is still an incurable and unstoppable process that we cannot develop measures to contain or avoid. We need more information."

Greenwood shook his head. "But listen to me prattling on! Please forgive the lengthy preamble. However, I believe it was necessary to understand what we need from you. *Do* you understand?"

Kathy, Rodriguez, and Markham shook their heads.

"We are fairly certain that Dr. Rodriguez is a carrier. This means he is immune to full-blown infection, but not its nasty little mind games. Exposure to the entities in the residence where Dr. Rodriguez was staying suggests that Ms. Ryan and Sgt. Markham may also be carriers, the effects of which we are working to negate as the four of us talk in here." He gestured at the room around him. "This quarantine chamber emits certain magnetic vibrations which may give you a headache or possibly make you feel a little light-headed, if you feel it at all. That's okay; that's just the room doing its thing. We perfected it following data received after the medical examination and release of two police officers involved in the Van Houten incident. We hope to refine and expand the process to remove the infestation of these entities pending information we receive from you.

We think a little fine-tuning might even be able to reverse, to some degree, their alteration of people's thinking and functioning."

"These entities…what are they, exactly?" Kathy asked.

Greenwood cocked an eyebrow. "Exactly? We can't say at present. We understand you see them as faces in inanimate things—fabric, wood grain, and the like. And hear them whispering. We suspect they require non-organic materials to inhabit in order to act on their environment, but are capable of pulling up stakes, so to speak, and hitching rides with mobile organic entities."

Rodriguez looked genuinely scared then. "So, they're like, what, demons that possess curtains and couch cushions?"

"We believe they're a kind of parasite," Greenwood said. "The physics of the world from which they come are contradictory and indefinable, and so, in large part, are they. Beyond what we can observe here…" He shrugged.

"What are you leading up to, Dr. Greenwood?" Markham had been so quiet throughout the conversation that Kathy had almost forgotten he was there. His stony expression suggested to Kathy that he anticipated confrontation in Greenwood's answer.

"Pardon?"

"My assignment was to bring Ms. Ryan and Mr. Rodriguez here for debriefing. With all due respect, you've done more talking than listening, and you've indicated that the reason for this is that it's leading somewhere. Somewhere that includes me, evidently. I would like to know what the end game is, as it was not part of my initial orders."

Dr. Greenwood dropped his hands to the table. "Fair enough. Regardless of the future direction of the project, we need information, and you want answers. We would like a team to gather data, this time with eyes wide open to the nature of the environment, and with certain protections in place. We want to understand as fully as possible what we're up against, so we can take every possible precaution to protect and heal the employees in this lab who were exposed, and their families and communities, which were exposed unknowingly by extension…So much of this happened because we just didn't have enough information to correlate all the possibilities. You can change that. You can bring the Green Team home, and they can change it. The best way to meet all of these objectives is for us to send you through the gate."

For several moments, no one spoke. Three pairs of eyes were fixed on Greenwood, three jaws slack with surprise.

"Oh no. No no no," Rodriguez said, sliding his chair back. "I'm not going back."

"You can't be serious," Kathy said.

"I won't do it!" Rodriguez said, his voice and body both rising.

"Mr. Rodriguez, please, just sit and—"

"I'm not going back there!"

"Jose, sit," Kathy said, extending a hand to calm him.

"Are you hearing this? Are you *hearing* this?!"

"Yes, Jose, I am. Let's sit and hear what the doctor has in mind, huh?"

"Hear him out? Are you crazy?"

"We'd give you every possible chance for survival—" Dr. Greenwood interjected.

"Bullshit!" Rodriguez slammed a fist against the nearest Plexiglas wall and Kathy was surprised to hear a faint vibrational hum. For several seconds, the hum was the only sound in the room, or indeed, anywhere on the floor. Then, more softly, Rodriguez said, "You couldn't protect us before. You couldn't protect John or Warner. And you can't protect us now. We thought we opened a gateway to a new Eden, but we didn't. You know that. We found hell, a quiet kind of hell, and that's the worst kind. It's insidious. It attacks the safe places in your own head and then kills you from the inside out. And you're out of your goddamned mind if you think I'm willingly going to set foot in that place again." Finally, he sank into the chair, his whole demeanor deflating.

Dr. Greenwood paused long enough to make the appearance that he was considering Rodriguez's words, and then said, "Mr. Rodriguez, I can't begin to imagine what you must have gone through—"

"No, you can't," Rodriguez interjected huffily.

"But I'm sure you can understand how important it is that you join this expedition."

Rodriguez opened his mouth to protest but Greenwood held up a hand.

"I understand you're scared. And honestly, you should be. You all should be. Because you're right, Mr. Rodriguez. It poses a risk both personally and professionally to say so, but I must agree with you. There is insanity on the other side of that gate, insanity that, despite our best intentions, we may have introduced to this world unknowingly. I have to carry that with me. I have to sleep with the knowledge that my shortcomings here could have let a poison into our world. But I can't right any of these things without Ms. Ryan and Sergeant Markham, and they will never survive a trip to that world without an experienced guide like you."

Greenwood turned to Kathy and Markham. "I need all of you. I'm not asking you to give a pass to an old man's wrongs. I'm asking you to help me prevent this company making any more of them." He leaned in. "It's asking a lot of you to trust me, I know. But the three of you are the best possible chance Claire Banks and her colleagues have for rescue."

"How do you even know they're still alive?" Kathy said. It occurred to her that she could have phrased the question more sensitively, and added, "I mean, if your job is to assess risk, I'm assuming you must have reason to believe sending us wouldn't be a wasted trip."

Dr. Greenwood nodded. "We do. Mr. Rodriguez may remember the medical exam he and Ms. Banks and the others underwent before their first trip through the gate?"

"Yeah," Rodriguez said. "What about it?"

"The Green Team was given a number of inoculations against disease. One of those inoculations had a nanobot that tracks vital signs and relays the data back here to the lab. The information feed regarding location is corrupted—it's coming through completely garbled—but the feeds indicating brain wave activity and respiration are active in all missing Green Team members. It was, of course, how we knew you were alive, Mr. Rodriguez, but not where to find you. Not right away."

It was a lot to digest. It didn't really surprise Kathy that there was information the Paragon Corporation had kept hidden from her, at least until now, but it was frustrating. She also resented the sudden changes to the parameters of the job they had hired her for, particularly because her involvement thus far seemed designed to make sure she couldn't say no to those changes. That people somewhere had opened a gate they couldn't close and had let things in that didn't belong here…well, that was par for the course in her line of work. That was her bread and butter. But something about the whole situation didn't sit right with her. There was some missing piece somewhere, some other facet to the proposed scenario that Greenwood was holding back. Kathy didn't like it.

"So if you can track vital signs, what about my squad over there?" Markham asked. "They were my people under my command."

A shade passed over Dr. Greenwood's features, and his hesitation was enough of an answer, but he replied, "We held out hope, Sergeant. Memorized the names and implant numbers of every one of them. I'm sorry."

Markham remained stony, but Kathy could tell pain in a tough man's eyes when she saw it. She almost reached out to touch his arm, to offer sympathy, but decided against it.

"It was, perhaps, their weapons," Dr. Greenwood offered gently. "If your people, trained fighters all, met with something that maybe the Green Team unleashed or awoke somehow, or something they left in their wake… what I mean is, something killed them but not an unarmed, untrained group of scientists and researchers. It's possible that whatever it was took the weapons as a sign of aggression. Honestly, we don't know. All we can say is that we believe a different approach to rescue is necessary."

"And we're your different approach?" Rodriguez said.

Greenwood met his gaze. "Just tell us what happened there. Help us understand."

Rodriguez sighed. "Okay. I'll tell you what I told Warner and Kathy. Then you'll see. We're all just screwed."

Chapter 5

It was twilight and the lights came on in the dead city.

As bluish clouds stretched long and a violet night stained the alien sky of Hesychia, a lone cry from the city depths echoed around the stony, silent buildings. The aimless wind stirred the foliage that had begun to reclaim the streets like a hand absently ruffling the hair of a small child.

On the far outskirts of the city, the multitude of trees grasped at the sky, their long fingers casting bony, arthritic shadows out over the edge of the plains. The limbs creaked in the wind, but otherwise, their silence was as thick as the dense underbrush of the forest floor.

Where the dirt was exposed, there was a new set of footprints, a marvel in and of itself for such a place. The soft, dark soil hadn't held prints of any kind in millennia, not until the humans from beyond the gate had come, the Green Team of Paragon Corporation, and those footprints had been swept away over time by the shivering of tree roots beneath the soil and atavistic gales of wind.

The fairly recent set remained, though, in part because the trees had watched with genuine curiosity the desperate flight during which they were made, and in part because the prints had run so far out of reach—from city to woods, then back across the plains toward the mountains.

They stopped suddenly before the steep gray face of the rock, without evidence of backtracking or a scuffle. It was as if something from the sky had swooped down and carried away the maker of such prints. And yet, to those who had once roamed those plains, conversing with the trees and gazing at the mountains as if they were great stone gods long before the true gods came, that would not have been so strange an ending to the prints or their maker. Of course, those beings were long gone, as were the beings which ruled the air.

In the land of Hesychia, once called Xíonathymia, only the gods and demigods remained—them, and the silent trees.

Once the twin moons rose fully overhead, the trapezoidal crystals in the city center began to vibrate.

The Wraiths were awakening.

* * * *

Night was settling over the road. It seemed to Carl that it was still early to be getting so dark, but shadow had already gathered thick to either side of the road, definite shapes blurring into indefinite voids as Haversham gave way to the woods beyond.

"I think I should take you to the hospital," Carl told Lefine. When the other man didn't answer, Carl glanced away from the road. Lefine was slumped against the passenger side door, lightly clutching his arm, but his eyes were open and his chest was rising and falling.

"Lefine? You hear me?"

"I heard you," Lefine muttered. "They don't think it's a good idea."

"What?" Carl frowned at him. "What do you mean?"

"I don't think it's a good idea," Lefine said.

"Why not?"

"Because I—stop the car!" Lefine's hand shot out to grab Carl's arm, causing them to swerve. Carl cut the wheel to regain control and pulled over onto the side of the road.

"What the fuck, Lefine?"

"I—I'm sorry." Lefine looked genuinely shaken. "I thought I…I saw…"

"What?"

"In the road…I thought I saw something."

"What did you see?"

"A piece of fabric in the wind. Like a bed sheet, only thinner. And the way it moved…"

Carl stared at him. "You nearly wrecked us over someone's old laundry?"

Lefine shook his head. "No, not laundry! It was a sheet. Like…a shroud. It melded into a shape with a face and hands, and it—" He dropped his face into his hands. "There's something very, very wrong with me, Carl. I—"

Suddenly he looked up from his hands, evident alarm tightening his features. "Wait...is this the dream, or is it real?" He turned to Carl. "Are you real?"

"Lefine, what're you talking about? What's gotten into you?" Carl said.

"The million dollar question," Lefine mumbled, then suddenly opened the car door and ran out into the darkness.

"Darryl! Wait! Where—" Grabbing a Maglite from the glove compartment, Carl tossed his door open and ran out into the dark after Lefine. For a moment, the robed figure loped ahead of him, and then the darkness swallowed them both.

"Lefine? Come back here!" Carl turned on the flashlight and ran in the direction that he'd seen his partner heading. The light pushed the darkness around, shoving it out of the way but only temporarily. Carl shined it over the ground, looking for footprints, but there were none. He searched the wooded area ahead of him. There was nothing but darkness and the occasional tree. And where, exactly, was he? He'd been by Lefine's place hundreds of times, been up and down the very road he'd pulled off of, but none of this area looked familiar.

"Lefine! Goddammit!" A root caught his foot and he stumbled forward, sure for a second that he was going down face-first. He managed to balance himself, though, by catching hold of a nearby tree-trunk, but the Maglite was jarred out of his hand and rolled a little ways down a hill.

Carl was a big man, not exactly fat, but bigger than he would have liked and paunchy around the middle. He hadn't realized though how out of shape he was until just then. For several moments while he caught his breath, he leaned against the rough bark of the tree. Total darkness enveloped him. The night had cooled, and when it stirred, it turned Carl's sweat cold.

"Lefine!" he called when his breathing had returned to normal. "Where are you?"

"Help me, Carl." Lefine's voice came from somewhere several feet to the right of him. Beneath it was the low hiss of multiple whispering.

Carl swooped toward the glow of the Maglite and picked it up, then charged off in the direction of the voice.

"Lefine, come on, man. Tell me where you are." As he jogged along, Carl swung the light around in front of him, cutting through the darkness. The beam of light fell then on a hideous, silently shrieking face of a beast and Carl cried out, skidding to a stop. He repositioned the beam and saw the face was nothing more than rough clumps of bark half-peeled away from their trunk.

The whispering had grown, if not louder, than fuller, surrounding his head, forcing its way into his ears, shoving its way down his throat and into his chest like a noxious smoke. He could almost taste it, taste the whispering, as crazy as it seemed, and it tasted bitter and faintly coppery.

It was like the dreams...

Carl turned, swinging the Maglite, and the beam came up so suddenly on Lefine's back that Carl uttered a little cry of surprise. Lefine's head was bent. He just stood there, swaying a little in the dark.

"Darryl?" Carl took a few steps closer. He couldn't have explained what kept him from rushing to his friend, just that it was that gut instinct again, telling him something was wrong. "Hey, buddy," he said softly. "It's me. It's Carl. Why don't we go back to the car, huh?"

Lefine didn't answer. If he heard Carl at all, he didn't acknowledge it. He just swayed.

Carl took a few more steps forward, close enough to touch Lefine if he reached out, and frowned. His heart began to pound in his chest.

Lefine wasn't there at all. It was only his robe, hanging from a nearby branch.

Carl looked around, confused. He'd been sure he'd seen Lefine, sure he'd made out the man's head and legs in the darkness, or their silhouettes, at least. But how—

"Darryl?" He shined the light at the robe again stirring lightly in the breeze, swaying in the dark, and saw something else he hadn't noticed before. The ground beneath was dark and wet with blood.

* * * *

The gateway on Paragon's thirty-first subfloor rippled unsteadily from late afternoon into the night. Ravi Varma, the researcher on night shift, noted with some worry that the gateway had been doing that a lot lately. He marked it down in the electronic log on the company laptop as he had been instructed to do, then went back to watching the monitor. Ravi had been at it eleven hours already, with only two half-hour breaks to eat. He was developing a faint headache from the monitor's screen light and his eyes were getting heavy. He hadn't been sleeping well the last few nights—ever since the gateway had begun to ripple, in fact—and wasn't used to working the night shift. If anyone asked after his well-being, Ravi chalked up his lack of sleep to being busy and a little stressed.

His real thoughts on the matter he kept to himself. When he could finally fall asleep, the bad dreams woke him right back up. He was forgetting simple things, like the names of people from college and movie titles, or where he'd put his car keys and his favorite pen. He'd developed a small but odd rash, a tiny patch of gray under one arm. Twice now, he thought he'd heard someone whispering his name when no one else was in the lab, and it had happened once at home as well. All day he'd felt watched, like someone was standing behind him. He'd noted that in the log as well; he'd been told to write it all down, every weird thing, no matter how small or seemingly insignificant.

What he had yet to put into words, though, were the hands and the faces.

He'd heard Rachel and Corey mention them earlier in the cafeteria as they'd eaten their second meal of the night. Well, Ravi had eaten; the other two had just poked their food around their plates with their forks. Ravi thought maybe what they'd told him had gotten under his skin a little bit. It wasn't what they had been saying; he'd stubbornly maintained that most of that was absurd. It was *how* they'd told it, how their eyes darted and their voices shook a little when they mentioned seeing faces in the toilet paper sheets in the rest rooms or in the cafeteria's Formica tabletops. Both of them had been jumpy, too, like they were waiting for something bad to happen any minute. In fact, it had struck Ravi with near-ridiculous specificity that they were like two people blindfolded and left to navigate their way out of a room crowded with hypodermic needles and other sharp things tipped with corrosive poisons. It was a visual that sprang uncomfortably to mind as they'd told him about the faces, and even after they'd picked up their lunch trays and left, Ravi couldn't get the image out of his head.

He had known Rachel for six years and Corey for almost as long. He'd never known them to be imaginative or nervous or to pull pranks. Neither was the type to partake in any of the drugs from Pharmaceuticals and Chemistry, one floor up. They genuinely seemed to believe what they were telling him, and also seemed earnestly upset about it. They asked about the gateway, if maybe it was leaking radiation or some chemical…but Ravi had assured them it was contained and carefully monitored, that he saw to maintaining the safety protocols himself, and besides, Rachel and Corey had never even been near the thing, not really, not without a thick pane of glass between them and the gate, so how could it have anything to do with the toilet paper in the ladies' room?

The two junior researchers were a little younger than Ravi and a little less experienced at Paragon, so they had seemed to accept his logic and look a little less shaken. Before they'd gone back to work, though, they'd confided that now they were starting to see the faces everywhere, and thought they heard whispering too.

He'd nearly broken down and told them about the dreams then, about the whispering he'd been hearing himself, and about the strange vibes he'd been getting in the lab all afternoon and night, but he didn't. Some underlying voice in his brain suggested that to admit to it out loud and compare notes would confirm the experiences were more than just stress-induced weirdness. They would fuel the notion that the wrongness they'd all been feeling lately was external…that perhaps it really *was* a symptom of prolonged exposure to the gateway…or a possible taste of what was on the other side. Rachel and Corey were scared enough, and didn't need what was probably just coincidence making things worse and distracting them from their work.

Truth be told, Ravi didn't think he could manage that kind of distraction just then, either.

Luckily, there weren't many nuanced surfaces in the lab. Mostly, the instruments and equipment were smooth, sterile, and metallic and not conducive to imagining faces. Nonetheless, on his return to the lab after lunch, Ravi had thought for just a second that he'd seen an odd, distorted face in the reflective metal corner of the security doorway leading to the gate. When he'd looked again, there was, of course, nothing there. What he'd probably seen was his own reflection, or part of it, or some other part of the lab that, at just the right angle and with the right movement, had formed a kind of distortion his brain translated into a face.

That's how he'd explained away the first face. The others were harder.

There was the one he thought he saw doodled on a napkin, half-hidden beneath his boss's coffee mug, but when he'd lifted the cup, sloshing some of the cold liquid onto the desk, he'd seen the scribbles for what they were—scribbles. There was the one he thought he saw in the smudges of glass between the observation control room and the lab proper, though that, he'd insisted to himself, was just a trick of the overhead fluorescent lights. There were ones he'd seen at home, too, in the bedsheets and the shower curtains, scowling and sneering and growling. Usually, the faces were silent, just frozen masks of stiffened fabric. Sometimes they weren't silent.

And of course, there were the ones he'd see from time to time in the substance of the gateway as it rippled and churned. That thick oily stuff had begun to pinch, stretch, or swell out toward the lab, just a little—that was new, and duly logged—and sometimes, those movements seemed to make a face. Even if he could dismiss the dreams, the whispering, and the glimpses of faces all over the lab, he knew he had to tell his superiors what the "gateway goo," as the researchers had been calling it, was doing.

He'd heard rumors about John Van Houten and he'd seen the state the recon guy had been in when he'd come back through the gate. He didn't want there to be anything more wrong than his just being tired, but he didn't want to neglect a genuine potential problem, either. Ravi was not a brave man, but he was a responsible one.

He crossed the control room to the laptop and tapped a few keys to start a new entry in the log. He typed "is making faces, 4:47 a.m.," looked at it, and then backspaced. The words looked insane. Worse, the words suggested insanity—his own. They suggested he wasn't functioning at 100% mentally or professionally, and that worried him. He had worked really hard to get the position he held in the lab and to work so closely on the Ostium project. He couldn't afford to look like he was cracking up.

Then again, if what he was seeing was true, it absolutely needed to be recorded. He couldn't be the only shift researcher to see the faces, right? He had the brief sensation again of being watched, and his body tensed. The faces did that sometimes. They had no eyes, not really, but they watched. They watched and they judged and then whispered things into his brain until he wasn't sure if the thoughts he was having about cutting Rachel and Corey with razors and sticking them with hypodermic needles were his thoughts, or those of the faces.

Rachel and Corey weren't the only ones in the room of sharps, he supposed.

He leaned over to retype what he'd deleted. "Forming vaguely human facial features, possibly mimicking human face, 4:47 a.m." The entry looked more scientific that way, he thought, and felt a little better about it.

He looked at the gateway over the computer screen. It had stopped rippling for the time being. In fact, it was just about as placid as he had ever seen it. As he stared at the dark burgundy, he thought he could hear a faint hum in the background, and for just a second, he thought it turned white, almost clear. The white engulfed his sight and he turned away, leaning on the desk for support and blinking heavily to clear his vision. He bowed his head and took several deep breaths, and by degrees, he felt clearer, more present.

Then he heard a cry from the lab. He looked up and gasped.

Something was trying to pull itself through the gate.

Ravi could see a head and torso up to the waist, with arms grasping at the air in front of it as if looking for something to hold onto. Whoever it was, the figure was covered in the gateway goo, sheathed in it, painted in its swirling oil-slick colors. Ravi couldn't make out any of the facial features, but...

He hit the alarm. A woman's voice announced in jarringly calm fashion that there was an Emergency, the senior staff needed to return to the lab at once, Emergency, and between each repeated announcement, a blaring wail like an air raid siren.

His shocked gaze fixed on the figure, Ravi crossed to the door of the observation control room and pushed it open. It seemed to be struggling, wiggling toward freedom from the substance of the gate. Jogging across the lab, Ravi called out to it. "Hello? Hey! Hey, there!"

The gateway rippled behind another glass enclosure about twelve feet square, jostling the figure like a rag doll. The door, a few feet out of the range of those flailing arms, rattled as if caught up by some unseen wind.

"Help me." The voice coming from the bowed head of the figure was hoarse and deep. Ravi figured the gateway goo had slid down the poor guy's throat, and he thought again of that room of syringes and sharp things.

Ravi could barely hear anything else but the blaring alarm. The figure's head raised again, the arms gesturing, and its voice seemed to cut through the noise somehow.

"Please, help me," the figure said again.

Ravi glanced back at the door. Where was the rest of the senior staff? What was taking so long? He held up his hands in a placating gesture. "Uh, help is coming, buddy. Just hang in there—"

"No time! You need...to get me out of here."

"Ah, I can't. See, it's against protocol. But help is on the way I swear! Just hold on one—"

"They're coming! Please!"

Ravi hesitated. "Who's coming?"

"There are things here, Ravi. Terrible things. And they don't want to let me leave."

Ravi frowned. The voice sounded familiar, now that it was shaking off some of its scratchiness. The eyes...he knew those eyes. "Do I know you?"

"It's me, Rav. It's Rodriguez," the voice said. "Please, take my arms and pull. I'm stuck."

"Dr. Rodriguez? Oh shit. Hold on," Ravi said, and opened the glass door. "I'll get you out of there."

He took hold of one of the outstretched hands and pulled. He was so intent on getting Rodriguez out of the gateway that it took a few moments to realize his own hand was sinking into the dark burgundy goo. What had felt like flesh a moment before now felt like jets of liquid movement bundled into muscle. He looked up at the face and saw it wasn't Rodriguez at all, that those eyes weren't and couldn't be familiar because *it had no eyes*, no real teeth or tongue. And it was grinning, just like the faces in the metal and glass—like the faces in the gateway. This thing with its iron grip on his wrist wasn't trying to escape the gateway. It *was* the gateway.

The face of the figure imploded with a splash in reverse, returning to the rippling, swirling burgundy. Before Ravi could pull free, the hand holding onto him yanked him forward, throwing off his balance, while the opposite arm and torso melded back into the gateway like liquid silver.

Panicked, Ravi struggled against the strength in that one remaining arm, but it was dragging him toward the gate. He heard shouting and the frantic rush of feet pounding across the lab to him. He tried to look over his shoulder, but he couldn't turn his head or neck enough to see whatever assistance might be coming.

"Help me!" he shouted, but was dismayed to find his own voice sounded hoarse like the figure's had, nearly too weak to be heard over the alarm. He tried to lock his legs but another sudden yank pitched him forward. "No!" he shouted, and then that cold, almost-wet stuff was engulfing his face, his ears, his whole head. His arm shot out much like the figure's had, trying to find something to hold onto to pull himself free. There was nothing to grab, though, and his arm plunged in after his head. All around him was an almost-wet darkness, cool and tingling against the skin, and then he felt like he was falling.

He thought maybe he felt someone try to grab his foot before all of him was gone—he was pretty sure one of his shoes slid off—and then Ravi Varma was pulled through the gateway.

* * * *

When the alarm went off, Kathy, Rodriguez, and Markham were still in the Plexiglas quarantine room on Subfloor 24. Greenwood had left them there to discuss their options after Rodriguez had retold his story. They'd gone around in circles for hours, discussing the pros and cons, with Kathy and Markham leaning toward going and Rodriguez still vehemently against. It was well after four in the morning, and the conversation had petered out to occasional mumblings some time before. Rodriguez had finally nodded off. Kathy was feeling sleepy herself, and had just closed her eyes when a blaring sound like an air raid siren sliced into the silence. They all jumped, Rodriguez sprawling out of his seat with a small cry.

In between bleats, a mechanical woman's voice provided instructions. "Emergency. All relevant personnel, please return to subfloor 31. Emergency."

"What is that?" Kathy asked, rising. Markham was at the door in seconds, trying to force it open.

Rodriguez picked himself up off the floor with a wince and said, "That...sounds like an alarm. Or, you know, a steel knife through the head. Could be that."

Kathy and Markham both cast him a glance. Markham replied, "It's a security breach alarm. Subfloor 31, Rodriguez. It's the gate."

The other man's eyes grew big. "Oh, right. Shit."

Kathy joined Markham at the door. "We have to get out of here."

"Working on it," Markham said, feeling for an edge he could pry open.

"Move over," Rodriguez said from behind them. They turned to see him with a chair raised.

"Dr. Rodriguez—" Markham began, backing away.

Rodriguez swung the chair at the Plexiglas gate, but it only bounced off, one of the metal legs clocking Rodriguez just above the right eye. It split the skin above his eyebrow, drawing blood.

"Ow! Fuck!" Rodriguez dropped the chair, cradling his eye with one hand. He stumbled to one of the other chairs and flopped into it. "You're up, Sergeant. I'm out of ideas."

Markham looked on the verge of saying something, but decided against it.

Kathy turned to the sergeant. "What else can we try? That won't fail spectacularly like that, I mean?"

Markham was about to reply when the door swung open. For a moment, the three of them just stared at each other. In the next, they bolted from the glass enclosure before the door could close again.

"How..." Kathy watched the slow swing of the Plexiglas door behind them as it returned into position.

"Failsafe, maybe. More likely, another glitch Dr. Greenwood didn't account for, since usually alarms cause quarantine lockdowns." Markham shrugged. "As long as we're out, it doesn't matter. Let's get moving."

They took off for the elevator.

"Will the elevators work if the alarm is going off?" Kathy asked as Markham pushed the Down button.

"All the elevators keep working. They're on separate circuits. They're meant to protect and convey employees to safer floors in the event of a crisis," Markham said.

The elevator dinged and the doors opened. The three piled inside and Rodriguez hit the button for Subfloor 31.

"We're...doing this, then?" Kathy said after a moment of silence. "We're going through the gate?"

"Looks like it," Markham said reluctantly.
"Guess so," Rodriguez grumbled.
"Okay, then," Kathy replied.

Chapter 6

It took a long time for Carl to find his car. He hadn't run far into the wooded area on the side of the road, but it was as if the way back had been stretched and twisted out of shape, looping away from the car and the road. Carl was tired, he was frustrated, and, if he were honest with himself, he was scared—scared for Lefine and scared for himself. He had never seen his partner act like that. Why had he run off? What had he seen?

"Lefine?" he called half-heartedly. He didn't expect Lefine to answer, but was frustrated all the same when he didn't. "God damn it."

He kept shuffling through the darkness. Every time he thought he found the path, a tree would loom suddenly in front of him, its branches scratching at him and catching his clothes. An unseasonably cold wind had picked up, blowing across the back of his neck and the places where he had sweated through his shirt, making him shiver. The wind carried the whispered voices and they surrounded him, telling him all the things in his body that were slowly dying. They told him all about what they had done to Darryl Lefine, and how much what was left of him was suffering...

He shined the Maglite ahead of him and saw the car.

"Finally!" he said, just to hear a real voice, and jogged toward his car. He opened the driver's door, but before he could get inside, a hand clapped him on the shoulder. He jumped and turned, expecting to see Lefine.

It wasn't Lefine, though. It was a tall man whose face was vaguely familiar. It came to him a moment later. He knew the man from the Paragon quarantine facility. He looked around the man and into the darkness behind him. Carl thought he could make out silhouettes but his head was starting to hurt and he felt dizzy. The whispering wouldn't go away.

"Lieutenant Hornsby," the man said, "we'll need you to come with us."

"Where's Lefine? What did you do to him?" Carl said. His service revolver was in his glove compartment. The whispering told him to grab it. He glanced in that direction, just briefly, before fixing an angry gaze on the man.

"I imagine you're considering going for the gun in the glove compartment," the man said. "We've relieved you of it already. You left your door unlocked." The man held up and jingled Carl's keys.

The man was right; he hadn't bothered to lock the door when he'd bolted after Lefine—hadn't even grabbed the keys, in fact. He felt anger stirring in his chest. The whispering was like a rush of wind in his ears. It told Carl to peel off the man's eyelids with his teeth.

Perhaps the man could read his mind, because he spoke with slightly less smugness in his voice. "Lieutenant, we don't intend to hurt your partner or you. We just want to get you both somewhere safe, and quickly. You may remember meeting Dr. Greenwood? He thinks he can treat Lt. Lefine's condition, but we'd like you there to keep him calm. Would you please come with us?"

"I saw blood," Carl said. "Lefine is hurt."

"We know, Lieutenant."

"What did you people do to him? He was out there…Did you find him?"

"We can help him if you come with us."

Confused and exhausted, Carl nodded, and allowed himself to be led to a white minivan parked behind his car. When Carl glanced back, the man at his elbow said, "One of our guys will get your car home safe," and tossed Carl's keys over the hood of the minivan to another equally tall and imposing man on the other side.

Carl was ushered to the back door of the minivan and assisted up into the back seat. Despite the circumstances, it felt good to sit. The whispering receded until it finally subsided altogether. The man he had been speaking to got behind the wheel.

"Where's Lefine?" Carl asked.

"On his way to our facility. Now, Lieutenant, I have a lot to explain to you before we get to Paragon, so please listen carefully. You're about to be part of something very important."

* * * *

The elevator opened on subfloor 31, a vastly different floor than the previous one. This floor was fully constructed, with pale gray walls, drop ceilings, and overhead lighting. A long hallway lined with doors stretched out before the elevator, ending in a corridor running perpendicular. The alarm seemed to be coming from the left hallway.

Now that they were on the same floor as the gateway, the three moved with a little more reluctance toward their destination. The alarm, still calmly calling relevant personnel back to the lab in between blasts, grew deafening as they turned the corner. Kathy and Markham followed Rodriguez past offices and glass windows with drawn shades until they reached a door labeled "Suite 40 – Research." Rodriguez tried the door, but it wouldn't open.

"Lost my key card," he explained sheepishly, and Markham stepped up to use his own. Once they were buzzed in, the door opened onto pandemonium.

In the lab room, researchers were running toward another Plexiglas enclosure, this one surrounding an upright six-by-four-foot rectangle of some strange dark burgundy viscous liquid framed neatly in polished metal. Kathy assumed it was the gateway. Each portal to another dimension she saw astounded her, proof that there was so much beyond human knowledge and understanding. She wished she had more time to inspect it, but in the midst of the chaos around her, professional instincts took over, and she assessed the situation.

A solitary shoe lay just beneath the gate. The substance within rippled. Several feet away, people in lab coats conferred with others, who in turn, hurried off to confer with others. Behind and to the right of Kathy, the observation control room was a frantic crowd of researchers and scientists tapping at keys and peering into computer monitors, over shouts of confusion and frustration. No one stood near the gate, and no one noticed Kathy or her companions, who made their way uncertainly toward it.

The alarm stopped mid-shriek as a voice from the observation room came over the loudspeaker, carrying across the lab. "We lost him! He's gone! His stats went blue!" and then "Wait! Oh God…they're black. Repeat, Ravi's stats went black."

The words slowed the whole chaotic process to a defeated crawl. Markham tapped a military-looking young man of probably no more than twenty-one or twenty-two on the shoulder. The soldier snapped to attention as Markham asked, "What happened?"

The young guy answered, "We lost Ravi, sir. Either he fell, or something sucked him through the gate."

"What?" Rodriguez stepped up to the young man. "What do you mean?"

"We're not sure exactly how it happened, sir. We lost contact with the subject entirely. Best if you ask them." The young man gestured toward the observation control room.

"Dismissed," Markham said absently, and the boy saluted and walked off.

Evidently Rodriguez's professional instincts had taken over as well; he stalked off toward the observation room, Kathy and Markham at his heels.

"What happened?" Rodriguez said as he swung through the doorway. "Where's Ravi?"

For a moment, the other researchers just stood there, staring at him in awed silence. Finally, one young woman in a ponytail stepped forward. The ID badge around her neck showed a picture of her smiling, with the name KETTERING, ABIGAIL printed beneath it. "Dr. Rodriguez? Is that really...really you?"

It occurred to Kathy, as it must have occurred to Rodriguez just then, that most of Paragon probably hadn't even known Rodriguez was back, let alone expected to see him there in the lab. Rodriguez held up a hand. "Yeah, yeah, sorry. It's me. I'm back. Long story. Tell me what happened here."

Responding to the urgency in his voice, the younger researchers scurried into action, gathering the data they had been printing from the observation control room computers.

"See those black lines there?" Abigail pointed to one of the monitors. "Those are Ravi's life stats. Ravi Varma. He's a junior researcher here and—"

"I know Ravi," Rodriguez broke in a little more gently. "What happened to him?"

"He was...alone in here. We're not really sure what happened. When we heard the alarm, we came running, and..."

"And he was on the inside of the quarantine zone," said another young researcher, whose name tag read FERGUSON, GEORGE. "It looked like he was being pulled through the gate."

"Pulled through, or voluntarily passing through?"

"Pulled through," Abigail said. "By the time we got here, we saw—well, we thought we saw..." She looked to George for confirmation and he nodded. "A hand, sort of, made of that stuff from inside the gate. It had his arm all the way up by the elbow, and was pulling him."

"It was whispering," George added softly. "Like the faces do."

"His vital signs," Kathy broke in. "You said they went black. What does that mean, exactly?"

Abigail and George looked startled by her presence, as if only just noticing her standing there with Markham.

"Abigail, the signs," she repeated.

"Oh, right. Well, our monitors can only determine four statuses for implanted personnel on the other side of the gate. Honestly, I'm surprised it works at all. We tweaked those things for months—"

"And even now, they can't track *where* you are, just *how* you are," George added.

"Yes," Abigail replied. "When the researchers are alive and okay, the data appears on the screen in green. When someone dies—" Abigail's voice fluttered just slightly and she gave Markham the tiniest guilty glance, "the lines go red. That means the vitals have stopped entirely. If for some reason the implant is no longer connected to its host tissue—if it were removed, say—the lines would go black. We'd be disconnected. And then there's the status of the lost team members. Ms. Banks and her team all have blue lines."

"So what does blue mean?" Kathy asked.

The junior researchers glanced at each other and then Rodriguez before answering.

"We don't know," George said. "We aren't sure how to qualify it quite yet. We designated blue as a catch-all for..." He seemed at a loss to explain further.

"For 'Status Unknown,' right?" Rodriguez sighed. "If an individual is not able to be read as either alive or dead, for example, but somewhere in between."

"I don't understand," Kathy said.

George cleared his throat. "Well, if an individual was to be materially altered, say, or assimilated with other DNA, that would be blue. Essentially, it was meant to determine if a significant percentage of decay or alteration to the DNA caused confusion in identifying the host. We didn't really expect anyone to show up like that, though."

"But my team shows as blue? I was blue?" Rodriguez tried to meet the gazes of his junior researchers, but their discomfort was evident.

Finally, Abigail answered. "You and the rest of the team would flicker—blue, green, blue, green, then blue for a while with a burst of green, then vice-versa. It was inconsistent, hard to follow. Now they're all blue."

Kathy raised an eyebrow. "Could blue still mean they're alive, though?"

"I...I guess it could, but it would be unlikely that they would consider it much of a life," Abigail replied. Even minor alterations to our genetic code can cause fatal mutations, tumors, that sort of thing. For the nanobots to report blue, there would have to be changes so significant that the technology doesn't recognize them as fully human anymore."

"What if the people showing up as blue had parasites?" Kathy asked. "Parasites which could attach themselves in such a way as to confuse the nanobots but otherwise avoid detection, even on return trips through the gate?

"Parasites?" George looked bewildered. "Initial studies showed no signs of single- or multi-cellular animal life, no bacteria or viruses, and nothing like parasites. Plus, we already proved nothing organic survives coming through here."

"Depends on how you define organic, kid," Rodriguez replied. He turned to Kathy. "I'm sure of it now. They let me go. The Wraiths. They sent me back because it was the only way to come through."

"Sure sounds that way," Kathy said.

"What are they doing now?" Markham asked suddenly.

"I'm sorry?" Abigail looked startled again. Kathy decided those poor junior researchers probably often looked startled or confused in a place like that.

Markham looked at her impatiently. "The Green Team. Dr. Rodriguez's team. What are their statuses doing now?"

"Oh, right. We're monitoring them over here," George said gesturing to a laptop on a corner of the observation room counter. Another junior researcher, a blond boy with round, nervous eyes behind thin-rimmed glasses, looked nearly panicked by their approach.

"Owen, show them," George said.

The blond boy muttered unintelligibly to himself as his fingers darted around the keyboard in front of him. The monitor pulled up several lines in peaks and valleys reminiscent of a lie detector printout. Each line was labeled with a name and number:

Banks, Claire 032764
Gordon, Richard034519
Rodriguez, Jose037683
Vogel, Terrance032280

Jose's line was black and flat. The others offered a steady output of jagged blue line, out of unison and with no seeming pattern, rhyme, or reason. Kathy watched her companions study the screen. Markham's face betrayed nothing of what he was thinking. Jose, however, looked dismayed. Kathy suspected he was staring at his own line, gone black. He was there, alive and well, and to the best of their knowledge, still carried the nanochip inside him. He should have come up green, but he didn't. To the computer, the technology that he had no doubt trusted his whole professional life, he was lost, still missing in the world beyond.

"We have to go back," he said softly, then turned to Kathy and Markham. The look in his eyes was sad and sort of desperate. "We have to find them."

"You're sure you want to? No one would blame you for bowing out," Kathy told him. "They can't compel you to go."

"No," Jose agreed, "but they can." He nodded at the screen. "It's right there, Kathy. They aren't the only ones who are lost, you get me?"

Kathy nodded. She believed she did understand him. Some might have called it closure that Jose needed, but it was more than that. It was the need to know for sure just how much of himself was left on the far side of the gate, and if he could—or should even want to—reclaim it. He needed to know in a figurative and maybe even literal sense how much of his own line had really gone blue.

Markham clapped a meaty hand on Jose's shoulder. "We've got your back, man."

"We'll be watching out for you," George slipped in softly. "All of you, if you're going back through."

"We'll do everything we can on our end," Abigail added.

"Let's go, then," Jose said, and strode out into the lab.

The defeated slump had passed, and once again, the lab was a flurry of new activity. All around them, scientists and researchers rushed around with clipboards and instruments which, to Kathy's untrained eye, they seemed to bring close to the gateway's quarantine chamber but never inside of it. Kathy guessed they were looking to evaluate the new data and possibly run some tests. Their excitement was quickly eclipsing their fear. Something had made contact from the other side, or from within the substance of the gate itself, and that was big news. To them, it was probably not unlike a piñata filled with mysteries of other universes, just waiting for them to crack it open.

Kathy wondered what Ravi's disappearance would mean for their little scheduled trip through the gateway. Clearly, there were forces acting on the situation that Paragon would have to reevaluate.

She didn't have long to wonder. The three of them hadn't covered much ground between the observation control room and the gate when they saw Greenwood heading their way with a confused-looking middle-aged man in tow. The man was paunchy and balding on top, but had a pleasant enough face, the kind of face that could be warm when he smiled. Kathy bet that pleasant face could also look intimidating when he wanted it to. The man moved like a cop, took in his surroundings like a cop, and was regarding Greenwood like a cop might regard a murder suspect.

"Oh, you made it," Greenwood said, as if their escape from his quarantine chamber had been no more impressive a feat than their showing up at his house for dinner. He didn't look annoyed or even surprised, and again Kathy felt the jarring aspect of his unconventional personality. The odd half-smile that accompanied his words only served to reinforce to Kathy that there was something wrong with the man—wrong with the whole situation. Cases that were recommended to her through the Network, the covert group of occult specialists she was affiliated with, were always vetted for her protection, and she trusted the Network implicitly. Still, she couldn't help finding that she most definitely did not trust Greenwood or where this case was going.

"Please don't let that most unfortunate business with Mr. Varma alarm you," Greenwood said as he approached with the confused man in tow. Behind them, four very large and well-armed men hovered in silence, each with a backpack dwarfed by the meaty hand that held it. "We have our best people on it. It doesn't affect anything regarding the important matters we've discussed."

"You just lost a researcher to a force you know nothing about," Jose said, eyeing the large men behind Greenwood with suspicion. "Not on that side of the gate, where anything can happen, but over here, where you're supposed to be the first line of defense. How can you say it doesn't affect anything?"

"Dr. Rodriguez has a point," Markham said. "I'm no scientist, but I would think proof that there's something from the other side capable of crossing through, of making unwanted, even hostile contact, would warrant some re-evaluation."

"It doesn't change the urgency or importance of your mission," Greenwood replied in that disconcertingly calm voice. "Preliminary evidence shows that what took Mr. Varma is simply another incarnation of the faces, a manifestation of the parasitic infection. It was a unique occurrence. Mr. Varma's proximity to the gate and individual genetic predisposition to the substance therein led to another unfortunate but unforeseeable incident, but one, as I stated, that was particular to Mr. Varma. If anything, the incident underscores the urgency of your departure."

"What about our safety?" Jose asked.

"What about it? I don't see how anything has materially changed in that regard."

Jose threw up his hands. "Do you understand the bullshit that falls out of your face, or do you just keep throwing words together until the people around you stop talking?"

"Jose—" Kathy cautioned, glancing at the big men, but inwardly, she was smiling. She'd been pretty close to saying something similar herself.

Greenwood ignored them. "I understand your renewed anxiety regarding the journey. I do. However, it's more important than ever that you cross through and make contact with Claire Banks and her colleagues. Obviously, the situation on both sides of the gate is growing more complicated. Of course we want you to be safe, but we need you in there, gathering information—information, I might remind you, which is crucial to the protection not only of the Green Team, but of humanity in general." He gestured to the man behind him, whose expression of confusion had fully morphed into suspicion beneath a veneer of genuine awe and unease. "This is Officer Carl Hornsby. You may be aware that Officer Hornsby and his partner were first responders on the scene when poor Dr. Van Houten expired. Officer, this is Kathy Ryan, Dr. Jose Rodriguez, and Sergeant John Markham. You'll be going with them."

Carl, who had still been taking in the details of the lab itself, pulled his gaze away from the gate and shook hands with each of them. "Is…is that it?" he asked, pointing toward the gate. It was quiet now, a placid upright pool of dark burgundy with static swirls of color. It was the first time Kathy had gotten a good look at the gate herself. She had seen gateways before—too often for any one person, if she thought about it—but she'd never seen one quite like that. She supposed it was because most of the gates she'd seen were ones opened from the other side, through magickal means. This was, perhaps, the first she'd seen opened from this side, through scientific procedure.

"That's it," Greenwood said.

"Okay, so why me?" Carl asked. "These three, I understand. You explained that much, but I still don't see how I fit in here. I'm not a scientist or a military guy, and I don't know anything about all this occult stuff… about dimensions and whatever."

"Certain…less scientific but perhaps more experience-driven data—that occult stuff—suggests four of you stand a better chance than three, and my superiors have instructed us to integrate all data into our research. Further, Officer Hornsby, much like them, you appear to be immune to the infection's mutation," Greenwood replied. "And you are a man of questions that need answers."

"Look, you've been feeding me bullshit since before I even got here," Hornsby said. "Your men told me I was here to help with Lefine's treatment. I went against my gut and trusted them and let them bring me here. Then you bring me here and tell me that the only way to cure my partner was to go through the gate and gather information to fill in the gaps of your knowledge. I'm not an idiot. Of course I see the absurdity of sending a townie cop to do the job of trained military and scientific personnel. But again, I went with it to get some answers, to try to understand what the hell was going on. Now you're telling me that some voodoo plan of yours has magically added me to the roster of other people you're lying to and screwing over?"

Greenwood sighed, and his expression darkened. "You know, Lieutenant, you've been a problem from the beginning. We assumed you would succumb to the physical infection like your partner did and save us the trouble of figuring out what to do with you, but you surprised us. Luckily, the occult data gave us an option—helped us kill two birds with one stone, so to speak."

All four of them turned to Greenwood, surprised. Kathy's instinct for trouble ratcheted up.

Greenwood tapped a couple of buttons on the device around his wrist, and the glass door enclosing the gate opened. Kathy noticed that suddenly, the very large men, larger even than Markham, surrounded them. Each of these mammoth men took hold of the left arms of Kathy and her group and pressed something circular and metallic against their shoulders.

Markham, who had been assigned the largest of the men, evidently because of his size and strength, made to yank his arm free, but his handler held him fast. Jose managed, "What the fu—" and then there was a brief little gust of wind from inside the metallic things. In the next second, Kathy felt a tiny spot on her skin burning, and in the moment after that, the large men and their devices had retreated to their original position behind the old scientist.

Markham drew his service weapon and pointed it at Greenwood, but the scientist looked unperturbed. Immediately, the big men had their weapons drawn as well and pointed at Markham.

"Please don't make this difficult," Greenwood said. "You've only been inoculated and implanted with the vital stats chip. You've also been implanted with an updated data chip which we believe will relay information about your environment as your body and mind perceive it, allowing us to map the world a little better and keep an eye on your whereabouts."

"Who the hell said you could implant us with anything?" Beneath Markham's practiced military calm was a smoldering anger. The look in his eyes indicated that he very much wanted to pull the trigger.

"Sergeant, please, lower your gun," Kathy said. She didn't think the men would hesitate for a second in taking Markham down, and she didn't want to see that.

"It's for your protection," Greenwood said, looking nettled.

"And what does any of that have to do with protecting us?" Jose interjected. "Your chips—they don't work so well."

Greenwood smiled. For the first time, Kathy thought, it was genuine—and she hated the smug, seething disdain in it. "You really are exhausting, the lot of you. I have one goal, Mr. Rodriguez, and that is to get you through that gate by whatever means necessary. I tried to be pleasant, to allay your fears and project genuine concern for your well-being, but you are all beginning to try my patience. The fact is, you are four uniquely qualified information gatherers, both because of your evident immunity to progression of the entity-driven infection and because of your individual training and background. As far as some of the prevailing cooler heads at Paragon are concerned, our sending you through the gate is a win-win. If you survive there on the other side, that is beneficial to us. It is in our best interest that you stay alive as long as possible, so that you can bring us back more information about that other world. If you don't, it would be a loss to science, but then four loose ends who know way more about MK-Ostium than anyone at Paragon is comfortable with would have been dealt with. Nevertheless, believe it or not, the company does want you to return. I, personally, don't care one way or the other about any of you. I believe we can develop all we need from what we already have. Of course, your recovery is not my problem anyway—that's the yellow team's concern. I'm content to let your little sycophantic underlings scurrying about like mice in the observation control room worry about that."

"And you think you can coerce us into helping with any of this?" Markham held the gun at Greenwood's face while he kept close watch on the men whose guns were pointed at him.

"Oh, I think you know I can."

"He knows we're carriers," Kathy said. "Even if we weren't before, he can see to it we are before we leave here. We can infect our loved ones, family, coworkers. We can't leave the facility without neutralizing the entities, or we'll infect every place we go. And Greenwood here will hold the quarantine and neutralizing processes over our heads until we bring him what he wants."

Greenwood winked at her. "Smart girl," he said. "Of course, if you do this for us you have the word in writing of the CEO of Paragon himself that we'll neutralize the parasites and eradicate all elements of the infection before you leave this facility. Either way, the problem will end with you."

Markham finally lowered his gun, but that simmering rage still lit his eyes.

"I knew something about this didn't make sense," Rodriguez said. "If you can neutralize the parasites now with tech we have in the lab, what information are we really going through the gate to get? You can't tell me you actually care about Claire, Terry, and Rick, so what are you looking for over there?"

Greenwood glared at him. "We need to know for sure what the blue status means. Your personal data isn't enough. And we need to know how the parasitic carrier system works."

"Jesus," Markham said, the dawn of realization in his voice. "You *want* us to bring something else back through. You said it yourself. You need carriers because it's the only way anything over there can survive here. You want to weaponize whatever we carry back to this side of the gate."

Greenwood didn't answer. He didn't have to. The superiority in his expression had hardened in defensiveness.

"You son of a bitch," Jose said.

"You're all just making this up as you go along, aren't you?" Kathy said to Greenwood. "Paragon hired me to keep casualties to a minimum, until you saw an opportunity to repurpose me. You just couldn't give up the chance to make money off a biohazard."

"It's not about the money," Greenwood said, and strangely enough, Kathy believed he thought he was being sincere. "If not us, then someone else, some other corporation or country less interested in our well-being will come along and thoroughly explore every part of the place, every stone and overturned leaf, for profiteering. We got here first, but do you think the member states of CERN are far behind us? We're simply staking a claim and protecting our interests before the real people holding the purse strings do."

For Greenwood, it might very well have been the scientific discovery he was after, and the misguided belief that Paragon might really be able to use alien biological agents to protect the country. He didn't strike her as that naïve, but she supposed it was possible.

"If you've genuinely convinced yourself that you're doing this to protect the country, then I feel sorry for you."

"Don't feel sorry for me, dear lady," Greenwood said, that unnatural, unflustered expression returning to his face. "I'm not going through the gate."

While they had been talking, the five large men who had inoculated them had encircled them again. All of them still had their guns drawn, and were still carrying small backpacks in their free hands.

"Greenwood, think about what you're doing," Kathy said. "Think about what sending us through is going to lead to. You've lost control of this whole project."

Greenwood regarded her coldly. "Thank you, Ms. Ryan, but for the time being, your input regarding the future direction of the project is not needed. Your consulting might be better utilized beyond the gate."

The large men turned their guns on Kathy and Jose, who reluctantly backed toward the gate's open quarantine doorway. Markham and Officer Hornsby held their ground despite the guns pointing at their faces. However, seeing Kathy and Jose ushered into the quarantine room and so close to the gate ended whatever standoff Markham and Hornsby were planning. They grudgingly took the backpacks they were handed and then they, too, joined Kathy and Jose inside the gate's quarantine chamber.

"I sincerely wish you luck," Greenwood called.

Jose flipped him the middle finger.

"Who first?" Kathy asked.

"I'll go," Markham said, and with a short, quick breath, he plunged into the swirls.

"Age before beauty," Hornsby said, smiling awkwardly at Kathy. He, too, took a breath and then dove through the gate after Markham.

"Ladies first," Jose said, gesturing to the gate. He looked terrified.

"See you on the other side," Kathy said and gave him a small smile. Then she forced herself to move forward, to surrender to crossing the gateway. She felt the wet-not-wetness as the swirling fluid engulfed her, obliterating sound and light, and then she was falling.

Chapter 7

The falling sensation lasted only a few seconds before she found herself on the spongy, mossy floor of an immense forest. She hadn't landed, exactly, but she was on solid ground. A quick inspection reassured her that all her body parts were present and intact and that there were no injuries, and she exhaled in relief, the tension in her chest unknotted. It felt good to let the air out of her lungs, as if finally emerging from beneath the depths of an ocean and into the air again.

Markham stood nearby, brushing himself off, as did Hornsby. A moment later there was a flash and a little pop and Jose was crouching next to her. She and Jose rose, and each were handed a backpack.

"Everyone okay?" she asked, unzipping the little canvas bag. In it were bags of nuts, granola bars, bottles of water, baggies of vegetables and fruit slices, and packages of jerky as well as a few small rolls of self-stick bandages, a small sewing kit, tiny flashlights, and a tube of antibiotic salve.

"Fine, I think," Hornsby said. "Is this...are we...?"

"This is Hesychia," Jose said spreading out his arms. The terror in his face had dissipated some, but it had been replaced with a loose, almost reckless look of despair. "Welcome to the new world."

It was just like Claire had described in her journal notes. Kathy took in the large, fern-like plants tucked against the ivy-laced trunks of enormous leafless trees. Plump fruit hung from the bone-white branches of most of the trees, fleshy in color and appearance, with a soft white fuzz. There were no sounds of birds or animals, nothing but the gentle breeze swaying the branches.

Here, Kathy, noticed, there were no discernible faces in the vegetation, which seemed to her like a very good sign. The woods, at least, seemed safe.

The four made their way to the edge of the forest and gazed out on what looked like a limitless landscape, with a great indigo ocean to the east and sharp, steely mountains to the north. There was a small bright green flag at the edge of the woods, ostensibly put there by the Green Team to mark the location of the gate so that they could return. Between the forest's edge and the mountains were a few miles, at least, of brilliantly-colored wildflowers of uncommon shades of pink and purple and blue. The air smelled faintly like jasmine and honeysuckle, though so far as Kathy could tell, neither flower grew in the field before them.

It was the sight to the northwest, though, which ultimately arrested their attention. There was the immense stone city, the dead city, that Claire had mentioned in her notes and Jose had described getting lost in.

Hornsby gaped. "Oh my God."

"What?" Markham's hand was on his gun.

"I've dreamed of that place. That city—the city with the twisting streets and the faces and whispering and—" Hornsby turned to the others. "That's where they want us to go, huh? Right into the mouth of the monster."

"We thought it was abandoned a long time ago. I mean, I guess it was, but it isn't empty. Something else lives there now." Rodriguez gazed at the great stone walls. "That's where I lost my team."

"Then I guess that's where we start," Kathy said. "The sooner we give them what they want, the sooner we can find a way out of here. Jose, you want to lead?"

Jose shrugged. "Won't do much good," he said. "We were lost the whole time we were in there."

With a small smile, Kathy began walking.

"Whoa, wait," Jose said, jogging to catch up. "Fine. Fine, I'll lead. Just hold up, huh? No one goes anywhere alone." He turned to the two men following behind him. "No one, got it? No heroes."

They came up on the massive stone wall that Jose had described. The individual stones, a kind of charcoal gray with faintly glowing, translucent blue veins that tapered to green, struck Kathy as ancient, piled high and mortared by some long-gone masons. Some stones were worn smooth, while others retained an uneven roughness, almost like pockmarks, catching the waning light from the sun as it sank toward the horizon. Kathy estimated that the wall had to be hundreds of feet high, imposing and impressive at the same time. She couldn't resist the urge to reach out and touch stone that had been handled once by sentient inter-dimensional beings.

There had been so many cases where she'd seen the destructive work of such beings, but rarely did she get to admire any of their creations. So much of her job was spent keeping them out, and it was strange for her to be let in, such as it were, to invade their world and to glimpse their notion of home and the everyday, even if it was simply an echo of the past. These were not the structures of beasts intent on destruction. There was permanence here, not the work of dimension-hoppers looking to suck a new world dry. In a way, it made her sad, or at least wistful, that there had once been a civilization that Earth might have been glad to invite in, to exchange ideas with and learn from.

Whatever claimed the dead city as its own now—whatever the Wraiths were—was something Kathy had experience with, most likely. The kind that fed, that destroyed, that ravaged whatever it touched. It should have been a relief, she supposed, to know her experience would probably prepare her for what they were up against, but it ignited that despair, that hopelessness that even vodka lately had trouble putting down.

The stone vibrated almost imperceptibly beneath her fingertips. Almost.

"You okay, Ms. Ryan?" Markham was at her shoulder, and the other two men were looking at her with concern.

She forced a smile. "I'm fine. Let's get moving. It's getting dark."

The gigantic city gate was parted like arms reaching out to embrace them—or crush them—and it, too, was as Jose described. A complex series of scrolls and arabesques, its iridescent blue metal caught up the dusky light in its swirls like the colors of the gateway had swirled in the burgundy. Kathy couldn't be sure, but she thought the city gates might have been emitting a faint hum, like they, too, were vibrating.

The four of them paused at the opening, taking in the height of the gates. They were dizzying from that angle, so much so that they seemed to cause the illusion of unnatural slants and bends.

"Is it me, or does anyone else feel like that opening is a trap? Like we'll go to step through and get zapped or smushed or something?" Hornsby rubbed his gut. "Like the city knows we're here, and it's waiting for us."

"You're not wrong there," Jose replied. "It knows we're here. I'm sure of that. But those gates will let us through. The city wants us to come right in. It can't do anything to us out here."

"It's just ruins," Markham said. "Just stones, and correct me if I'm wrong, Dr. Rodriguez, but the stones didn't test as living entities."

"No," Jose agreed with reluctance. "They didn't, Sergeant. But that doesn't mean the city isn't alive." He glanced at Markham. "In a way."

The rose and lavender hues of the sky had begun to fade toward a dark purplish-blue. From beyond the gates, the lights came on in the dead city. They cast a soft bluish glow on the stony streets, stretching disjointed—

dismembered, Kathy thought—shadows around the buildings in such a way that it was difficult to gauge the shape of them. They were enormous, though. There was no doubt about that.

"Come on," she said, and led the party between the gates and under the immense stone arch. There was a moment as they passed dead center of the arch, between twin bars of metal, that the humming got louder, and Kathy could almost see or imagine she saw, the metal scrolls vibrating. Then they were inside the city.

A thunderous clang behind them made them jump. They turned to see the gates had closed. Kathy guessed they were also on some mechanized timer, since she hadn't felt any wind strong enough to blow them shut.

If the gates had been disconcerting with their size, the buildings of the city certainly continued the pattern. Kathy understood what Jose meant when he'd said it was hard to tell how tall they actually were. Staring too long at them, trying to put their lines and angles right in her head, hurt Kathy's eyes after a while. They leaned at impossible angles that changed as soon as she shifted her point of view. What she thought might have been doorways or arches pinched in the middle until she stepped a foot or so to the left or right. Few of the buildings had doors, and although the interiors were dark, Kathy could see bare walls and some furniture, mostly tables and chairs, towering over stone floors.

The streets were wide as well, and so far as she could see, none of them ran a straight line for more than a few hundred feet or so. Like the buildings, trying to follow the curves of the streets for too long was dizzying.

Still, the more she looked at the irregularly smooth- and rough-hewn surfaces of the buildings and the rises and dips of the stones in the streets, the more she was sure of something else Jose had mentioned—the notion of movement, of life, of being watched by…by what? The twin moons had risen, and the way certain surfaces caught the light, they did look like faces—scowling, laughing, talking faces that pulled together in one step and fell apart as soon as her perspective changed. She wanted to believe it was just a trick of the moonlight, an optical illusion like the face on Mars, but she couldn't quite pull it off, even just to herself. She thought it was more like those pictures places like Spencer Gifts used to sell, the ones that looked like nothing but lines of patterned color until you relaxed your gaze and caught it just right, and suddenly, there was a picture under the picture, a face, maybe, a thing that had been there all along, waiting to be seen.

As she looked at her companions, she got the impression from the way they warily eyed their surroundings that they were seeing the faces, too. Greenwood had called them an infection, a kind of parasite, but here in their world, their natural habitat, they were more like predators stalking them silently, camouflaged by the strange stone, following their movements and waiting for a chance to whisper their nightmares on the wind.

"How you boys holding up?" Kathy asked.

"This place is wrong," Hornsby said. "Everything about it—the shape of it, the texture of it, even the colors—it's all wrong."

"I agree with Officer Hornsby," Markham said.

"We shouldn't be here," Jose added. "None of us should. Greenwood was wrong about this. About us." He didn't specify what Greenwood was wrong about, not that there wasn't plenty to choose from, but Kathy noted that he stopped short of mentioning that Greenwood might have been wrong about any of them truly being immune. Prolonged exposure, the old man had said, made no difference to those who were simply carriers. Was that true? Did Greenwood know that for sure, or had he just told them what he thought they needed to hear to pacify them before coming to Hesychia?

Jose turned to them suddenly. "I'm sorry," he said. "I'm sorry any of you are involved in this at all. This was our fault—Paragon's, the Green Team's. My fault. We meant to do good, and…" He shook his head. "I'm sorry. I just…I'm sorry."

Markham nodded. "You couldn't have known about all this."

"No one blames you, Jose," Hornsby said. "You didn't put us here. Greenwood did. And he's going to pay for that."

"Yes," Kathy agreed. "He is. You can't carry that kind of guilt around with you, Jose—not in this business. I've been doing this a long time, and you know what guilt becomes?"

She thought Jose glanced at her scar; to be fair, she couldn't be sure, but she expected him to, and might have assumed he had. People always had questions about the scar across her eye. She went with it anyway. "Scars," she said. "Scars and vodka bottles stashed around the house, and taking suicide jobs just to see whether it will be your guilt or your stubbornness that will wear you down first."

Jose didn't reply, but his thoughtful expression suggested she'd sent him off thinking of his own scars, and what inter-dimensional work did to the body and soul after a while.

"Speaking of scars," Hornsby said, "I don't mean to be rude or insensitive, but…" His voice trailed off.

"But you're wondering about my scar?"

He looked sheepishly at her and shrugged. It might have been the earnest, un-police-like, almost boyish innocence in the question, or the fact that he was candid enough to ask instead of staring or going to obvious lengths *not* to stare. Whatever it was, Kathy smiled.

"I was a teenager. I'd been poking around in my big brother's closet, and I found his trophies."

"Like, sports trophies? What, was he particularly protective of them or something?" Jose asked. The other men said nothing, but they were listening just as intently.

"No, not sports trophies, but he certainly was protective of them. My brother…he, ah…he kept finger bones. One each from the women he raped, mutilated, carved, stabbed, and dumped like trash in the woods. In the end, I think they convicted him of six, but he claimed there were sixteen of them. The cult he belonged to encouraged him. Facilitated his hunting."

Hornsby nodded slowly. The look on Jose's face was of pained sympathy. There was no shock in Markham's eyes, either—a man like him had probably seen his share of evil—but there was empathy, she thought. Empathy, and not pity—no pity from any one of them, and Kathy appreciated that. It was encouragement to continue.

"Anyway, it had been hot and humid one night and my t-shirts were in the wash, so I went looking for one in my brother's closet where he kept his little box of human finger bones. He caught me. He knew, I guess, from the expression on my face that I'd found them. I think he wanted to kill me that night. He said he didn't, that he only wanted to cut me." She took a breath. "And he did cut me. I think if my dad and the sheriff hadn't come home when they did…" She tried to chuckle, but it came out as a dry, brittle sound. "Anyway, I had no idea until then what he was. My dad suspected, but not me. Most people don't really believe family members could just not know, but it's true. He was my big brother, and he usually looked out for me. I loved him. I'd tried to take care of him after our mother…anyway, I had no idea. I moved out and went to college for criminology and he's been locked up in the Connecticut-Newlyn Hospital for the Criminally Insane ever since. It was his ties to a cult, I think, that landed him there and not in jail. Like his fellow cult members, he possessed a genuine, honest belief that forces outside of space and time had protected him in his killing for so long—made him sort of invisible. Once, he told me a story about them, and gave me reason to believe it. It's one of the reasons why I do what I do."

"Do the scars and vodka or the suicide jobs?" Markham asked.

"All of it. It's all one and the same, really. Jose, is that your library over there on the right?" With that, story time was over. She didn't know why she'd told these three strangers anything about herself or her brother or her scar. Normally, even close friends, the few that she had, wouldn't have unearthed so much information from her. But here beneath alien stars and within the empty corridors of the dead city, she felt disconnected from the old world and its little personal brutalities. The usual mortifying regret that would have accompanied sharing so much of herself was utterly absent there.

Still, she was done talking about it and thought the tone of her answer conveyed that effectively.

Jose followed her gaze to a large, left-leaning building slouching over the street and his face lit with recognition. None of the buildings they had come across were marked with anything like writing, pictographic or otherwise, but that building featured something like a sign. The library was perched at the top of broad steps that ran beneath an arch between pillars, and on the arch was something vaguely resembling a slate lined with runes, all carved in stone.

"That's it! I mean, we shouldn't have come across it so soon, but yeah, there it is." Forgetting his mistrust of the place, a little of what Kathy assumed was the old Jose—the scientist and researcher excited by discovery—returned as he studied the exterior of the building. Turning to the others, he said, "Want to pop inside for a sec? Really, just for a second. Just to look around." At their hesitation, he added, "To be thorough in our search, of course," and grinned at them.

Even Markham cracked a small smile. "Not too long. Don't know if I like the idea of being...enclosed in any of these buildings overnight."

"Sure, let's take a look," Hornsby said. "How many people can say they got to visit a library on an alien world in another universe?"

The three men turned to Kathy. "Lead the way," she said to Rodriguez, who nodded and headed for the arch. As Kathy passed under it, she got a sense of what Markham had meant by being enclosed in the stone. Despite its large spaces and lofty openings, passing through structures like gates or arches left her with a feeling of being crowded, of being herded toward something. She also felt a sense of finality, as if all decisions from that point on were irreversible and probably wrong. She could only imagine the cloying, claustrophobic feeling that passing *into* a structure here would induce.

She kept those ideas to herself, though, as they crossed the door-less threshold of the library building. In the gloomy interior, she thought she caught a humming like that from the gates, but at less of a tooth-grating frequency. This was more like the *ohm* sounds people made when meditating, and would actually have been somewhat pleasant, if not for a rumbling undercurrent of something deeper and rougher beneath. It seemed crazy to Kathy to think it, but she couldn't shake the feeling that the darkness itself was rumbling, weighing down the humming walls with its dourness.

Where they stood might have once been a lobby, although it was hard to tell for sure. There were great stone slabs that loomed over them like dream-distorted reference desks, and hanging above those were drop-shaped globules of what looked like cracked glass. These pulsed faintly with a turquoise light, but it was a weak glow that would only have illuminated part of the desktop; none of the globules' lights reached very far, and none managed to penetrate the shadow-swathed bases of the slabs.

In the far wall opposite them was another doorway, a mammoth irregular opening. If Kathy had had to pigeonhole the shape, she would have said a gothic arch came closest, but even that was not quite right. It made her wonder again what the architects of such a place had been like and what shapes they themselves might have been.

Beyond the opening, the darkness was too thick to make out anything. Similar doorways opened in the left and right walls.

"This way," Jose said, and led them toward the back wall arch. "Those other rooms just have broken shelving. Not much to see. But the books are through here."

Their footsteps, like Jose's voice, echoed in the cavernous front room. It made Kathy feel on display. Kathy wouldn't have been able to explain it well, but she knew she was being watched, just as she had known in the Müllers' living room and outside the library in the streets of the dead city; the walls were watching. And the ceiling. Their rough surfaces, as well as the massive tiles of the floor, did odd things with the scant light and the shadows. They stretched and pulled, pinched and shoved, until shapes that shouldn't have been shapes formed in the substances of the building materials. There were faces there sometimes, or parts of faces, slack-jawed, or laughing mouths and watching eyes. Sometimes, there were even outstretched hands, like something was trying to break through...

Kathy turned her gaze away from the surroundings and focused on Jose's back. It didn't seem healthy or wise to fixate on anything else just then.

When they entered the back room, the humming instantly stopped. The sudden silence left behind stopped them short. It was as if they had interrupted something. It was possible, Kathy supposed, that the acoustics in this world were different, but...

After several seconds of anxious waiting, they relaxed a little, and Kathy was afforded a chance to look around. The room was curiously hexagonal, its walls lined with rows of shelves which seemed hewn from the stone of the walls themselves. The rows spiraled upward for at least a hundred, maybe a hundred and fifty feet or more, so much so that the darkness gathered at the ceiling swallowed the uppermost ones. Some of the shelves had fallen, and Kathy could see that they were made of some kind of slate; the broken pieces had fractured into sharp layers of shards that stuck up from the floor like stalagmites.

Most of the shelves still standing were empty and somewhat reminiscent of the Paris catacombs, minus the bodies and coffins. But on some of the shelves were the book-like things Jose had described. They looked to Kathy like loosely layered slabs much thinner than the shelves, usually three stacked one on top of the other. Kathy assumed the two outermost, made of polished stone, were kind of like book covers, and the middle, which appeared to be made from something pulpier, like wood, must have been the page from which the three-dimensional runes Jose had described must have sprung. The book-things were enormous, large enough to squash a person if they fell from their shelves, but a scattering on the floor showed smudges where dust had been wiped away, presumably by Jose and the Green Team. Kathy found she was excited to check them out, to see the records of that ancient civilization even if she couldn't read them.

Jose reached the books on the floor before the others, and put his back into trying to flip open the front cover. He gestured Markham over. "Sergeant, could you lend a hand please?"

Markham shouldered the other side of the front cover, and together, the men heaved the book open. Right away, the woody texture of the inner page-slate began to ripple, and tiny fireworks of light shot up off the pages. These flickered a moment and then formed faintly shimmering three-dimensional runes.

Kathy frowned. There was something familiar about those runes. What was it?

"See? This was the first one we found. I'd kill to know what those runes say." Jose folded his arms over his chest, pleased in spite of himself, as he studied the runes. "Not that I'd read this out loud, of course. God only knows what would happen in this world or ours if those runes were read aloud. But I can't help it—I want to know."

Kathy thought she did. As she found individual characters she recognized, the pit of her stomach grew cold. This...this could be bad.

Hornsby reached out a tentative hand toward the runes and trickled his fingers through the nearest one. It rippled like water for a second and then regained its shape. "Incredible," he said. "I can see why Paragon would find this fascinating. These runes could be cures for diseases, solutions to energy and fuel shortages. Hell, they could be farming techniques that could feed the world."

"Or plans for superweapons that could destroy it," Markham replied. "Keep in mind, Paragon has interests in munitions manufacturing. They would weaponize those wildflowers out there in the field if they thought they could."

"Jose," Kathy asked, "did you check more than one book? Are they all in this language?"

"All the ones here," he answered gesturing at the spilled stacks of books around them. "We recognized a few recurring runes. Why?"

"It took me a while to recognize them, but I have seen these runes before. They predate nearly all worlds, all civilizations. They are the first language, used by the races of the first universes, the Travelers, even the greater and lesser creator gods. This language has been picked up by the newer creatures that move between dimensions—Hollowers, Scions, Hinshing, those kinds of creatures."

She looked up from giving voice to her thoughts. She'd nearly forgotten the men there listening. They looked confused, and reasonably so. This was far beyond even Jose's experience. "What I'm saying is, this could be bad. These Wraiths, whatever they are, could be much older than anything I've ever dealt with. Much more powerful. Paragon has no idea what they might have tapped into here."

For several moments, no one responded. Finally, Jose said, "Can you read these runes? Do you know what they say? Maybe there's something here that can help us."

"Like what?" Markham said.

"Medical books about illnesses could, theoretically, serve as a primer for those looking to make people sick, right? Books about volatile chemicals can be used to build explosives. We do it to each other all the time. Maybe these ancient writers gave us something to work with—something we can use to fight back when we come across the Wraiths." To Kathy, Jose said, "So, can you read any of this?"

"Very, very little of it. I know a few basics about the language but very little specifics. For example, I know the runes generally stand for complex concepts, such as notions about emotion, communication, and interaction. Some, it's believed, stand for concepts about the nature of time and space that we have no understanding of yet. We've determined that some are male characters and some are female, some are aggressive, some are passive, and some are neutral."

She considered the runes that hovered in front of her a moment, and then pointed. "Given their structure, those two are opposites. We think that one means some kind of beginning or birth, a predawn, maybe, or darkness before something is. That one over there would be the end of something, the fire of sunset, the end glow. Those two took us years, literally, to translate and we're still only guessing based on context of placement. Now, this one we think might be a verb—to run or to dance, something with active movement. And that one we're pretty sure is referring to the Convergence, the space between dimensions. But beyond that..." Kathy shrugged apologetically. "The language is still pretty new to my colleagues and especially to me. I can't really make out most of the specific ideas different runes stand for."

"Wow," Jose said, floored. "That's fucking amazing. We could have the story of the creation of a universe here, or the birth of a god..."

Kathy didn't want to dampen Jose's excitement; she knew what he was feeling. It was because she understood, though, and because she had seen that same look in his eyes before that she added, "My colleagues and I only learn them so that we can prevent the inevitable disasters that would result from people using them. Many old occult books refer to these as the language of doing and undoing. The characters themselves have power separate from the phrases and sentences in which they might be used. It may well be the language of creation, but it's also the language of destruction. And like you said, we can't begin to know what kind of power we'd be trying to wield in speaking them."

"Like a toddler trying to control a firehose," Hornsby said.

Jose nodded. "I get you. I do. And don't worry. It's proof enough for me that there's more to life and death than just coincidence and accident and atoms bumping into each other. In the end, what more does a scientist strive for than that?"

"If we're talking about a scientist like Greenwood, it won't be enough until all the words in all these books are translated," Kathy said. "Weaponizing those face-things would be bad enough. Could you imagine if any one power got its hands on a word that could undo the existence of an entire country?"

"Let's get out of here," Markham said. He looked at the book and the runes like they were vipers. "I think we've seen enough. And to be honest, I feel like I'm drowning in here."

"Wait a sec," Hornsby said. He was eyeing the upper shelves suspiciously. "Let's just hang back a minute."

"Why? Kathy asked.

"Because I think there's something up there that's been watching us, and it seems attracted to movement," Hornsby said.

"What are you talking about?" Rodriguez asked. "There aren't any faces in here. This whole goddamn city is one big mindfuck, yeah, but we were in here for hours last time, and—"

"I can see them," Hornsby said, his voice hushed. His gaze was fixed on the gloom far above their heads. "When we move, they move. They don't seem to be able to hear or see us—at least, not see us very well—but they do seem to respond to movement."

"What are they?" Kathy asked. "The faces?"

"No...no, I don't think they have any faces at all."

The others followed Hornsby's gaze and waited in silence. The gloom did seem to be moving up there, ebbing and flowing, waxing and waning like a tide over the upper shelves. Kathy didn't think that was what Hornsby had meant, though. Then out of the corner of one eye, she saw a blur of mushroom-paleness dart from one stone slab to another.

"See? See that up there?" Hornsby was pacing in a small back-and-forth line, his eyes on the spot where Kathy had seen the shape.

"I saw it," she said.

"Where? What was it?" Jose crossed the room to the lower shelves below and looked up. "I don't see anything," he added, turning back to them.

Suddenly, the shape above him screeched. The blur leaped off the shelf, landed without a sound between Jose and Kathy, and looked up at her.

"Oh my God," Markham said.

The thing crouching in front of her did not, in fact, have a face. Instead, there was a gaping black hole in its bulbous head. The jagged edges looked singed and shriveled, yet they rippled and waved, each on their own, as if testing the air for scent or sound. Within the black was a gullet ringed with muscles sinking down into darkness. There didn't seem to be any teeth.

Its head twitched on the thin stalk of a neck, its emaciated limbs trembling as it turned itself around. Its sunken chest and swollen abdomen swelled and shrank, exchanging sizes, its mottled skin stretching and wrinkling ostensibly with its breathing. Its long, multi-jointed fingers, six of them each and something like a thumb, looked split at the tips, and sharp shards of bone scratched against the floor tiles.

"What the fuck is that?" Hornsby asked. He moved to reach for something—most likely his service revolver—but then realized it wasn't there. The creature turned its twitching head toward him and screeched again, the ragged flaps of its face waving outward. From the dark pink interior of its mouth, long, needle-like fangs extended from the muscled rings. They looked like curved ivory, but they, too, waved in and out. The thing arched its back and spikes shot out along its spine.

"No idea," Jose said breathlessly.

"I thought there were no living animals in this world?" Markham said. He was watching the creature warily, and as he spoke, the head jerked in his direction, twitching wildly. The teeth opened outward.

"There weren't before," Jose said. The thing whipped around toward him and he flinched.

"Jose, don't move," Markham said. He had grabbed a narrow sliver of broken shelf and was brandishing it like a knife. "Hey! Hey, kitty!"

The creature whipped its head back around toward Markham. Its back spikes rippled along with its oddly pulsing back. Markham backed away slowly, and the thing skittered after him, its twitching head chirping in frustration.

"Come on," Markham said. "That's right. Come this way."

Markham led it several feet away from the others, keeping his guard up and talking in a low, soothing voice to it the whole time. "That's right. That's right. This way." He had almost made it to the doorway when an errant slab of broken shelf caught him at the back of the calf and he tripped. He fell backward over it and landed heavily on the floor. The creature let out an ear-splitting shriek. It leaped at Markham, its overlong fingers splayed, as the others rushed to him. He raised the shard of stone as the creature landed. It shrieked once more, flailing its arms frantically, then stopped moving.

"Markham! Are you okay?" Kathy and Hornsby each took one of the thing's arms and rolled it off Markham. The feel of its skin made Kathy bristle with disgust. The sensation was like the gateway, chilly and wet without being wet, almost oily. Its chest, now that it wasn't expanding and contracting, had shrunk some, and its bones were visible beneath that awful skin. The shard of stone was jutting from its shriveled chest, but there was no blood. Rather, the wound had turned a charcoal gray and had begun to disintegrate. As it turned to powder, the chest cavity began to fall in on itself until the decay had engulfed the entire creature. In seconds, the stone shard clattered to the ground.

Jose reached out a hand and helped Markham up. "You okay, man?"

"I'm fine. Thanks. It just scratched me up a little as it was dying." Markham dusted himself off with one hand. The other he clutched close to his body. Deep furrows ran from the back of his hand and across his forearm to almost his elbow. When he saw their looks of alarm, Markham pulled down his sleeve and applied pressure over the wound. Blood welled up despite his efforts, the drops pattering onto the floor.

"Jesus, man, are you sure? Those are pretty deep." Jose looked from the blood soaking through Markham's sleeve to his face and back again.

Markham waved him off with his good hand and stooped to unzip his backpack. He took out a roll of bandages, shoved his sleeve up again, and wrapped up his arm. "Let's get out of here. If there's one of those things, there could be more."

"I'm sorry. There never should have been that one," Jose said, more to himself than to Markham. "But yeah, I guess you could be right." He led them back through the doorway to the outer lobby, glancing back a few times at Markham along the way.

Kathy could feel the hum again, as well as the tension Markham's suggestion had ignited. They hadn't been expecting one creature like that in the dead city, let alone—

Something that could have been a screech echoed from one of the huge side rooms.

They froze. A moment later, another high-pitched wail reverberated through the library, and then another and another.

"Run," Kathy said. "Now!"

They took off through the lobby toward the front doorway. Behind them, there was no sound of the creatures' footsteps, but the humming got louder. Kathy could feel it in her legs, rising up through the floor. She glanced back. The faceless creatures were crawling across the ceiling and down the walls, pouring out of the side doors. She saw some of them drop to the floor and scramble toward them. They moved very fast. "Run!" she screamed.

Chapter 8

The lobby room seemed much longer than it had as they ran across the floor. Behind them, she was sure the creatures were dropping silently to the floor. She could only hear them when their bone-claws scraped the tiles. They could have been twenty feet away, or ten, or maybe ten inches. They could have been close enough to grab her by the hair and yank her back, sinking those flesh-rending talons into her body. She wanted to look back, but she didn't. She couldn't afford to lose any ground.

After what seemed like a disproportionate amount of time, the doorway loomed ahead of them. Kathy and the others shot through it—she wished there was a door to close behind them–and tumbled out into the street. They staggered away from the building, and only then did they finally turn to see the progress of their pursuers.

There were dozens, maybe hundreds, of the creatures clamoring toward the doorway.

"Shit!" Rodriguez shouted, nearly tripping himself over street debris as he backed away. "Shit! Shit!"

Then the creatures stopped short in the doorway. Kathy and the others held their breath, waiting for the outpouring...but it didn't come. They crowded the top of the doorway, a whirlwind of flailing, multi-jointed limbs and twitching, cratered heads of waving jagged skin and spiny teeth.

"What are they doing?" Hornsby asked.

A few of the creatures reached around the door frame to move out into the night, but then they skittered back, as if the outside air hurt them.

"They stopped. They...I don't think they can come out here." Kathy took a step toward them and their keening rose until it was deafening, the shrieks of a multitude. They didn't come out, though.

"Let's go. Whatever's holding them back might not be permanent."

"Good idea," Markham said. He looked pale, and was bleeding through his bandage a little.

They took off away from the library, following the moonlit street until it banked to the left and they found themselves on a side street. It was hard for Kathy to shake the feeling that they were still being followed, and as they leaned against a wrongly-slanted building to catch their breath, she watched for signs of those creatures, but there were none. Whatever kept them in the city library seemed to be holding.

"Think we're okay for now," Jose said, panting, his hands on his knees. He straightened up. "Where to now?"

Kathy peered down the long side street. It was devoid of debris; there was no one there to leave any. She gestured toward the other end. "That way, I guess? You said you found the city center when you got lost, right? So let's get lost."

In agreement, Hornsby and Jose made a move to follow her suggestion, but stopped when they saw Markham. He was leaning heavily against an obtuse angle of the building across from Kathy, almost laying on it, cradling his bad arm. His forehead had broken out into a sweat and he looked even paler than before.

"Sergeant, you okay?"

Markham, whose eyes had been closed, opened them suddenly. He looked as if he'd been caught doing something wrong. "I'm fine, I said. Just a little warm from running."

"Sit," Kathy told him. When he looked about to protest, she commanded it; her tone leaving no room for argument. "Sit down, Sergeant Markham."

He regarded her a moment, nodded, and then sank to the ground. She went to him, opening her backpack as she did so. He seemed to have lost his in the flight from the library. She handed him one of her little bottles of water. "Drink that," she told him in the same inarguable voice, and he did. Then she took another small water out of her bag and knelt down beside him, unwrapping his bandage.

"What are you doing?" he asked, weakly trying to pull his arm away.

She kept unwrapping the bandage anyway. "We should clean those scratches." She was going to add, *"to prevent infection,"* but she didn't think either she or Markham was quite ready to admit out loud that particular ship had sailed. Infection had begun to take root, she was pretty sure, and although she didn't really think pouring water on it could help, she was pretty sure it wouldn't hurt, either.

The skin around the scratches had taken on a pale, washed-out bluish tint, the skin there thin, almost like tissue paper. As she poured water over the scratches, black blood streamed over his forearm onto the ground and was replaced by new red rivulets. That, Kathy thought, seemed like a good sign. Maybe infection hadn't gotten such a foothold yet. She took the antibiotic salve out of her backpack and squeezed a generous amount from the tube onto Markham's scratches. With his free hand, he rubbed them in.

"Thanks." He smiled weakly at her.

She took out the sewing kit. "Would you like me to sew those up?"

"I've got it." Markham took the sewing kit and offered her a weak smile. "Not the first time I've patched myself up."

Kathy helped him thread and rethread the needle when he needed it, but otherwise, he did an admirable job of sewing closed those angry furrows. Kathy could see the pain in his eyes and in the tension of his body language, but he said nothing the entire time.

"Let's get that rewrapped," she said, and, replacing the salve and sewing kit in her bag, she pulled out a roll of bandages.

"Thank you, Ms. Ryan," he said.

"Kathy. Just Kathy is fine." She found herself blushing a little. Caregiver was not a role she had ever really been comfortable with, nor was it one she thought she did well, so the genuine gratitude in his voice threw her a little. Still, she managed a small smile at him. When Markham's arm was rewrapped and he'd had a few more sips of water from the bottle she'd given him, he looked a little better. Although he was still pale, his color had begun to come back a bit, and he'd stopped sweating.

Jose and Hornsby helped Markham to his feet.

"Let's keep moving," Markham said. "I'll feel better putting one foot in front of the other."

They moved as a group down the side street in the direction Kathy had suggested, trying to look for significant landmarks or indications of life without looking too closely or too long at the building faces. Particularly on the street onto which they emerged, a main thoroughfare judging by the width of it, the buildings hemming them in from both sides had that disconcerting stucco surface. In the moonlight, faces leered and bore stone teeth. The wind had picked up some, too, and as it rushed past their ears, it sometimes sounded like whispering. At first, Kathy could only catch occasional words—*slaughter...rape...eviscerate...betray...*but as they made their way further along the desolate avenue, the words came faster, and she could understand more of them.

They suggested terrible things. Unthinkable, unspeakable, stomach-turning things amidst hiss-like chuckling and high-pitched, mad giggles.

Slaughter her...rape the little ones...eviscerate...betrayal of...peel off layers of the eyes...flay the back slowly...break the souls...

One of the voices whispered, *to break you...make you just like me.*

"Do you guys hear that?" Hornsby asked tentatively, but the whispering had grown surprisingly loud. It wasn't just in Kathy's ears now; it felt like a buzzing inside her whole head. Was this the beginning of infection, or were they just surrounded by those things, those parasite faces? She looked at the others. Jose was blinking and shaking his head and Markham was pinching the bridge of his nose; both looked to her like they were consumed by the whispering as well. The one who seemed the least affected was Hornsby. By his expression, Kathy guessed he realized that, too. He didn't waste time with the information, though; as Markham staggered forward, he bore the man up with a shoulder under his arm.

"Rodriguez! Kathy! Let's move!" He hurried Markham down toward another side street.

Kathy could tell he was right, that they should get out of there, but the whispering was telling her other things, and she found it exhausting—so much so that her legs and arms felt heavy. It was easier just to stand and sway. There were so many whispering voices in her head now that she didn't even have to hear the awful things they were saying. She got the gist of it, but the terrible mind-movies the thoughts suggested had run their reel.

She noticed Hornsby had come back without Markham and meant to comment, but it was too much effort to talk. Deep in her mind, she knew this was wrong, this lethargy. Alarms were going off in the distance of her thoughts, and although this sent part of her brain on lockdown, another part was fighting not to lose herself, to follow after Hornsby, who had taken both her and Jose by the arm and was half leading and half dragging them in the direction in which he'd taken Markham.

As they moved, the air seemed cooler, freer, and the whispering faded. By degrees, Kathy felt more alert, more herself, and by the time the three of them reached Markham, who was sitting hunched over on a large front stoop, the whispering had dissipated entirely. Jose seemed better, too, and Hornsby looked relieved.

"Thank you," she told the police officer. "I think you might have just saved our lives."

"Any time." He was eyeing Markham, and that concern had crept back into his face again. To her and Jose, he said, "I don't think he's doing so well."

"I'm...fine," Markham said. It seemed like a strain to talk. The wound on his arm had begun oozing again, both fresh blood and something that looked like bronchitis phlegm.

"You need more antibiotic."

"It won't work," Markham said, looking up. His expression was laced with pain. "It's gone deep, whatever it is."

"What can we do?" Jose asked.

"The arm should come off," Markham replied. "Stop the infection before it spreads."

"Are you serious?" Jose looked at him as if the fever had already begun to boil Markham's brains.

"No way to do that," Hornsby said. "Between the four of us, we have, what? A pocket knife?"

"There are shards of broken stone in the buildings—not just the library. They'll cut through muscle, I'm sure of it. They might even be heavy enough to break through the bone. Like a guillotine." Markham coughed hard. When he recovered, he studied the skeptical looks on their faces and sighed. "Look. I don't know if that thing was poisonous or if it was just filthy with alien germs, but these wounds are deep, and they're infected. The infection is spreading. I can feel it. It's going up my arm, and if it makes it to my brain or my heart...Cut off the arm, and I might still be able to fight it off."

"Markham, man, I'll be honest with you," Jose said. "I don't know if it's in me to do that. I don't know if any of us can do that."

Markham turned to Kathy. "You have to," he said. "Or I'll die here."

All three men watched her, waiting.

"Sergeant, we have nothing to dull the pain, and—"

"It can't hurt worse than it already does," he said through a grimace.

"And no way to cauterize the wound. If you bleed to death—"

"We'll make a fire," Hornsby said.

"And what if the laws of physics here don't allow for fire to exist?"

"There is oxygen in the air here," Jose said. "We tested for that, to make sure we could breathe."

"How far up would we have to cut?" Kathy asked.

"Above the elbow should do it," Markham said.

Kathy nodded. "We can search this building here. We'll need to find wood to make a fire. If we find an appropriate stone, we can sterilize it in the flames, and cauterize his wound. We'll need to pool our antibiotic salve. You guys okay with that?"

Jose and Hornsby nodded.

"Can you guys get Sergeant Markham to his feet? Let's get out of the street."

"Kathy." Markham grabbed her arm with his good hand. His grip was still surprisingly strong. "Again...thank you."

"Don't thank me yet," she said softly. "I've never done an amputation before."

* * * *

The building they entered was bigger inside than the library had been, although the first room they entered looked as if it had been swept clean. Immediately, they were on guard. If a place that looked as if time and space had abandoned it had been teeming with monsters, then a place far less dusty and cluttered with debris seemed even less likely to be empty.

It was hard to tell what the building might once have been used for. Unlike the library or what Kathy thought had been residences, this place had no furniture whatsoever. The walls were smooth, much smoother than anywhere else; there were no faces here, no whispering or humming. The silence within seemed so intent on remaining unbroken that even their footsteps were muted, and their voices, when they did speak, were hushed.

There was only one doorway, and that was on the far wall, about three football fields away.

Remnants of a door still hung from the doorway under which they passed, swinging a little on perfectly silent hinges attached to the top of the frame. The fragment of door looked heavy and very loose. Kathy hoped it would hold at least until they were out from under it.

Beyond the doorway was a stone antechamber just before a staircase curving down into the ground. It reminded Kathy of the throats of those library creatures, a gaping maw and stone-ringed gullet spiraling toward the pit of this world's gut.

They exchanged glances with one another and one by one, they filed down the stairs.

Kathy wouldn't have thought it possible, but the silence deepened as they descended. There was no echo, no shuffling sound. They couldn't see, either. They had pulled out the tiny flashlights they had been given in the backpacks, but found that each offered a brief flicker of light before giving over to darkness, and not one of the four could be induced to light up again. Jose made a comment about Paragon technology, but the stairwell nearly swallowed it up.

They did their best to feel their way, that same smooth stone winding around and down, but after a while, the texture beneath their fingertips changed from smooth to rough and back again, and then on to no real sensation at all. At first, Kathy thought the wall had dropped away, that they were balanced uncertainly on a staircase suspended over an endless chasm in the all-encompassing darkness, but she found she couldn't extend her arm. Something structural prevented it. It wasn't any less disconcerting, though. It felt to Kathy as if they were slipping down into a kind of waking unconsciousness.

Kathy and Jose supported Markham, with Hornsby bringing up the rear. She could hear Markham's breathing growing more ragged. That she could hear it at all surprised her...and struck her as a bad sign. They were losing Markham fast.

"Are you okay, Sergeant? Need to stop a minute?" Her words sounded muffled in her own ears, snatched out of the air.

"Keep going," Markham said. At least, that's what Kathy thought he said.

She did keep going, following the massive stairs down into the depths of an alien world. The buildings, sizable as they were, had felt like they were pressing on her, but the stairwell felt suffocating. She was breathing the place in, and it was crushing her.

She was just about to suggest they turn around and go back up, get out of that heavy, choking, crushing nothingness, when she rounded a bend and saw a faint light blue glow lighting up what looked to be the bottom of the staircase.

"I think we found the bottom," she said. She could feel the rock again under her fingertips and could hear her own voice normally. When she reached flat ground again, a tension she hadn't realized she'd been carrying eased, and she could breathe again. Markham stumbled a little on the bottom step, but seemed better than he had on the staircase. Jose and Hornsby emerged from the dark. They had made it.

"So now what? Keep going and hope to find something sharp?" Jose looked around.

They were in a dirt tunnel supported by wooden beams. One of the beams had fallen and begun to splinter on the ground. There was promise there—broken wood for a fire, possible jagged rocks beyond it, unearthed by whoever had dug the tunnel.

"Let's keep going a little farther, see what we can use down here," Kathy said.

The tunnel looked longer than it actually was. They closed the distance within minutes and emerged into a room the size of a suburban neighborhood with a ceiling six or seven stories high. Inside, it was several degrees colder than the tunnel. Like everywhere else in the city, the room was made of stone, but it was utterly smooth—flawlessly so. It was clearly octagon-shaped, another architectural anomaly in the dead city. Set into six of the walls were countless massive metal drawers with T-shaped handles, arranged in rows. Against one of the free walls was a kind of counter slanting downward, and on it was laid out a number of bright silver instruments at least as large as Markham, if not larger. Although none of them was recognizable to Kathy, she saw that many had scroll-shaped handles and s-shaped blades. The light blue glow was coming from orbs in the ceiling, and unlike other light sources around the city, these were extremely bright, almost harsh. They were focused in groups over enormous stone slabs with crisscrossed legs on wheels. The slabs had grimy fabric sheets draped over them, and Kathy could see that a few covered irregular contents laid out on the slabs.

"Oh my God," Jose said, crossing himself. He had figured it out just as Kathy did.

"It's a morgue," Kathy said flatly. "We found a morgue."

Chapter 9

The silence made sense to Kathy now. So did the smooth walls. What she and the others might have thought of as physical discrepancies or anomalies elsewhere most likely meant the presence of the parasites or some other creature in the city, which wasn't really dead at all. There was life in the uneven, rough surfaces of the buildings and streets, in the hums and buzzes and whispering. It might not have been life as human beings thought of it, but the physics were different here. Senses worked differently because the elements acting on them worked differently.

But silence—total silence—and the absence of triggers for the senses... that meant death. The absence of life. These parts of the city truly were abandoned, even by whatever existed elsewhere now.

Whether that made them safe, though, or was an indication of places where even devils dared not tread remained to be seen.

"There are tools there," Markham said after a long silence. He was looking at the instruments suspended against any notion of gravity on the slanted counter. His skin had gone pale again, and he looked as if he was having trouble keeping his eyes open, as if every fiber of his will was stretched in keeping him standing.

"Yeah," Kathy said. "Why don't you sit? We'll get what we need."

Markham nodded, stumbled toward one of the wheeled slabs, and sank to the ground, leaning his back against the legs.

To the others, she said, "If we don't get that arm off, he's going to die. We need to find a way up to where the tools are, and we need to find a way to sterilize and cauterize. Any ideas?"

They had been making their way to the counter where the tools were, and as they reached the lowermost edge, they looked up. Perspective had caught up with them, it seemed, revealing that what had looked human-sized and accessible from across the room was anything but. The bottom ledge of the shelf was at least ten feet above their heads. Even if they could find a way to access it, it was on a slant. Those tools each had to be at least six feet long, and who knew how many pounds. If they'd had more time, Kathy would have suggested scrapping the whole idea and going somewhere else to find a cutting tool. As it was, though, she didn't think Markham could make the trip back up the stairs.

Making this work might be their only chance to save him.

"I suppose we could boost each other up?" Jose said.

"If we were circus performers, maybe. We'd have to stand on each other's shoulders to make it up there," Hornsby said.

"Is there something we can climb on?" Kathy asked, looking around. "Maybe a box or something?"

The room had been swept pretty clean, though. There was nothing on the floor.

"Hey, what about that wooden beam in the tunnel? Do you think the three of us could drag it back here? If we could prop it up against the edge there, we might be able to walk up."

Jose shrugged. "Can't hurt to try."

They made their way back across the room. As they passed Markham, Kathy noticed that his eyes had closed. If he heard them, he showed no sign. His chest was still moving up and down, though, so that was good.

"Do you think one of us should stay with him?" Hornsby said, following Kathy's gaze.

"Yeah, I do, but honestly, I think it's going to take three of us to move that wooden beam all the way back to the counter," she replied. Seeing Markham pass out of sight as they re-entered the tunnel, though, made her feel ill at ease.

They walked for what seemed like too long a time. Kathy was beginning to wonder if they had missed it in the gloom when it resolved itself from the shadows a few more feet ahead. It was disconcerting how distances and angles were so inconsistent in this world. There was enough to make her feel like she was going crazy. She supposed she should feel lucky that the beam was even still there, and not moving and shifting and distorting with the rest of the city.

It might as well have been back on Earth, though, or on Earth's moon, for all the good it was going to do them. They found that out as soon as they tried to move it. Even with the concentrated effort of all three of them, it was way too heavy to budge, let alone drag back across the morgue.

"Damn it!" Kathy kicked the thing, and the wood cracked where her foot made impact. She kicked it again and could have sworn that the crack healed itself. "That was a fucking waste of time."

"It was a good thought," Hornsby offered, and she tried to smile, but it just wouldn't stick. She hated that she'd blown a half-hour at least of the few Markham had left.

Disappointed, they made their way back to the room. Kathy thought about the amputation. She supposed she could use the backpack straps or some of their clothing as a tourniquet. They had the sewing kits and the antibiotic, and despite its unwillingness to budge, she thought they might at least be able to use that damned timber for fire. It was the cutting instrument, really, that was holding up the works. They would just have to scour the place and see if there was anything they could use either to access those instruments or cut off Markham's arm. It occurred to her then that her own bag with the handgun in it had been lost some time between the Subfloor 24 quarantine room and the morgue of a strange city on an alien world; her gun was gone. Markham still had his, though. Three, maybe four shots would sever enough flesh and bone that they could get the lower half of his arm off. It would be incredibly painful for Markham, but it would probably do the job…unless, of course, the physics of firearms were distorted, too.

As they re-emerged, Kathy glanced over to check on him, and swore again. The men turned.

"Jesus," Jose said, looking at the empty spot and pool of blood where Markham had been moments before. "Where the fuck did he go?"

"This is all my fault," Kathy said, fighting the urge to scream. "Fuck." To Hornsby, she added, "You were right. We never should have left him alone."

"It's not your fault," Hornsby replied. "You were trying to save him."

"Why didn't he say something? Shout if he was being attacked?"

"Maybe he wasn't," Jose offered. "I don't mean this to sound sarcastic, but maybe he got up and walked away. Markham's strong and he's stubborn. If he's also delirious, he might think he can help himself. Look—the blood's still pretty fresh."

Jose was right. The blood pooled by the giant gurney where Markham had been sitting hadn't begun to congeal yet, and a smeared trail of it moved away toward the far wall. It was possible that Markham had gotten up and walked away, although Kathy couldn't imagine how, in his state. Still, nothing in Hesychia followed any kind of known logic, so maybe it was foolish to try to apply any to the situation.

"You could be right. Let's follow the blood."

The trail was irregular, formed from smears a few inches wide. They struck Kathy as the smears a severed arm might make if dragged off by a wild animal. She hated to think that they were tracking an arm and not a man, but there was no other choice. The blood trail was the only lead they had. They followed it until it petered out, but then they saw it continuing several feet away, and picked up the trail again. It took several inexplicably circuitous routes across the vast floor tiles, but ultimately, it led straight to one of the bottom cold chamber drawers. A semi-palm print with fingers splayed reached for the bottom left edge of the drawer. It was big enough to be Markham's, Kathy supposed.

Up close, the drawer faces were enormous. Kathy estimated them to be about three stories high and three times as wide. They looked to be made from the same metal as the gates, although they didn't glow. The drawers didn't appear to have any means of distinguishing one from another—no labels, no markers, nothing Kathy could see that might identify one body from the next. There didn't appear to be any way of opening them, either. Kathy saw nothing that could be construed as a handle. In fact, the surfaces of the drawer faces were more or less smooth.

"He couldn't have gotten one of those open himself," Hornsby said. "Right?"

"I don't see how," Kathy replied. "Damn it. We need to find him."

They crept up to the drawer. None of them voiced it, but a creeping doubt made them cautious.

Maybe it was Markham's blood smeared across the floor like that... but it maybe it wasn't. The latter possibility kept them from shouting for him. Sure, he needed help and they wanted to find him, but they wanted to find him alive, if they could. It seemed wiser not to draw attention to their search...just in case. If Markham had staggered off somewhere, he'd be safer if nothing knew where he was.

Kathy put her ear against the cold metal surface and listened. Hearing nothing, she knocked gently and in a quiet voice, said, "Markham? It's us. Are you in there?"

She waited. Jose threw his hands up, silently asking, "Well?" and Kathy shook her head.

"I don't hear anything," she said after a moment, moving away from the metal. "Think we can get it open?"

Hornsby stepped forward. "Let me try something." He searched around the side edge of the drawer—all of them protruded a few inches away from the wall—and finally uttered a small "Aha!"

A moment later, there was a heavy grinding noise.

"We should step away," Hornsby said, and backed off to the side. The others followed.

"What did you do?" Kathy asked.

"Had a dream about this place once. This particular building, I mean. Had a lot of dreams about this world, all of them bad. Anyway, in the dream, hands came out of the walls and pressed these circular indentations on the sides of the drawer, and they all opened." He shivered. "It was pretty awful, that one. I used to think the worst part of my job was seeing the bodies of dead children. No dead body is pleasant, but with children... anyway, a decomposing human body, even a child, is nothing compared to what the bodies of otherworldly things do after death."

The grinding stopped, and they could see a long and badly dented drawer extending out onto the floor, beneath the glow of the orbs above. Cold air poured out of the top of it, along with an unpleasant whiff of something stale. Kathy waited. Hornsby's retelling of the dream, in that tired way cops had of only lifting the lid off a trauma, had left her uneasy. If he had been right about the mechanism for opening the drawers, then he might be right about what he had seen inside them.

When, after a few minutes, nothing dead or otherwise scrambled over the top of the drawer to meet them, they spread out and began to examine the length of the drawer's side.

"Hey! Hey, come here! I found a crack in the metal. I think we can get inside," Jose called from the far side of the drawer. Kathy and Hornsby made their way around to meet him. Sure enough, close to the wall, there was a six-foot-high dent in the metal, the center of which had split open. It looked just wide enough to squeeze through.

"Okay, let's go, then," Kathy said.

"Wait." Hornsby glanced around the empty morgue. "We have a potential issue here. A mechanism on the outside of the drawer opened it, right? If we all go in there and the drawer closes again, that crack is going to be blocked off, and we'll have no way of opening the drawer again. I mean, I can't imagine there's a way to open it from the inside. Who would need it?"

"Good point," Jose said.

"We could split up, but if—I'm just saying if—Markham didn't just get up and walk away in his delirium, I mean, if something took him, then it probably picked him off because he was alone." There being only three of us, if we split up, someone's going to be alone. I'm not saying not to do it. Just saying there's a risk."

"No, you're right," Kathy said. It almost struck her funny how quickly they'd gotten used to the level of risk already present just by being in that world. Hornsby did bring up some solid points, but in Kathy's mind, the new level of risk couldn't be avoided. "Maybe you and Jose should stay out here and guard the door, and I'll go in there and look for Markham."

"Kathy, if that was his blood, he's in bad shape, and you can't carry him back here by yourself. You need someone to go with you," Jose said.

"Listen, I'll stay here." Hornsby leaned a hand against the metal. "Jose's in better shape than I am, so you two go in there and find Markham. I know how to work the mechanism over there, and if it closes, I'll just let you back out."

"Are you sure?" Kathy asked. "It was this side of the drawer Markham disappeared from."

"I know. I'll shout if anything funny happens."

"Good." Kathy squeezed his shoulder. "We don't want to lose you, too, Carl."

He smiled at her, blushing a little. "Go on then. Find Markham."

She gave him a nod, and then followed Jose through the crack in the drawer.

"Be careful!" he called after them.

They slipped into the drawer. The length of it exposed to the glow of the orbs was fairly well lit, and it was clear from a cursory search that it was empty. Markham, if he was in the area at all, was not in the drawer proper. That left the interior recess of the wall.

It was dark, like the stairwell had been.

"Sergeant? Sergeant! If you can hear me, let us know where you are!"

No response, no signs of movement. The recess yawned before them like the mouth of a cave. It smelled funny too in the drawer; it wasn't a smell she would have normally associated with death, but it was unsettling all the same. It reminded Kathy of the breath of sick people, the slow rot of gangrene, the flesh forgotten under a plastic bandage, the—

"I'd kill for a flashlight," Jose said, breaking into her thoughts. He smiled at her. "And a hot roast beef sandwich."

"With gravy," Kathy added, glad to focus on anything but that smell.

"Of course. And maybe french fries."

Kathy smiled, too. "Maybe there's a stash of sandwiches down there."

"I suppose the only way to find out is to go look," he said.

The smile slipped off Kathy's face. "I hope Markham is okay. That *was* a lot of blood."

"We'll find him."

Kathy didn't answer; it was the kind of thing people said to comfort others, but while it was a nice gesture, there was no real promise behind it.

Kathy thought there was a strong possibility that Markham was already dead. She didn't say that, though. Instead, she headed for the recess in the wall.

She felt Jose moving closer to her as the darkness swallowed them. She was glad not to be alone in there. She thought of Reece back at home. He knew sometimes she couldn't call to check in, but it didn't stop him from worrying. Ever since the murders up in Connecticut, when he'd gotten a glimpse of what she really did for a living, he worried. He was easy going by nature, but what he felt, he felt with passion—love, anger, joy, worry, all of it. He said it was his Irish blood, and that she was the kind of woman worth feeling every bit of those feelings for. Still, she hated to put him through the worry. He wasn't a jealous type, not really, but she wondered how he'd feel about her leaning on another man in the darkness a whole other universe away.

It was a strong possibility she wouldn't make it back to Earth. That was her line of work, case after case of strong possibilities she wouldn't make it out alive at all. Was he worrying about her now? She felt guilty. She loved Reece, possibly more than she'd ever loved anyone, even her own family, but she couldn't help feeling sometimes like his life would be a lot simpler without her in it. He didn't agree about that, and it was another reason why she loved him, but it wasn't lost on her that even his love had to have limits.

Jose must have been on a similar thought track, because he suddenly said, "You know, I always liked Claire," in a wistful kind of voice that, despite its softness, echoed in the drawer. "I mean, really liked her, as more than just a colleague."

"Oh?"

"Yeah. She was the whole package. Beautiful, smart, enthusiastic, funny. She was my boss, though, and Paragon has this thing about interoffice dating, so I never said anything. Well, to be honest, I told myself that was why I never said anything. The truth was, I was always the kind of guy who got by on wit and a big mouth. I got the girls who liked to laugh, you know? And Claire...well, she was always dating these really smart, wealthy stiffs..."

They tried the flashlights again, working the feeble light around the drawer, but the light didn't go far. So far as they could see, there was no sign of Markham.

"I used to think about it, though," Jose went on, "about telling her how I felt. I mean, we were here more or less alone together in this beautiful world, like it was made especially for us, you know? And we'd watch the sun set and the moons rise together and I thought, *if this doesn't bond you to someone, this once-in-a-lifetime experience, nothing will.* I'd watch her every day and find another new little quality about her to like. To love. I thought I loved her, actually. I was going to tell her that, the night we went into the city. Was going to tell her on our way back to camp."

"Do you think she knew? Some women are pretty perceptive that way."

The flashlights wavered and went out, but they kept moving. The far end of the drawer was some distance away yet.

"I don't know. I don't think she did. Like I said, I have a big mouth and I'm a wise-ass—I used to tell her she got the sarcasm from both ends—so she didn't take me that seriously. I think that was one of the things I liked about her."

"Well, you can tell her how you feel when we find her."

She felt Jose beside her, heard him walking, but couldn't see his expression.

"I just left her here." His voice was soft.

"It wasn't your fault."

"She used to tell me she could always count on me when she needed me, and I just…I left her here."

Kathy stopped suddenly, and Jose bumped into her. She found his shoulder in the dark and gave it a squeeze. "Jose, none of this is your fault, okay? None of it. You were working hard, dedicated to doing your job, and people higher up in the company took advantage of that. That's on them. All of this is on their shoulders, not yours."

He patted her hand. "Thanks, Kathy."

"Sure. Now, I think if we keep taking this path down the middle here, we can break at the far back end and sweep up the sides. If Markham hasn't collapsed on our way, then he's likely leaning against a wall." She thumped the side of the flashlight with the palm of her hand and it flickered, spit out a faint beam of light, then sputtered out.

"Sounds like a good plan," Jose said. "I—"

Just then, a moan came from somewhere off to the left. It sounded like Markham.

"Hey! Hey Markham, is that you?" Jose started toward the sound.

"Jose, wait—" Kathy began, but Jose was closing the distance.

"Help me." It was Markham's voice, weak and shaky. Kathy jogged to catch up to Jose.

"We're coming, buddy," Jose said. "Hang in there. Keep talking. We'll find you."

From somewhere farther off in the darkness, there came a giggle, like that of a small child.

Something else was in the drawer with them.

"Kathy, I think I found him." Jose's voice was close, right in front of her. She reached out until she felt his shirt, and he took her hand and pulled her down toward Markham.

"Let's get him back into the light," she said. They managed by touch alone to each get a shoulder under Markham's arms and lift him. It was awkward, but he was surprisingly light, lighter than he should have been. She'd expected dead weight, more or less, but given the shuffling of his movements, he was trying to do the work of standing and shuffling along on his own.

"We got you," Kathy said as they moved him out of the darkness. "Stay with us, Markham."

"My arm," he murmured.

"Stay with us," she repeated.

Over their shoulders, bouncing between the walls of the drawers, came the echo of the giggling again. Even if acoustics didn't have their own arbitrary rules in this world, it would have been impossible to determine a more specific direction, or how close behind the source was to them. Kathy got the sense that whatever it was, it was holding back deliberately, amused, watching them struggle with their friend.

"Bleed, bleed, bleed!"

Kathy flinched at how close the giggling voice was to her ear. It only partly registered that there was no accompanying breath...

"It's...it's got me," Markham's voice said, weak but tinged with panic. "Go on. Get out of here."

"No!" Kathy said. "We've got you. We'll get you out of here."

She and Jose moved faster. Markham was heavy, and they could barely see. Behind them, the giggling grew louder. It seemed to come from everywhere.

"Almost there," Jose said, breathing heavily.

They emerged into the light and set Markham down. Before they could feel any sense of relief, though, reason began to splinter and fall away. For starters, Markham's bad arm, which had been draped across Kathy's shoulders in the dark, was gone—all of it, right up to the elbow, just gone. It wasn't bleeding; rather, the end of the stub was crusted with a dark purple scab. Second, what was left of Markham was clearly in no shape to have talked to them at all; the bottom half of his face was gone, as well as most of his throat. The ragged, torn flesh of what was left of his head waved like fingertips, like the open maw of those things in the library. His eyes were wide, fogged over in death, and his clothes were torn. He was also missing a foot.

For several seconds, Kathy and Jose could only stare in horror. It made no sense. He'd been okay. They had found him and he was going to be okay, and—

Just beyond the edge of the darkness, a misshapen silhouette giggled again.

"Tricked you," it whispered. "Tricked you tricked you tricked you..."

The remains of Sergeant First Class John Markham began to twitch as if laughing along with the creature in the shadows. All around the silhouette, high-pitched laughter echoed through the drawer.

"Trickedyoutrickedyoutrickedyou..."

Kathy glanced at Jose. He had a look in his eye she'd seen before; people on the verge of breaking looked like that. She grabbed his hand and tugged him away from the twitching thing at their feet. They ran for the crack in the drawer.

"Wait! Wait for me!" Markham's twitching remains called out behind them, and fresh peals of laughter erupted all over the drawer.

Kathy and Jose squeezed through the crack, then took off around the length of the drawer toward the other side.

They found Hornsby propped casually against the wall. When he saw them running and took in their expressions, he looked alarmed, and pushed off from the wall to join them.

"What? What happened? Did you find Sergeant Markham?"

"Well...we...we found..." Jose managed between panting breaths.

Kathy shook her head. "We've got to go."

Without another word, Hornsby nodded. Kathy and Jose moved quickly across the room, Hornsby hurrying to keep up. The three of them made it to the tunnel and trudged its gloomy length in silence. Kathy figured Hornsby had questions, but he kept them to himself.

The trek back up the stairs required supreme force of will, and it was exhausting. A combination of disappointment in not being able to save Markham and the sensory deprivation of the stairwell created a weight on them, pulling them down, dragging at their feet until it was all they could do not to just sink onto the steps and stay there. It took a very long time—it seemed like hours—but they finally made their way to the top. The smooth, empty room stretched out before them, silent as a tomb. They crossed it and trudged out into the street.

"You two okay?" Hornsby finally asked.

Neither Kathy nor Jose spoke, but Kathy offered a half-hearted shrug. The moons overhead had shifted in the sky. It was late, and they were all tired.

"I'm...sorry about Markham. He seemed like one of the good guys."

"Yeah." Kathy looked around the empty street. Across from them were ruins of a building that Kathy couldn't remember seeing before. Most of the first floor was there. It looked like it was open to the sky, but the stone was smooth, and Kathy held on to that as a sign they might be safe there for a while. "Listen guys, we need to rest. We can't keep going on fumes."

"Where? Backtrack to the forest?" Hornsby asked.

"This place isn't going to let us leave now," Jose said, and flinging an arm out in the direction they'd come, he added, "Look."

They turned back toward the road they'd come up...how long ago had that been? Hours? The library was gone. The buildings there looked completely unfamiliar.

Kathy turned back to the ruins. "How about holing up there for the night? It's better than being out on the street...or shut up in one of the buildings."

Jose shrugged. "Fine with me."

"Me too," Hornsby agreed.

"Okay then," Kathy said. "Let's get some sleep."

Chapter 10

Most of what had crumbled off the building had been reduced to debris, but it was empty debris devoid of anything resembling a countenance, and for that, Kathy was glad. There was no whispering in the ruins, and there was something comforting about the stars overhead. Kathy watched until she was sure both Jose and Hornsby were asleep, and then felt herself begin to drift off as well.

When she awoke again, the sky was a deep pink, and for a few seconds, she couldn't remember where she was. It came back to her as she sat up, her body stiff and aching from the hard floor, and looked around. She was far from home, far from Reece. Jose snored lightly nearby, his face pressed into the uneven contours of his backpack, which he had been using as a pillow. Hornsby's coat and backpack lay in a crumpled heap by the doorway.

Hornsby was gone.

No, no, no. Not again, she thought. *This can't be happening again.* "Jose!" She leaned over to shake him awake. "Jose! Hornsby's gone."

"Huh?" Jose rolled onto his back and blinked.

"Hornsby's gone! Wake up." Kathy rose to her feet.

Her words took a moment to penetrate Jose's haze of sleep, but then his eyes sprung open and he sat up, taking in Hornsby's things by the door. He hopped up, brushing the dust of the debris from his clothes and looking around the ruins.

"Hornsby? Where are you, man? Hornsby!" Jose started toward the door.

When Carl Hornsby swung through the doorway, he nearly collided with Jose, and both jumped.

"Jesus," Jose said shakily. "You scared the hell out of me."

"Out of *us*," Kathy said. "Where were you?"

"Just stretching my legs," Hornsby said. "I thought my couch at home was hell on my back, but that floor..." He shook his head. "Sorry. Didn't mean to alarm you guys."

"We're just glad you're okay," Kathy said. "Did you eat? We should probably eat something and get moving again."

"Yeah, we should probably find the center of town, if we can," Jose said, picking up his backpack. "I've been giving it some thought. When I was here last, the Wraiths only came out at night. If we could get there during the day, we might have an opportunity to look for Claire and the others safely."

"Sounds good to me. Any idea which direction we should try?" Kathy gathered up her own backpack and slung it over her shoulder.

Jose hung from the doorway and looked from one end of the street to the other and back. He turned to them and pointed to the right. "That way?"

"Sure. Let's go." Kathy filed out of the ruins behind Jose. She turned back to see Hornsby reach down and grab a sharp fragment of rock. A flash of unease spiked through her. "Hornsby? You ready?"

He smile at her, holding up the rock fragment. "Just in case, right?" He put the fragment in his backpack and added, "I mean, I'd rather we do everything we can to avoid having to cut off anybody's anything, but... just in case we need something sharp."

"Fair enough," Kathy replied as he joined her in the doorway. "Better to have it and not need it than need it and not have it, right?" She managed to smile at him as he passed by into the street, but that unease lingered. Hornsby was an okay guy—he and Jose both were—but there was no real way to measure the effects of this place's stresses on someone. That it changed people was without question. Was it changing Hornsby?

They started up the street together. The morning was cool, made more so by the insistent breeze that tugged at their hair and clothes as it blew by. To Kathy, the air was sharp, almost electric. The city was humming with anticipation. Something was happening, or about to happen.

The sun had made its way to the center of the sky before they reached the end of the road. It wasn't so much that the road was that long, but rather that the sun that day was moving fast, hurrying along like it was trying to defy Jose's plan to get to the town center before dark. When a cloud passed in front of the sun, Kathy was surprised to feel a moment of panic that dusk had somehow snuck up on them. Then the sun emerged again, its rays sweeping the shadows aside. It did little to warm the streets, though...or else Kathy's shiver had been internal.

Kathy noticed as they walked that despite the height of the city's protective stone wall, which the night before had remained almost constantly on their left, there was no sign of it now beyond the buildings in any direction. She hoped that meant that they were winding their way inward toward the city center. She also noticed, when looking up at the sky, that the sun seemed to have backtracked in its path. She, Jose, and Hornsby had been moving steadily in one direction, or at least Kathy thought they had, but the sun, which should have been in front of them, now shone on their backs. She pointed it out to her companions.

"Could we have gotten turned around?" Hornsby asked.

"I don't see how," Jose said, but he didn't sound convinced. "It could be the city. Or the sun. Hell, nothing in this world works right."

"I think we should keep going anyway," Kathy said. "I don't see the city wall out there between the buildings. I think, as impossible as it sounds, that we actually are getting closer to the center."

"I don't think it matters which direction we go," Jose said. "We'll get there when the city is good and ready to have us." He had that look in his eyes again, the one Kathy had seen in people just before they broke. She didn't like it.

"Maybe," Kathy said, meeting Jose's gaze. She needed him present, pulled together, and with them. "But we decide the direction. We can have that much control, at least, okay?"

Jose nodded. "Sure. Sure, yeah, you're right."

They kept moving for what felt like a very long time. Kathy's feet hurt, and her muscles were still sore from sleeping on that hard stone floor. What kept her going was imagining how to get revenge on Dr. Carter Greenwood. She wasn't often given to such thoughts—in fact, she probably tried harder than others to avoid them. Creative visualization and numerous schools of magic posited that thoughts given time and focus were manifestations of will, and her experience with her own family bore that theory out. She didn't want to be like her brother; he must have thought about doing all those horrible things before he'd done them, hurting and raping, maiming and killing. She believed that when his thoughts, his visualizations of violence in all its vivid detail, weren't enough anymore, they had become the catalysts for his actions. She had the same genes that he did, and so the same possible weak spots in the boundary between thinking and doing.

However, it felt good to imagine getting revenge on Greenwood, and as they trudged in relative silence down another city street, the revenge scenario blossomed into a bouquet of violent ends. Greenwood losing an arm seemed most appropriate. She was so lost in that particular outcome that Jose's voice at first sounded very far away, a buzzing nuisance whose volume and insistence grew until it snapped her from her thoughts.

"Kathy! Come back to us, huh? You okay?"

She blinked, looking around. The whispering in her head and in her ears subsided...which was disconcerting, since she hadn't realized there had been any whispering at all. Those parasite things were getting to her, and she didn't like it.

They were in an open pavilion encircled by tall, distended buildings. The street beneath their feet was paved with uneven stone, but there was more of a sense of precision to this area than anywhere else in the city. That precision was echoed and amplified by the center of the area, a hexagon whose six points were nailed into place by massive stone pedestals. Atop each pedestal was a statue facing the center of the hexagon, in all respects identical to its five other siblings, and the nature of the statues immediately incited a kind of soul-sick horror. There wasn't an individual feature that Kathy could point out as the reason, but the terrible culmination of every sculpted plane and curve moving one into the other, of the detailed realism of the anatomy, of the implicit suggestion that such sculptures had been carved not only from shining stone as replications from living models, but possibly from the models themselves. It was, Kathy thought with a grimace of revulsion, as if reality and art were vomiting into each other's mouths, and these sculptures were the spillover.

The figures stood upright like angels, their shapeless bodies draped in long robes. They had immense outstretched wings, taloned on the ends, which were neither bat-like nor bird-like, but managed to exhibit features of both. Their heads reminded Kathy of flames, flames of stone and flesh whose tongues were drawn up and out behind them by the same unseen icy wind that had frozen them in place. Their outstretched arms reached for the sky above, bearing in claw-like hands inverted trapezoids of sparkling blue crystal.

Kathy and the others stood on the very edge of the open pavilion, still some distance from the hexagonal city center, but she could feel a different kind of energy coming from the space between the statues. To say that it was a breath wouldn't have been quite right, but it was the energy of something living and breathing and aware of its surroundings. A living doorway, maybe, in a world beyond a living gate.

"Is that it?" she asked. "The city center? Are those the trapezoids?"

"Yeah," Jose said. "That's it. We found it."

Kathy looked up at the sky. It was dusk already. Impossibly, the sun was already beginning to sink below the city skyline. "How..."

"I don't know," Jose said. "I have no idea how, but we made it."

"Where did the rest of the day go?"

"I don't know that, either," Jose said more softly. "The length of days and nights is arbitrary here."

"Possibly less arbitrary than we think. Maybe this place is done playing with us," Hornsby said, "so it let us in."

Kathy glanced around the city and then returned her attention to the statues. The lights had not yet come on. The Wraiths, she thought, might still be asleep. "We're losing daylight. Let's go look while we still can." She started for the statues.

"Now?" Jose asked.

"Before they wake up," she called back over her shoulder. "Come on." She heard them hurry to catch up to her.

"Are—are you sure we shouldn't just wait until tomorrow?" Jose sounded genuinely scared.

Kathy glanced at him. "We'll stay alert. We'll be out of the city center before dark. But it isn't dark yet. We can't let this place fuck with us, Jose. Because you know it will; it'll keep trying to confuse us and exhaust us and thwart our plans at every turn if we don't just jump in and wrestle what we want right out of its hands."

"Okay." Jose exhaled. "Okay, yeah. Let's do this."

As they got closer to the hexagon of statues, that feeling of nervous anticipation heightened, and so did the feeling of being watched. Those sensations intensified further as the three explorers passed by one of the statues and gathered in the center of the hexagon.

"This is it. This is where we were." Jose was looking at various items on the ground, the detritus of human trespassing the first time around. The Green Team's belongings had aged and in some cases, begun to decay, although the progress of both varied from item to item and was incongruent with normal timetables. The women's clothing was in fairly good shape, but one of the sets of men's clothing had been reduced to fraying tatters. The other set had large holes in the shirt, but otherwise looked intact. Two watches lay on the ground next to the clothes. Both had stopped, but at different times, hours apart.

Two of the three backpacks looked like savage wild animals had torn them to pieces. Whatever contents they had once contained were gone now. The other backpack looked untouched, but when Kathy picked it up, it disintegrated in her hands. She wiped her dusty palms off on the seat of her jeans with a grimace of distaste and kept looking.

As Jose had mentioned, there was more intimate evidence of the Green Team there in the dirt and dust of the ancient city, things that unsettled Kathy far more than their variably decomposing gear. Little chunks of metals and resin—their dental fillings—had been scattered some by the wind, but lay in groupings near the clothing. She recognized the anchor-shaped birth control IUD lying near Claire's jeans, and an oblong metal plate with an accompanying handful of screws nested in the tattered shreds of khaki pants. Perhaps most disturbing of the lot was the stent. She'd seen pictures of coronary stents before, little tubes of latticework like tiny chain-link fences rolled up. It bothered her to see a real one lying in the street. It suggested a number of possibilities regarding the fate of the Green Team, and not all of them were good. A woman could live without her IUD. A guy might be crippled but likely wouldn't be killed by the removal of the plate and screws in his leg. And she supposed the removal of a stent wasn't necessarily fatal, but…

If she were to assume that Claire and Rick and Terry hadn't just been vaporized on the spot and that the blue lines on the Paragon printout sheets did indicate *some* kind of life, then it was possible that the three missing Green Team members had been…supplemented in some way to keep them alive. If they were being kept alive, for what purpose? And if they had, indeed, been supplemented, would it be wise to try and get them back?

The clicking of plastic against stone drew her attention. Jose, clearly frustrated, had chucked his flashlight at the base of one of the statues.

"Piece of shit," he muttered. "You'd think a company like Paragon could afford to give us flashlights that worked."

Kathy was about to point out that the flashlight was more likely malfunctioning due to the strange physics of Hesychia than poor craftsmanship, but decided against it. It wasn't about the flashlight, Kathy decided. It was about fear and frustration and missed opportunities with Claire. Jose was looking for an outlet to vent through.

The men continued searching the bases of the statues, which were big, but not big enough to house doors or stairwells, Kathy noted. Seamless and smooth, they were probably solid stone with no indication of so much as an inscription. Their distortions were less apparent, but they had also been devised with the same slanted surfaces and skewed perspective as the rest of the city. Their function genuinely seemed to be just to serve as pedestals for the monstrosities on top of them.

For Kathy, it was the statues, or more precisely, the trapezoids they hoisted into the air, that held the real fascination. They were the key to discovering what had really happened to Claire Banks and her team. In a way, she wanted the night to come on faster. She wanted to see those trapezoids glow and get her first glimpse of the Wraiths and how they used the crystals.

In thinking of the oncoming night, she looked upward. The dusk had grown brilliantly red and was blending into purple while they had been searching the city center, and Kathy realized they had lingered long enough. "We should get out of here," she said. "Night's coming."

As if her words were a command, the lights began to come on in the city. Jose watched them for a second, alarm tightening his features. "Move," he said, tugging at Hornsby as he passed. "Move!"

They ran from the hexagon of faceless statues to the pavilion just as the trapezoids began to glow. A strange thing happened then—strange even by the standards of this new world. Kathy was suddenly aware of the face-things, the parasites, crowding the edges of the pavilion. She couldn't see them but she could hear their whispering…so, so many voices whispering that it had created a hiss, a low buzz of unintelligible syllables that pushed madness around in the air as if it was its own breeze. What struck her as so strange was that they weren't focused on her or her companions. In fact, if they noticed the presence of human beings at all, they didn't seem to care. They remained at the outskirts of the hexagon, waiting. Their whispers were fervent, anxious, the buzz and murmur of a gathering crowd, unsure what to expect. Although she couldn't recognize the language, she could feel the meaning of the words.

The Wraiths were coming. The eyes of the gods.

"This way," Jose said, and she and Hornsby followed him to an odd double awning made of some sturdy-looking fabric, the Hesychian equivalent of leather, maybe. It jutted over one of the surrounding building's doorways, its uppermost flap draping like a small tent over the lower, thicker one. Boxes haphazardly stacked along the side of the doorway gave them relatively easy access to climb up to the awning, and they slipped between the two heavy pieces of fabric.

"I hid here last time and they left me alone," Jose whispered, peering through one of the vertical rips in the overhang. Through another, Kathy could see the trapezoids. Their formerly clear interiors had grown cloudy, and those clouds swirled within the confines of the crystal like small, contained storms. What Kathy had initially taken for veins of lighter blue had become small bolts of lightning creating an intermittent glow over the flame-like countenances of the statues.

The whispering grew as the light increased until for several minutes Kathy's senses were engulfed by both the light and the voices. Then it all suddenly snapped off—the lights, the sounds, the churning storms inside the crystal trapezoids.

"That's it?" Hornsby asked. "I expected…I don't know, more otherworldly fanfare. More trouble, I guess."

"Are they gone?" Kathy asked. She, too, was surprised. She'd expected the Wraiths to manifest as entities in some way, even if only for a moment. She'd imagined flickers of spectral things not unlike the statues that held their trapezoids. It wasn't so much that she was disappointed by the anticlimax, but rather, she was suspicious that maybe she'd missed something vital, something necessary to finding Claire and her team members and getting the hell out of there.

Jose gestured for them to lower their voices, patting the air between them to tamp down the noise. "They're here. Give it a minute. You'll feel them."

The three sat in silence, feeling the air and listening.

At first, Kathy noticed nothing, but then gradually their voices found her, like the first intrusions of wakefulness after a long sleep. To say she heard them at first wouldn't have been quite accurate, because it was more the impression of sound, an association with sound, than anything she could actually hear. If glass had a voice, it would have sounded like the Wraiths, high and sharp and brittle, tinkling, echoing, musical but haunting. Like the whispering, the Wraiths' language was unfamiliar but she thought she understood the sentiments behind it. She wondered briefly if the last inhabitants in this world all spoke a variation of the First Language, the language of the books in the library. The idea terrified her…but it made sense. Words that could create, alter, and destroy across language barriers, across time and space, words that could unmake people or remake them, drive them insane or change their very DNA…

Kathy peered through the rip in the upper awning again, looking for the source of the voices. She expected not to be able to see them, not in any traditional sense, and she was right. She knew about creatures whose physical bodies vibrated at higher or lower frequencies or occupied spaces between known physical matter. She'd read in old Network files about other creatures from universes where physicality existed beyond just the 3-D directional features of length and width and breadth, and so possessed an extra personal direction that human eyes were not sophisticated enough to see. Kathy suspected the Wraiths might have been of the latter category, present but more complex in structure than the physical limitations of sense could perceive.

"Can they see us?" she whispered to Jose.

"I don't know. They can sense us, though. I don't doubt they know we're here."

"But they haven't tried to take us like they did your team members, or kill us like they did the recon team. Why?"

"We're not blue lines yet," Hornsby replied, thinking aloud. "Maybe we're missing something…or have too much of something, like whatever makes us immune to infection from the faces."

"You may be right," Kathy said, keeping her voice hushed. "Maybe what we need to do is take a good look at the abductors before continuing to look for the abductees. Maybe get the Wraiths' attention."

Jose shook his head. "Are you crazy? Haven't we gotten enough attention from the things in this place?"

Suddenly, Kathy was aware of a change in the air. It was not the presence of something new but the absence of the voices and reduction of the anxious electrical charge to a barely perceptible hum. "Are they…gone already?"

"They go quiet sometimes. It could mean the day is coming on already." He peered out through the rip. "Sky's still dark, though. I don't know… it happened a few times when I was here last. I never could say for sure, but it's almost like they go to sleep or meditate or something. They don't do it often, but when they do, it's eerie. Feels kind of like waiting for the other shoe to drop."

"Maybe they're praying." Hornsby peered around Jose's head and out through the rip. "Could be even Wraiths have gods."

Kathy smiled at him. "You're pretty good at this occult detective work, Carl."

His big cheeks blushed as he grinned. "It's pretty fascinating. Or would be, if we weren't, you know, so close to constantly being killed by it and all."

"You bring up a good point, though. It's a behavior pattern to consider. In fact, there's a lot to unpack here. Jose, the first time you found the city center, it was just as the Wraiths were coming through the trapezoids. Where were you all standing?"

"What difference does that make?" Jose looked confused.

"Because your positions might have made the difference between disappearing and remaining. Could proximity to the statues have been a factor? Were they closer than you were? Maybe those trapezoids work like vacuums, expelling one entity and then rushing to fill it with another."

"We were…kind of all spread out," Jose said, trying to remember. "I was standing in the middle of the hexagon, sort of near Claire…and the others were probably closer to the statues, yeah."

"Okay, so that's a potential factor. Maybe timing was, too. Maybe we should consider the possibility that their abduction might have been accidental or just coincidental."

"No, I heard them, the Wraiths," Jose said, sounding nettled. "It wasn't an accident. They knew, Kathy. They took my team on purpose."

"Okay, so then they were chosen. Why? Was it random, or were they looking for certain traits?"

"They never said why. Just told me terrible things in those awful glassy voices."

"What did they say?" she asked.

Jose thought a moment. "It's hard to remember now. They tried to fill my head with...worst case scenarios, I guess. I tried to block it out, but I couldn't. They told me stories, night after night, of what was happening to the others, that they were naked, afraid, each of them alone in the dark—" Recollection dawned on his face. "In the dark—I'd forgotten about that! The Wraiths said Claire and the others were alone in the dark somewhere."

"Where in the dark?"

Jose's face fell. "I—I can't remember exactly. A place...without stars, I think they said. Which...doesn't help at all." He sighed.

Kathy patted his shoulder. "Everything helps, even if we can't see how yet. Any of the little details, no matter how strange or contradictory they might seem, could offer an answer." Another inconsistency in their situation suddenly occurred to Kathy, and she was surprised she had only just now realized it. "Like, for example, the bodies of the recon team."

Jose and Hornsby gave her blank looks.

"They were killed in or near the hexagon, according to the surviving member, Lt. Briggs. I heard a recording of his debriefing. He couldn't remember much other than that he'd lost the others 'back by the statues.' He said the Wraiths from the trapezoids brought light and that there was blood. And Jose, you said you never saw the Wraiths leave the hexagon except to return back through the trapezoids, right? The recon team had to have been killed in or near the hexagon, and yet, there are no bodies here. Given the evidence so far of the uneven passage of time and irregular rates of decay in this world, statistically we should have found at least one body or one skeleton, and if not bodies, then clothes, weapons, dog tags, something of their having been here. But there's no trace of them. And so again, it brings up the question of Lt. Briggs's survival, at least until he got back through the gateway. Why him? What was different about him?"

"I don't see how all this is going to help us find Claire and the others," Jose said, still prickly. He folded his arms across his chest defensively, gazing out through the rip in the fabric again.

"Not that Greenwood was right about anything else," Kathy replied, "but he was right about one thing. We need more information. We can't find anyone or fight anything if we don't understand anything about our situation, even just superficially. These aren't meant to be just philosophical questions, Jose. They're practical considerations for developing a combat strategy. If the Wraiths are lesser gods, there may be intelligent design at work here. That means guns and slivers of rock probably won't work, but certain words and incantations may be useful in protecting ourselves or binding them from doing more harm. If they are just as physical as the library monsters or just as insane as the faces and their infected victims, we might have to consider other methods. The point is, in these situations, weapons work only within specific parameters and by understanding the nature of the beast. The wrong weapon will only make the problem worse. And to be honest, some of the behavior of the creatures who live here is outside of my experience. My usual arsenal of spells and incantations at best would do nothing at all. At worst..." Her voice trailed off.

"Okay, so you want to study the Wraiths. I get it. And like I said, I'm not a scientist," Hornsby interjected after a moment, "but it takes years of observation and study and interaction to come to know anything about even the simplest species of animals. And those are animals we know work by the same laws of biology and physics that everything else on Earth does. But things like the Wraiths? Now, they could take decades, maybe centuries. Way more time than we have. What about them, exactly, do you need to know?"

"You're right, Carl," she said. "We can't hope to know everything, but we don't need to. We just need to know where they fit in the occult fabric of the multiverses."

"Is that all?" Jose asked sarcastically.

"It's far more limiting than it sounds," Kathy said. "Look, bear with me. I told you, this is my line of work. It's fair to say that I've seen a lot of shit. As a colleague once put it, we've experienced first-hand things about both the architects and architecture of time and space that would destroy the psychological, emotional, and spiritual constants that have kept humanity going for thousands of years. Sound like a heavy bag to carry? It is. My job is to keep all that in check. But I'm good at what I do, and I've been doing it a long time, long enough to have discovered certain patterns of occult behavior that stretch across multiple dimensions and the universes within them."

"I believe you. You've probably seen and learned more than most can handle," Hornsby said. "But I'm still not seeing how all that effort is going to help us."

Jose said nothing, but his scowl softened.

"I do the best I can," Kathy replied. "I'm not so sure I handle it well, but I'm still standing, so there's that." Her voice softened. "No one who knows what is really out there beyond the walls of this dimension sleeps well. Those patterns I mentioned are all we have to even the odds against us. That's the effort we make…and it makes a difference."

"What do you mean by patterns?" Hornsby asked.

"Okay, let me try to break it down. There are certain systems of magick, for lack of a better word, which are attributed to the greater and lesser gods of each particular dimension. They have characteristics specific to the worship or imprisonment of those gods. They also take into consideration the physics, biology, history, spiritualism, transcendence, enabling energies, and limitations of the worlds in which they originated. Yeah, I know, it's complicated. For thousands of years, the organization I'm associated with has been collecting and collating data on those systems, studying every aspect, comparing and contrasting different systems. We master what we can, so we can protect our world from other worlds, other dimensions… and sometimes, from ourselves."

"So if I'm understanding all this, you're saying every universe has its own laws of physics and its own kinds of magick," Hornsby said. "And people like you, in your line of work, try to keep them organized and in the dimensions where they belong."

"Exactly!" Isolated in that awning-made-tent, Kathy felt that freedom from inhibition again, that release in finally being able to talk about her work without restriction. It felt good, so she kept going. "We've discovered that there's an unusually high compatibility between the particular systems of our universe and those of dimensions that would otherwise contradict or negate each other. We believe this is why so many entities try to cross from their dimensions of origin to ours—dimension-hoppers, Travelers, those that make one great leap across worlds to bear offspring, those that stumble through accidentally, and of course, those that are summoned. Luckily, those who cause problems can be dealt with along the same compatibility principles by modifying our systems of magick and science to affect theirs.

"Another lucky thing is that we don't see the crossing over of greater gods. Each stays in its own dimension, creating and destroying, just like ours. We don't know if that's by choice or simple impossibility, but it's a good thing. As a race, there are few of them—likely not more than one or two in any one dimension at any one time. Except in a single case."

Jose finally turned to her, his interest clearly piqued. "What's that?"

"A place called Xíonathymia. It's believed to be one of the oldest worlds in one of the oldest universes. It also has the dubious distinction of being the only world we're aware of in all the known dimensions to contain more than one greater god. Until we learned about it, we didn't imagine that such a thing could exist in one universe. But five of them were banished to that one world. From the stories that have been passed down through the eons, these greater gods were so powerful, and either so utterly indifferent to suffering or so actively looking to cause it, that it took the combined magick of five universes to cast them out into a sixth, far away.

"To get rid of them, it took spells crafted from the language you found in those books in the library, Jose. And even those spells only prevent them from returning to their own original dimensions; they don't affect the greater gods' ability to summon lesser gods and other servants who can act on worlds to which they are summoned, or cross into certain survivable dimensions themselves. In fact, under the right circumstances, with the right combination of occult keys and portals, those binding spells weaken. Many of the worst cults on Earth, like the Hand of the Black Stars, worship those five gods. They've tried everything to bring them across to Earth. Believe me, I know. I've seen their attempts."

"Why?" Jose asked. "Why would they want something like that?"

"All they see is the potential for power. They either won't or can't accept that those beings would use them up, body and soul, with empty promises of power."

The men in the small awning-tent with her looked exhausted. She couldn't blame them. They were underfed, dehydrated, scared, and tired. She knew she had probably told them way more than they could fully process just then, knowledge she'd had time to come to terms with and still found overwhelming sometimes. It had felt good to talk about it out loud with other people, to finally frame its vast implications and catalog its cosmic limitlessness. Maybe that was selfish of her, but telling them served another purpose. They deserved to know what they were truly up against. They deserved as many answers as she could give. Kathy needed them prepared, armed with knowledge, to help her figure out how to make it off that world alive. There was something about the place, some quality to it that was, if she was honest with herself, more than she could tackle alone. She didn't want to die there, nor did she want anyone else to be lost to this strange world, but without help, how could she expect to find lost people if being lost or being found didn't really mean anything anymore?

"What I've been trying to say," she said, feeling the full weight of exhaustion herself, "is that understanding these Wraiths is like studying a lock to figure out what kind of key you need to open it. If we ever want to get out of here, we need to make sense of this world."

"Nothing makes sense here. You're trying to apply logic to a place that doesn't have any."

"Everything has some kind of internal logic, even dreams," Kathy said. "Even insanity. I just need to—"

Outside, the world beyond the rip in the fabric suddenly darkened. Likely, all it meant was that clouds had passed in front of the two moons, but the three tensed all the same, their breaths shallow, while they waited for the light to come back. When after several minutes it hadn't returned, Hornsby reached around Jose's shoulder and looked out from the rip.

He said something Kathy didn't quite catch. When she asked him to repeat it, he said, "The stars are gone."

"What? That can't be possible," Jose said. He made his way awkwardly to the edge of the awning and climbed down their makeshift staircase of boxes, Kathy and Hornsby right behind him.

When the three reached the ground, they stared up into the sky in amazement. It certainly did look to Kathy like the stars had winked out; the sky had gone black all over, and there was no cloud cover to be seen. The only light now came from the twin moons, and from both, it was a pale, weak glow at best.

Then Kathy saw the tiniest of movements up there, the faintest bruise-purple twinkling and wobbling of distant celestial bodies. Hesychia's moons, which had picked up their pace across the sky as if ashamed by their poor light offering, reinforced Kathy's theory by passing in front of some of those darkly twinkling pinpoints and briefly changing their color.

"No, look – the stars aren't gone, not exactly," Kathy said, growing uneasy. "They're still up there, but they're emitting a different kind of light, if you can call it light at all. Maybe it's ultraviolet light or something. They're…"

"Black light stars," Hornsby finished. "I never knew…I didn't think such a thing was possible, that stars could do that."

"Looks like here, they can," Kathy muttered.

Jose's face lit up again. "Wait—*that* was what the Wraiths had said! I got it wrong. They didn't say Claire and the others were in a place with *no* stars; they said a place with *black* stars. Maybe…maybe this is some kind of eclipse or something and this black light will show us the Green Team location. Or—or maybe Claire and the others were always here, but now we can get to them!" His eyes scanned the hexagon, ostensibly looking for some kind of change—a new door or opening somewhere, a mechanism triggered by the black stars.

Kathy couldn't share Jose's excitement. Her whole body had gone cold. That feeling of unease in looking up at the sky had become genuine horror, a sour taste in her mouth. The signs had all been there. She wanted to kick herself for not realizing it before. "Jose, are you sure? Are you absolutely fucking sure the Wraiths said a place with black stars?"

"Yeah," Jose said, looking confused by her evident agitation. "Why?"

"Because only one world we know of is so far on the fringe of its particular universe that it is said to sometimes pass through a galaxy of black stars. Only one world in one universe—one place where rational science is skewed and ancient magick is unreliable. A first world in an early universe…remember?"

Both Jose and Hornsby considered her words, but didn't seem to be making the connection yet.

"Don't you see? This place you've been calling Hesychia…what if it isn't a new world but a very old one, one that already has a name and some unimaginably powerful inhabitants? Think about it, guys. If this is Xíonathymia," Kathy said, looking up at the sky again, "then somewhere on this world are the most malevolent forces in five universes, the god-monsters of countless worlds' nightmares…and us."

Chapter 11

"So, the Wraiths...are they these gods?" Hornsby asked. He was watching the trapezoids carefully now as if he expected them to belch out new horrors.

"No, I don't think so. Lesser gods, maybe," Kathy replied, her own gaze drawn to the trapezoids, "but nothing I've seen of them so far is consistent with our information about the greater gods." It wasn't lost on her that the Wraiths likely hadn't gone anywhere, only gone quiet. Hornsby had suggested that they were praying, and it made a lot more sense now in context.

"But they're still dangerous," Hornsby added.

"Apparently, even this world's equivalent of rats in abandoned buildings are dangerous," Jose said.

"I was raised to believe there was only one God," Hornsby said, a little sadly. He shook his head. "One God who created everything. A loving God."

Kathy softened a little. Part of her job was supposed to be to shield people from the bigger picture, to maintain faith in the security of the world where she could. She could tell that she had shaken a core foundation in Hornsby's character—probably in Jose's as well.

"None of this means that the God you believe in isn't out there," Kathy said, giving him a reassuring pat on the arm. "If anything, all of it means it's more likely that He is."

"Maybe," Hornsby said. "But He isn't here—not on this world, in this universe. Not here."

Kathy was trying to think of a response when a glassy squeal made them all jump. The air changed again, charged with a crackling electricity. The face-whispering started again, and out there in the open, Kathy could see subtle alterations in the surfaces of the stone-paved ground and the building fronts. This time, the faces that formed had moving mouths and wild, sightless eyes, and their whispering was both ecstatic and terrified.

The Wraiths had awakened from whatever prayer or sleep or meditation they had been engaged in. Ripples of movement in the air gave Kathy and the others glimpses of form, partial silhouettes in muted hues of gray as they swirled and danced overhead within the hexagon.

Then the Wraiths began to sing. To Kathy, it sounded like the music made from the rims of crystal wine glasses, and Kathy found herself compelled to move closer to the edge of the hexagon. A moment later, Hornsby and Jose appeared on either side of her, caught up in the hypnotism of the music as well.

It took some effort for Kathy to break the spell of the singing and reclaim her own thoughts. In a dazed and vacant voice, she pushed through. "They use the trapezoids to come from somewhere else...some other part of the world, maybe. And they go back to that place. I'd bet that Claire, Rick, and Terry, if they're still alive, aren't here in this city. They're wherever the Wraiths go when the trapezoids are activated."

"Maybe," Jose said.

"What they left behind...maybe the Wraiths consider those things superfluous, or maybe they can't be transmitted through those portals," Kathy murmured, still more to herself than Jose and Hornsby. To them, she said, "We need to know where those trapezoids go."

Jose cast her a sidelong glance. "Sure, sure I'll ask. Hey, creepy Wraith things? We know you're busy and all, flying around making weird noises and sending faces to fuck with us, but when you find the time, do you think we could hitch a ride with you to, I dunno, wherever creepy Wraith things go when they're not here?"

One of the rippling forms broke from the blurry whirlwind above them and stopped in front of Jose. It spoke a single word to him in that unknowable glass language. Jose tensed. It seemed to be waiting for an answer from him.

"Jose, try to talk to it," Kathy said in a hushed voice.

"What?" Jose's head snapped in her direction. "I was kidding, I—"

Another sound came from the rippling figure, a kind of shattering sound which might have indicated impatience.

"What do I say?" Jose whispered.

"Ask them if your team is alive. Tell them we want to bring Claire and Rick and Terry home."

Behind the form, the trapezoids began to glow. The whispering intensified.

Jose opened his mouth to speak but couldn't. He might have been thinking about Terry's coronary stint or the runes in the library book they'd found. Likely, he was thinking of Claire.

The figure rippled again, made a streaking sound, and flew back to join the others.

"I'm sorry," Jose said, exhaling a shaky breath. "I'm sorry, I just froze. I couldn't…I kept thinking about Claire, and…"

"It's okay," Kathy said, and gave him a gentle squeeze on the shoulder. "It's okay."

Before them, the Wraiths had slowed their movements. The trapezoids began to hum and each of the rippling, barely visible figures returned to one of them.

"Come on," Kathy said, and tugged Jose and Hornsby out into the hexagon.

"Kathy, I don't think—" Jose's words were cut off by the light pouring from the trapezoids. It grew blindingly bright, engulfing them until there was nothing but the dazzling whiteness of it.

Kathy made her best guess at the direction of one of the statues. She closed her eyes against the glare but it was no use—the light penetrated her eyelids, filling her, swallowing her, moving her along…

When the light went out, the sudden darkness dropped her to her knees, breathless and confused. It took several minutes for her eyes to adjust again, and when she did, she gasped.

She was no longer in the city center, but in some kind of cave. A lightless fire crackled with burgundy flames, offering no heat. Beyond it was a pile of what looked like fur pelts and hides.

Kathy herself was naked. And she was alone.

* * * *

Carl Hornsby opened his eyes, but saw nothing.

"Hello? Kathy? Jose?"

No one answered.

By degrees, the totality of the void around him faded, and shapes pressed through into his vision. He blinked until he could see, albeit weakly, in the gloom of…of some kind of chamber. He felt cold, and realized that his clothing was gone. His paunch, the seat of his gut instinct, hung over his bare feet, and he patted it, processing the situation.

The transportation to another place through the trapezoids had apparently worked. He had been pulled through, at least the organic parts of him.

His contacts, he realized, hadn't made the trip. That was why everything was a little blurry. That was okay, though. What he needed to keep breathing and thinking and walking and screwing—all those parts had come along just fine.

The first thing to do was to figure out where he was, and then hopefully find the others. He stumbled forward in the dark, aware that he probably should have been more scared than he actually felt. He wasn't, though, not really. The air in the chamber had a rose-like smell, a little like a perfume his wife wore, and it offered a sense of serenity he hadn't felt in a long time...if ever at all. Carl didn't think he'd ever met a serene cop, not even those working the 12 Steps, where serenity to accept the things they could not change was a kind of mantra. Well, except maybe Darryl Lefine—Lefine was about as serene as a man got.

Remembering his partner suddenly like that made him sad. Lefine would have been fascinated by this other world, and probably far more useful to Kathy and Jose than he was. Lefine was scrupulous with details, brilliant with connections...he was a great detective, and a great man.

Well, he had been, before. He was probably dead now, though who knew what that even meant anymore? Carl had never considered himself a religious man, but his mom was a die-hard, church-going Roman Catholic, and his uncle had been a priest. He'd been raised to respect the religion even if he wasn't the practicing sort, and until he'd been forced through a gateway into another world, he hadn't realized how much those tenets of religion had formed the foundation of his whole sense of the universe. His views had been so narrow, despite his willingness to believe in aliens and ESP and chemtrails and government cover-ups and everything else. To entertain the thought of those things was fun. It made the world interesting. But to see proof that the reality of everything was so much more complex than he could ever have imagined...it was overwhelming.

What did other worlds and other gods imply about an afterlife? Were there places to go after somebody died, and if so, were they just other worlds in other dimensions beyond our knowledge?

Worse, if scientists now could break into one other dimension, what would stop them from breaking into others? And what would happen if they broke into Heaven...or Hell? Didn't gates work both ways?

Maybe there were no atheists in foxholes, but who was he supposed to pray to in a universe ruled by other gods? Could his God even hear him? And if he died there in Hesychia or Xíonathymia or whatever the hell this world was called, where would his spirit go then?

It was more than his brain and his gut together could process, and it made his chest tight. He had to pull it together, get back to finding Kathy and Jose. His objective had to remain in the forefront of his thoughts—he had to get back home. He missed his wife. With effort, he had managed to keep her from his thoughts, because the idea of never seeing her again was more than he could handle. She had to be sick with worry, and he couldn't do anything about it. She was probably scared to be spending nights alone, had probably called the precinct enough times to drive his captain crazy.

She cared. She loved him, and he loved her. She was the perspective he needed, the only perspective that mattered. However small a piece of the bigger picture it was, however insignificant it might seem in the grand scheme of multiple universes, his life with Alison meant everything to him, and wasn't significance really defined by who loved you? For Alison, he wanted to make it home.

He took inventory of the room around him, blinking and squinting to try to get a better look. He was standing in the center of a large chamber which might have been a bedroom or living room, an assumption based on the uncharacteristically comfortable appearance of the objects in the room. Against the corner of the wall across from him was a large rectangular object draped in gigantic pelts whose silvery fur looked fluffy. Behind the rectangle where the two walls met hung a large burgundy cloth, shiny like silk. The room was warmly bright, almost cheery, but there was no visible light source. Aesthetically, it was a lovely room to look at. Practically, he thought if he could find a way to cut or rip a piece of fabric off of one of the objects, he could at least cover himself up. That was a start.

The only other item of furniture in the room was a piece of wood shaped like a slanted waterfall whose purpose was lost on Carl. As for other wall decorations, there was one. It drew Carl's attention for the sheer strangeness of it. He made his way over to it and gazed up.

The object hanging on the wall looked to be a sculpture of some kind, although Carl couldn't begin to guess what it was meant to represent. The thin plate of metal in the background was shaped like a Rorschach inkblot test, vaguely bird- or bat-like. Extending from the top just under the arc of the "wings" were two curving tentacle-like things with smaller tendrils branching off beneath, curling and waving in different directions. The main tentacles curved upward like the arms of those statues in the city center and wrapped around the hilt of a downturned dagger with three curved blades. The tentacles appeared to be made of some kind of clay, but the dagger blades and handle looked like glass tinted white. Carl supposed it could have been a coat of arms of some kind, but if so, it told him nothing he could understand about the family bearing it.

The longer he stared at it, the more it seemed to waver a little beneath his gaze. He blinked a few times and turned away. Nothing here was safe even just to look at—not for long, anyway. He shook it off. He had more important concerns, anyway, than alien art. He needed to find a door, for starters. The room didn't seem to have one.

What he had initially taken for an essentially box-shaped room he saw now to be somewhat round. There were no corners and nothing like the giant archways he'd seen all over the city. There were no windows, either. Unless people materialized through the walls, he couldn't see how anyone came or went.

As he scanned the place again, looking for other things he might have missed, he noticed an oblong box with an odd clasp keeping it closed. It looked to Carl like some kind of trunk, large by Earth-trunk standards, but tiny in comparative scale to everything else he'd seen. It was about six or seven feet long by four feet wide and high. *Just big enough*, he thought, *to hold a human being*.

He moved with caution toward the trunk, watching it the whole time to see if it would change somehow. Part of him was convinced it would spring open and this world's equivalent of clothing moths would come flying out and devour him like an Angora sweater.

When he'd gotten to within five feet of the trunk, it jerked, rocking a little. Carl flinched.

"Dammit, I knew it! I knew it," he said to himself. "This fucking place."

Still, he couldn't help creeping closer again. He could hear the occasional thump from the inside, but nothing violent enough to move it again. When he reached the clasp, it fell loose and the lid sprang open. He sucked in a breath, bracing himself for whatever might come flying out. He ticked the seconds off in his head...but nothing happened.

He peered in, then turned away with a sad shake of the head.

Two male human corpses lay in the box. The lower right leg of one was missing, but otherwise, the bodies were fully intact. In fact, they were more than intact; there was an abundance of extra bones that shouldn't have been there. They protruded from the desiccated skin, fused to the corpses' hands and forearms, ribs, and skulls. They didn't look like human bones. Carl couldn't tell for sure, but they didn't look like animal bones, either. Carl thought they might very well be the sort of thing that would cause Paragon readouts of blue lines instead of green.

No human could have survived those kinds of alterations without pain along with the hideous disfigurement. If the corpses were part of Jose's Green Team, then it was probably a blessing for them to be dead. Still, he didn't look forward to having to break the news to Jose. The researcher seemed like a decent enough guy, and Carl knew what it felt like to lose colleagues to violent and unfair circumstances.

He was about to turn away when one of them groaned. He looked down into the trunk again and saw one of the corpses try to lift its head, the shriveled eyes in their sockets straining to look up at him. The bottom jaw dropped to speak, but it only managed another moan.

"Oh my God." Carl could only gaze in horror at the pitiful things that had once been men. How had that happened to them, and why? And what the hell was still keeping them alive?

"Ki...ki..." the corpse-man begged from the trunk. "Ki uh. Ki uh." What was he trying to say?

Carl returned to the edge of the trunk. The mutated arm with its extra claw bones shook as it reached for him. "Kill...uz," it managed. "Please."

"I...I can't...I..." Carl looked around for something he could use to put the two out of their misery, but saw nothing at hand. "There's nothing here I can use. I'm sorry."

"Kill...kill..."

Carl considered his options a moment, swallowed his reservations, and climbed into the box. He put his arms around the neck of the one who had reached for him. The flesh felt like old, dry paper, and it flaked and crumbled under his touch. His fingers sank to the bone. The shriveled eyes jerked in the skull as they tried to look at him, and Carl's skin crawled. He put all his strength into snapping the neck bones. He heard a little pop and thought the job was done, but the bottom jaw kept working up and down, making those awful syllables that tried to be words.

Carl winced. He didn't understand how the neck bones crumbled beneath his fingers but the jaw and eyes kept working, begging him. A part of him detached from himself, while the seeing and feeling parts took over. There was no other thought in his mind except to make that monstrosity stop moving. Carl rose, revulsion driving him now. He lifted his bare foot and brought it down hard on the thing's head. The skull caved and his heel went straight down into something warm and mushy. He retched, lifted his foot, and brought it down again and again and again until finally the body stopped twitching and the reaching arm fell back. There was nothing left of the shriveled eyes or the jaw to move now. He turned to the other body and did the same thing.

Carl climbed out of the trunk, dragging his foot along the floor to wipe off as much of the corpses' brains as he could, then stumbled a few feet and threw up on the floor. He flushed hot and for a moment, he thought he might keel over and pass out right into his puddle of vomit.

Leaning over, his hands on his knees, he sucked in lungfuls of air until the heat faded and the sweat on him cooled. Then he backed away from both the trunk and the vomit, intent on finding something to wrap around his naked body and a door to get the hell out of there.

The room had changed again. It had grown somewhat darker and several degrees colder, he noticed with a whole-body shiver. The rectangular piece of furniture covered in pelts was gone, and so was the wooden waterfall that had stood opposite it. In the space between, there now stood a large statue of polished black stone, a figure of monstrous proportions. Lefine had once shown him pictures of bacteriophage viruses under a microscope—he was always reading science articles and showing Carl the strange ones—and the creature the statue represented looked a lot like one of those. It had a bulbous head, what Lefine had called an icosahedron, like a twenty-sided die, that was both hairless and faceless. Its torso was narrow, braided or twisted, and armless, and it sat on a tripod of spider leg-like appendages which held it up. In between the legs were other smaller tendrils, carved to look like they were waving, and on the end of each was a reptilian type of eye.

The statue stood on a stage between two massive stone pillars, with a chain leading from the top of each pillar to the "neck" area of the statue. Steps leading up to the stage were flanked on both sides by large stone bowls of a burgundy substance which looked and moved like fire but gave off no light.

The stage and the statue took up most of the chamber. Down where Carl stood, the trunk was gone. To Carl's surprise and unease, even the floor looked gone; he could feel a smooth, cold surface under his feet but saw nothing but black. His vomit was gone as well. There was nowhere else to go but up the steps.

Carl took a deep breath and climbed the first step, then the second. He felt his nakedness acutely, like he was on display. His legs felt heavy as he mounted the next step, and the next. There were twenty of them; he counted as he made his way up. When he finally reached the platform, he saw piles of fabric at the bases of the two pillars. Keeping his eye on the statue, he moved to one of the piles and found a few pieces of fabric to gird himself with. That made him feel a little better. When he turned back to face the statue, he saw the woman.

She was lying on her side directly beneath the body of the statue, the creature's legs surrounding her like thin bars of a cage. Since she had her back to him, he couldn't see her face, but he could see short blond hair and a drape of white fabric over her body. He tensed. She had been a blue line, too, and just because he couldn't see any obvious mutations didn't mean there weren't any. She was breathing, though—he could see the side of her chest rising and falling—so he had to go check on her. He jogged over to the legs of the statue and passed between them to its underside. It was warmer there, and Carl's gut logged the information, but his head pushed it away for the time being. He knelt beside the woman and turned her over onto her back.

Despite a few bruises, she had a natural kind of prettiness that reminded Carl of the farm girls and cheerleaders he'd grown up with in rural Pennsylvania. She had eased into her mid-thirties without losing that perky look of both, a combination of soft and athletic, of innocent and teasing. Seeing her made him think of Alison again.

Her eyes were closed, her mouth slightly open, but when Carl gently shook her shoulder, she stirred, blinked a few times, and opened her eyes.

When she fully regained her senses, she jumped and pulled back sharply from Carl. "Who...who are you?" she asked. Her voice was raspy and suspicious, nothing like the little girl's face it came from.

"I'm Carl Hornsby," he replied in his gentle-cop voice. "I'm a police officer, ma'am. I've come with a small team of people to find you and bring you home."

She blinked as if having trouble comprehending his words. "Paragon sent you?"

He stifled the sarcasm in his reply. "They made a compelling argument for us to come."

"Who? Who did they send?"

"Well, there's me, ma'am, and a consultant, Kathy Ryan, who has a lot of experience with, you know, other dimensions and stuff. We had a military man with us, but..." he saw from her expression that he didn't need to explain further about Markham. "And one of your team members, who managed to find a way out of this place once before. Jose Rodriguez."

The suspicious scowl on her face dissipated. "Jose? He's okay? He's here?"

"Yes, yes, and yes, the last time I saw him."

"Where...where are Jose and the lady—"

"Kathy," Carl offered.

"Where are they now?"

Carl regarded her sheepishly. "They came with me through the trapezoid, but...we got separated."

The woman nodded. She was shivering and clutching the thin white fabric, which Carl could see she had wrapped around her like a goddess in a myth. "They killed them," she whispered. "Terry, Rick...they did things to change them and then they killed them. They...changed me, too, but it was different. They killed Rick and Terry."

"Who?" Carl asked in that same gentle, soothing voice. "Who killed your team members?"

She stared blankly at Carl for a moment, and then said, "We have to get out of here. They could come back...This room changes..." She tried to stand, faltered, then tried again.

Carl stood, too. "Okay," he said. "Okay, let's go. Let's find the others, huh? Kathy and Jose?"

"Jose," she repeated. "Yes." She let him take her arm and usher out from under the statue.

"Do you know how to get out of this room?"

"There's only one door," she said.

"Right, right. I need you to show me where the door is, Ms. Banks."

"Claire. Call me Claire."

"Okay, Claire. Can you show me where the door is?" Carl led her gently toward the stairs.

"It's not in this version, not often. We usually have to wait until it changes again."

"Okay, we can do that. We just need to hang tight for a while then, right?"

"This version...this is the killing room." She hesitated at the top of the stairs.

"Oh?"

Claire glanced back at the statue and then met Carl's gaze. "The Wraiths are afraid of the Void. When I was under the Void, they left me alone."

"The Void...Do you mean...that statue there?"

"It's not always a statue. Just like the room isn't always a room."

Carl looked up at the thing again, looming over them, a purer black than darkness. It remained completely motionless, but if Claire was right and not delirious or delusional, it wouldn't stay that way. He turned back to her.

"Are you afraid of the Void?"

She looked away, into the gloom behind him. "I was a scientist once," she said with a wistful, faraway smile.

"I've heard," Carl said. "A good one."

"Now I'm afraid...of everything."

"It's okay to be afraid in this place," Carl said. "There's a lot to be scared of."

She leaned closer to him and whispered in his ear. Her breath was surprisingly cold. "The Void is a devourer of worlds. It doesn't think; it just eats. It eats. And it's waking up now."

Carl glanced again at the statue. So far as he could tell, it remained mute, unmoving. "How do you know?" he asked.

She pulled back a little and smiled to herself. "Because the Wraiths are coming to feed it."

Chapter 12

The light had torn the beginnings of a scream from Jose, but then it winked out, taking his voice and vision with it. For a few minutes, he was convinced he must be permanently blind, and cursed listening to that crazy bitch and her spiel about big gods and little gods and languages that could create and destroy.

But then Jose's eyes adjusted to a new darkness. The hexagon, the statues, the buildings were all gone. So were his clothes. When he tried sucking in a breath, he felt a small, sharp pain where he'd had a cavity filled a year or so before. It looked like he was in a cavern of immense proportions. Stalactites of glittering stone hung from a ceiling several hundred feet above, some of them as long as buses, while stalagmites reached up for them. Both gave off a faint phosphorescent light, though as he inspected one of the nearby stalagmites, he saw that it was a kind of moss growing on them, and not the rock formations themselves, which glowed. Jose listened for a moment and heard water dripping somewhere ahead and to the right. He heard no voices, though, human or otherwise. Was he alone here? And where, exactly, was "here," anyway?

He thought of the trapezoids, and of what Kathy had said: *"They use the trapezoids to come from somewhere else, some other part of the world, maybe. And they go back to that place."*

Maybe she had been right, crazy or not. Maybe his whole team hadn't been vaporized, as he'd secretly feared. Maybe they'd just been...moved. He found the thought comforted him a little—the first real inkling of peace since they'd originally discovered the city.

"I'd bet that Claire, Rick, and Terry, if they're still alive, aren't here in this city. They're wherever the Wraiths go when the trapezoids are activated."

He hoped Kathy was right…and found that he could actually get behind her way of thinking. He knew Claire; she was tough, a fighter. She wouldn't just lie down and give up, not if there was any way of surviving out here. And Rick and Terry, they were smart, resourceful—Claire had hired them for a reason. Jose allowed himself the tiniest cautious hope that he really would find his team again. Maybe, just maybe, he could make up for leaving them behind.

He began walking. He was aware of the parts of him dangling between his legs as he walked, and made a mental note to find something he could use for clothing, if he could. He circled around a grouping of stalagmites and then—carefully, as some of them were sharp and just about balls-height—stepped over some others, heading in the direction of the dripping water. At least, he hoped it was water that was dripping.

His backpack was gone, too, left behind in the city center with his clothes, and he felt surprisingly more vulnerable without the former than the latter. He could have used a snack just then or a drink. He didn't relish the idea of finding sustenance from any part of this mixed-up world, but realized he might not have a choice.

The cave beyond the rock formations narrowed into branching tunnels, not that such narrowing affected him any. The ceilings were still echoingly high. He chose the one to the left. The dripping water, he hoped, was coming from that direction, and although he knew he couldn't trust sound or any other sense completely, it was all he had to go on.

It was dark in those tunnels, and he wished again he had a flashlight, even one of those crappy Paragon-issued ones. No glowing moss grew on those walls, although something unpleasantly slippery, too smooth and too cold, did coat them. As he felt his way along, he grimaced at the sensation of the stuff being uprooted by his fingers and sliding across the backs of his hands.

He had walked just long enough to start doubting the direction he'd chosen when he heard the sound of footsteps. They stopped as suddenly as his own. He would have been inclined to chalk it up to echoes except that the faint green glow of the moss illuminated a bend in the path a few feet ahead. And the glow wavered a little. It was moving. Slowly, he crouched, feeling for something he could use as a weapon. His hand closed around a rock and he stood, edging as quietly as he could toward the wall.

After a few minutes of silence, the glow came around the corner.

Jose let out a battle cry made more of fear than bravery and hoisted the rock overhead. He was about to bring it crashing down on the head of the figure in front of him, controlling the glow, when he recognized Kathy. She flinched when she saw him, her hand fluttering up to her chest.

"Oh shit! Oh my God, I'm sorry!" He dropped the rock. "I'm sorry. Are you okay?"

She smiled at him. "Yeah, yeah, I'm okay. You just scared a year off my life, but it's probably one of the old waiting-to-die ones anyway, so it's okay. How about you?" She was carrying a stick whose tip was wrapped in the glowing moss. It looked to Jose like some kind of alien cotton candy.

"I'm fine, yeah." Jose knew it was probably rude to check her out, but she was wearing very little and had a nice body. She'd found some yellowish fur pelts and gray strips of hide, it looked like, and had tied a thin one across her breasts. Two others she'd made into a loincloth and thong, bound at her hips with the strips of hide. She'd even managed to fashion crude little fur boots, laced above her ankles. She looked a little like those women on old men's adventure books and comics.

If she noticed his ogling, she pretended not to. "We ought to get you something to wear," she said, turning back in the direction she'd come. "Unless you like your junk slapping around in the breeze."

He remembered then that while she was wearing very little, it was still more than he had on, and he blushed. "Oh yeah. Yeah, I mean, better to put all this away before these greater gods of yours take a look and make me one of them, huh?"

Jose heard her chuckle without turning around. "Sure, you don't want to embarrass them."

They turned another corner and emerged into a smaller cave than where Jose had first appeared. In the center of the cave was what looked like a fire pit with a stack of wood sticks. A substance danced and licked at the air above it, and although it gave off no light or heat, Jose assumed it was a kind of fire from its shape and the way it moved. Beyond that was the stack of strange animal pelts and hides. He made his way around the fire to them, playfully calling over his shoulder, "Want to turn around? I'm shy, you know."

She cocked an eyebrow at him but smiled.

He rooted through the pile of pelts. The furs and the skin under them both felt incredibly soft, and he wondered what animal they'd come from. Some of the hairless hides reminded him of the awning material in the city center. Others, he suspected, came from those terrible faceless things in the library. Those skins had been cut into strips, and although Jose had no desire to touch any part of those monsters, he saw that it was the most efficient way to keep the pelts in place.

"Have you seen anyone else? Hornsby?"

Jose shook his head. "No one yet but you."

"Yeah, same here." She glanced around the cave. "If you grab a stick, you can get a tangle of moss from that tunnel over there and make a kind of torch. And I think we should grab one or two of the smaller pelts. Maybe we can make waterskins or little packs to carry stuff."

"You're pretty good at this survival thing," Jose said. "Girl Scout?"

"Gamer," she said, and winked.

They gathered up three small skins and some strips of hide and managed to make three little pouches. Kathy tied one each around her thighs and Jose tied one to the belt around his waist.

"Ready?" Kathy asked.

"Ready," Jose said.

She picked up her moss torch and led him down a well-lit tunnel. There, the moss grew along the walls in abundance.

"I thought plant life might mean water, but I haven't seen any," Kathy said as Jose made a torch.

"Me either," he replied. "I thought I heard it, but—well, you know how sound is here."

She was quiet for a moment, and then said, "I'm sorry, Jose, for dragging you and Hornsby here. I'm used to just leaping into things, and I forget sometimes that certain situations call for a group decision."

"Kathy, you might be just about the craziest woman I have ever met." He grinned at her. "But I trust you, crazy or not. You have good instincts. Where you leap, I follow."

She smiled back. "Thanks."

Since the tunnel with the moss ended in a thick wall of rock fifty yards or so down, they backtracked again and chose another tunnel. It slanted downward and grew colder, which did not seem conducive to getting the hell out of there, but neither mentioned it. There was really no other way to go, and after a time, the tunnel leveled out and led to another cavern.

They moved through it slowly, navigating the stalagmites and ducking under those stalactites whose fang-tips reached low enough to graze them. Occasionally a chirping sound would echo against the walls and they would keep still, waiting and watching small undulating pathways appear in the moss, but nothing made a move to attack them. It struck Kathy again that Xíonathymia might once have been a beautiful, vibrant world. That so much had been wiped out, likely by the presence of those greater gods, felt like a genuine loss.

The cavern narrowed again into another tunnel, although this one looked like it had been deliberately excavated. Metal beams supported the walls and ceiling, glowing faint blue and providing just enough light for them to see their way. Occasionally, the rocky surfaces between the beams would catch the faint light and cast little shadows to form faces; although those faces watched them closely, almost contemptuously, given their snarling expressions, they didn't whisper. It was as if Kathy and Jose being there in that part of the world had somehow forced them into grudging silence. Whatever power to manipulate that the faces might have had over them in the city, that power seemed to be gone now.

"They're watching us," Jose said.

"I noticed," Kathy replied. "Just keep moving."

The tunnel widened and then turned to the left. They followed as it dipped and rose and bore to the left, narrowing and widening, until they turned a corner and the rock gave way to a hallway. It was so much like a standard, human-built American hallway that Kathy and Jose stopped short. It even ended in a rectangular wooden door about six and a half feet high, with a glass doorknob and key plate. In fact, the only thing alien about the scene before them was a single glowing orb, like a swinging lightbulb, hanging from the ceiling in front of the door.

"There's no chance that door down there is somehow the other gate you found, is there?"

Wide-eyed, Jose shook his head. "I don't think so. I don't remember."

Of all the oddities Jose had seen in that world so far, that little reminder of Earth was somehow the worst. It was cruel, in a way—like they were being teased with it, a photograph of water given to a man dying of thirst.

"Could be a trap," he said after a time. "What do you think?"

"Could be," Kathy said, "or it could be a way out."

"Why does it look like one of our doors? How could it?"

"I don't know," Kathy replied. "Maybe it looks however the person looking at it imagines it should look. Let's go check it out."

Jose followed her to the door. Upon up-close inspection, it certainly looked like a regular door to him, a single-panel pine interior door with a tarnished metal key plate and a polished glass knob. It even had mundane, human-made hinges, also of tarnished metal.

"We should open it," Kathy said, staring at the knob.

"Wait." Jose got down on the cold ground and tried to peer under. He couldn't see anything but more ground. He pulled himself up into a crouch and peered through the keyhole. Another strikeout – he saw only darkness.

"Anything?" she asked as he stood.

"Nope. Can't see a damn thing. You might as well open it. There's no other direction to go, right?"

"Right," she agreed.

Since he'd met Kathy Ryan back at Warner's house, she'd seemed to him either incredibly brave or incredibly reckless. She'd only ever seemed scared about discovering the true identity of the planet, and even that, she managed pretty well. She hesitated now, though, her hand reaching with maddening slowness, with reluctance, toward the doorknob. She was scared of whatever was on the other side of that door, and that made him scared, too. He had told her the truth about his trusting her instincts, so if she was worried—a woman who swallowed the knowledge of malignant greater gods for breakfast and then got on with her day—then he figured he ought to be damn well terrified.

She grasped the knob, turned it, and pushed open the door.

* * * *

Before Carl could ask Claire about the Wraiths, he heard a sound like glass breaking. It was them.

He glanced around the room, trying to keep his cool. He couldn't see anything but the half-changed room—the far side across from the statue had dropped away into deep space, glittering with a mix of those black light stars and blazing white ones, swirling nebulae in rainbow hues and faraway planets. A single thin platform of wood about four feet in width ran from the center of the stage's bottom step in a convoluted zig-zag across that endless space, down into the depths and up against, winding up and around again, and eventually arriving at a small wooden door in a jagged portion of sheetrock wall fifty or sixty yards across from the statue.

Behind the statue rose more stone pillars floating unevenly, their chains likewise connected to the creature's neck. On the stage at the base of the statue were five exceedingly large chairs set in a semi-circle facing outward.

"This is bad," Claire said. She was shaking badly, her gaze darting from the five chairs to the door across from them. "This is very bad."

"What's happening?" Carl asked.

"This is the room under the room, at the edge of the world. The Wraiths aren't the only ones coming."

She flinched and covered her ears as another glassy shriek tore across their little section of the cosmos. Carl could see them now, the Wraiths. They were pale gray slips of outline, a line of hovering ghosts following the ramps across the stars. They were making their way toward the statue, their voices like hundreds of glass things tinkling and splintering.

And then there was a groaning behind him, the sound a building might make upon waking up and stretching its legs. His heart pounding, he grabbed Claire and pulled her to him to protect her from whatever had made that sound, but she pulled away and ran as he turned in its direction.

He had suspected it would be the giant statue moving, but that made it no less terrible to see. Its head twisted from side to side as if it was working the kinks out of its neck and torso. It stretched its legs like stiff fingers against the stage. The myriad surfaces of the head blurred and stretched, splitting open to form a collection of mouths which in turn swam and stretched and melded with each other to form bigger mouths, then split apart again and swam on.

Beneath the behemoth creature, Claire cowered between its legs, covering her ears and squeezing her eyes tightly shut.

The Void had awakened, and the Wraiths had come. Carl thought again about Alison.

"I'm sorry, baby," he said to her, hoping somehow she could hear. "I'm sorry. I tried to come home to you." He turned back to the edge of the stage and looked down into the endless galaxies sprawling out below him. He wondered if it would hurt, jumping into that chaos. Would he freeze to death? Asphyxiate? Would he implode from pressure changes? However he died, it was preferable to being torn apart by all those hungry mouths or forced to mutate into a quivering, malformed monster by the greater gods of a world that had forgotten more than Earth might ever know.

A heavy grating sound, neither thunderous like the Void nor high-pitched and crystalline like the Wraiths, drew his attention across the chasm to the little wooden door. It was moving, swinging inward, and through it emerged two figures.

Oh my God, Carl thought. *They made it!*

"Kathy! Jose!" he shouted as loudly as he could. For several moments, their astonished gazes were fixed on the Void, and on the swirling slips of silhouette in a frenzied rush toward it. He called again and finally they turned their heads in his direction, their eyes lighting up in recognition.

"Carl!" Jose called. "You okay?"

"Yeah!" he shouted back. "I found Claire!"

"What?" Jose cupped his hand around his ear.

"I…found…Claire!" he called.

Jose's expression rippled with a number of emotions, not the least of which was relief. "Where? Where is she?"

Carl pointed toward the legs of the Void, where Claire, unharmed, had taken to hugging herself tightly.

"Claire!" Jose shouted. "Claire!"

She couldn't hear him. Carl knew the best chance for both of them was getting to Kathy and Jose and that door.

"Whatever happens, Alison," he said under his breath, beneath the din of the Wraiths, "I love you, and I'll find you wherever and whatever Heaven really is." Then he turned and ran for Claire.

* * * *

Kathy watched in mute horror and fascination as Carl Hornsby ran across the ebony stage toward the mammoth creature that looked like a virus. A blonde woman swathed in a flimsy white fabric shivered and hugged herself beneath it. It reminded Kathy a little of those disaster videos where people were told to brace themselves in doorways during storms. She had never understood the wisdom or seen the safety in such an action, nor did she understand now why the woman was giving Hornsby such a hard time about dragging her out from under the creature. Finally, he must have mentioned Jose; he pointed in their direction and the woman stopped struggling and looked. Jose waved and, apparently in shock, she offered a dazed wave in return. It was then that she let Hornsby tug her by the arm out from under the legs of the beast and toward the stairs. The wooden ramps connecting the stage to the platform on which they currently stood were narrow, and it was impossible to tell how soundly they were put together. She hoped they'd make it.

Already, the first of the Wraiths had reached the stage, and from the shattering sounds it was making, Kathy thought it might have spotted Hornsby and was signaling the others. The shining black creature with the multiple mouths was lifting its legs and crashing them down on the stage; Kathy didn't think it was meant as a hostile movement against Hornsby and Claire, but rather the impatient stamping of a hungry, agitated animal. That didn't make those spiky legs, easily eight feet per jointed segment and bristling with thorny protrusions, any less dangerous to the two on the other side.

"I should go help," Jose said, and started for the ramp.

Kathy reached out and grabbed his arm. "We don't know how stable those ramps are. If we go running, we can shake them loose and send them tumbling down to"—she looked down into a twirling galaxy coasting by— "to that. Plus, you'll draw more attention to Claire and Hornsby. That thing doesn't seem aware of them just yet."

"I think the Wraiths are. I can't leave her there. I can't leave her again," Jose said, his eyes and voice pleading.

"We won't. We're not going anywhere without her or Hornsby," she said. "We're going to keep the Wraiths distracted, and that thing, too, if we have to, so they can get across."

"And how're we gonna do that?" he asked.

"Give me a minute. I'm thinking," she said.

He shook his head. "You really are certifiably crazy, you know that?"

She smiled wryly. "Hell yes, I know that."

He smiled back. "Okay then. Leap away, crazy lady."

Chapter 13

Kathy stepped forward to the edge of the platform and began reciting the words of an old spell. She knew several of them, some in ancient Egyptian and Greek, some in Sumerian and Babylonian, a couple in Aramaic, ancient Hebrew, and Latin, and even one or two in the ancient tongue of the Celts. This one was different, though. It was a basic binding spell, but in the First Language, the language of beginnings and endings. She hadn't been entirely truthful with Jose, Hornsby, and Markham in the library when she said she only knew a few concepts and one or two words. It was true that her knowledge was extremely limited, but not as limited as she'd made it sound. She had been protecting them, and protecting creation along with them. Sure, she'd felt an inordinate amount of trust in those men, enough to confide important but ultimately harmless secrets about her brother, the nature of her job, and the complexity of the multiverse; none of those things could do much harm to anyone, other than maybe to the men's credibility and reputations. That language was another matter, though. Her professional instincts had kicked in and overridden trust.

That language could unmake galaxies.

She hoped that what she had learned, that simplest of binding spells, would be enough to hold the Wraiths and their pet while Hornsby and Claire made it across.

"Kathy...what are you doing?" Jose whispered. He kept glancing nervously at the stage, where Hornsby appeared to be trying to convince Claire to step onto the platform. Claire, meanwhile, kept watching the movement of the Wraiths, waving at them like they were angry bees. The Wraiths didn't seem to be able to touch them, not in a fully physical way, but flying around their heads like that, they were certainly distracting. They could make Claire and Hornsby fall if they followed them back onto the ramp. None of them knew the full capability of the Wraiths, either; their glass voices might be able to incite madness or introduce infection in ways the faces couldn't achieve. Worst of all, it looked to Kathy like some of them were trying to draw the big beast's attention to the humans' attempt at escape, and she was sure that thing could touch them and then some.

Kathy glanced at Jose and said, "The only spell I know that might bind them. We can't fight them all, but we can cripple them, at least, and increase our chances."

"Will it take long? To work, I mean?"

"I hope not," Kathy replied. We're on borrowed time."

"How's that?"

"See those five chairs over there?"

Jose looked and nodded.

"I'm good, Jose, but I'm not good enough to fight off five gods. We need to be out of here before they show up, dig? Now let me concentrate."

Jose nodded and backed off. Kathy closed her eyes and began mouthing out the chant, whispering, whispering like the faces, doing her best to make her mouth form the words. She was scared. She was downright terrified. She kept her hands clenched into tight little fists to keep them from shaking. She blocked out the sounds of breaking glass, of the groaning of moving mountains, of Jose's impatient fidgeting and the unintelligible syllables coming from Hornsby and Claire. On top of all that, the whistling of a source-less wind had begun to build, likely from the spell. She pushed it all away, found the cool, dark, empty stage in her mind, and imagined the words of the spell. As she shined a single light in her mind on the words, she pronounced them slowly, meaningfully, over and over, until she had recited them a total of nine times. Then she opened her eyes.

The sounds and sights around her came back to flood her senses. The Wraiths flickered angrily. They looked a little like overexposed images stuck in a film reel, jittering in place along the edge of the stage as their voices shattered across the chasm. The creature behind them had broken the chains that had linked it to the surrounding pillars, which had floated a little away from the stage. But the monster, too, appeared to be bound in place. Its legs lashed wildly and its head snapped back and forth, the many mouths working into fierce, angry shapes that emitted thundering wails. Hornsby and Claire were making slow progress along the ramp. He led her down a staircase and across a small platform there, then up another staircase and toward a ramp which swung out over the vast, star-swept universe around them. Kathy watched tensely as Hornsby turned to check on Claire, and sucked in a breath as he teetered on one foot misplaced too close to the edge, his arms pinwheeling. The wind had ramped up, whipping at their hair and the fabrics wrapped around them. And had the ramps grown narrower? Was that what the creatures across from them were doing with those wordless voices? It occurred to her again that maybe they weren't wordless at all...

"Come on!" Jose was shouting. "You're almost there! You can do it!" He paced nervously like an excited dog, anxious to get out onto the ramp and help. "This way! You've got it! Come on!" His reserve broken, he skittered out onto the ramp, his arms spread, looking to close the distance between them. Kathy saw Claire inch around Hornsby on the ramp and for a horrific second, she thought Hornsby was going to get pushed over the edge. He caught his balance again, though, and followed after Claire.

She reached Jose and rushed to hug him. The two clung to each other, stumbling uncomfortably close to the edge, the wind zipping around them. Jose managed to keep them balanced, and to help her back to the platform. Exhausted, Claire slipped from Jose's arms and sank against the piece of wall by the door, muttering that she had been safer under the Void and gesturing at the big monster.

Hornsby was about five feet away from the platform when the first of the greater gods of Xíonathymia the Great Far Place arrived. His arrival was heralded by a low rumble that shook the stage. The stairs crumbled and fell away, as did the stage all around the giant creature. The Wraiths screamed as they, too, dropped into the limitless gulf beneath them. A crack of blue lightning hit the stage, tearing it nearly in two, and the monster roared.

There were few descriptions in the old books of Iaroki the Swallower of Suns, but the creature that emerged from beneath the legs of the monster Claire referred to as the Void matched what Kathy had read. He was humanoid with the exception of his legs, which bent back at the knees like the haunches of an animal. He was very tall, about ten feet or more, and gaunt. His wiry gray musculature was exposed, and it writhed like worms on his frame. Each of his shoulders had three gray tentacles snapping at the air over his head, and the backs of his hands had long talons that curved up and out toward his long, clawed fingers. His hairless head had three faces, if they could be called that—one in front, and one to either side. These were little more than crisscrossed mouths, opening like Xs, and a single eye in the uppermost V of each face. From the top of the head, three twisting horns of black rose amid a crown of blue flame.

"Try not to look directly at him," Kathy told the others. "No one is meant to look into the face of gods for long."

Iaroki stretched out his arms and let loose with a shout so loud it brought Kathy and Jose to their knees. Claire covered her ears and cried out.

Hornsby was gone.

"Carl?" Jose said, searching around frantically. "Carl!"

"Help me," Hornsby's voice came from below. "I—I can't hang on."

Kathy and Jose crawled to the edge of the platform and saw Hornsby's fingertips, followed by the rest of him dangling over outer space. The fabric around him whipped around his waist and legs.

"Hang on, Carl, we've got you," Kathy said. "Grab our hands." She and Jose reached down for him, bracing themselves as best they could against the platform.

"I don't know if I can," Hornsby said. "I—"

"Carl, you need to trust us," Jose broke in. "Come on, there's not much time."

Hornsby looked from Kathy's face to Jose's. Uncertainty lined his features. With effort, he grabbed for Jose's hand.

"Gotcha, buddy," Jose said.

Kathy held out both hands to Carl. She could see the leap of faith he was making in his expression, and letting go, he snatched at Kathy's hands...and missed.

He shouted in fear and frustration, hanging by one hand to Jose, who was pulling, straining against his weight.

"Take my hands," Kathy said calmly to Hornsby. "Look at me. Look at me, Carl. Don't look down—look at me. And take my hands."

Hornsby reached up toward Kathy's outstretched hands and this time, Kathy was able to grab onto him. She and Jose pulled, but Hornsby was heavy. She put her back and thighs into it, pulling with all her strength, but still, she skittered forward on the platform. For a moment, she had a terrible vision of losing her balance completely and toppling over the side of the platform, taking Hornsby and, by extension, Jose with her momentum and dragging them down, down, down into endlessness.

Instead, she felt arms around her waist, and glanced over her shoulder to see Claire.

"Hi there," she said, and Claire smiled. It was a child's smile, but the eyes were steely. She was back with them, at least partly, at least enough to lend her strength as well in pulling Hornsby up. Between the three of them, grunting and yanking, they managed to pull Hornsby onto the platform up to his waist. He hoisted himself over the rest of the way, rolled over onto his back, and lay panting.

"How...how can I...ever thank...you guys?" he asked.

"By not dying on us," Kathy said, winking at him. "We need you."

"I'll see what I can do," Hornsby replied, winking back.

Kathy glanced at the stage, or what was left of it. The monster—the Void—was bobbing and swaying over the chairs. Iaroki paced back and forth in front of them with regal strides. Kathy supposed he was waiting for the others.

He didn't have long to wait. Another crack of lightning hit one of the nearby pillars, bounced off, hit the one opposite, than zagged toward the stage, striking the spot near Iaroki and splintering it.

When the dust settled, another being taller than the first stood appraising the landscape. This one Kathy recognized from her reading of old texts as Xixiath-Ahk the Blood-Washed. He, too, was humanoid, but massively built, a being of pure muscle, a warlord. From his groin hung a tattered loincloth, and his feet were wrapped in hides. His chest was bare, except for two long, smooth horns that curved outward from his pectoral muscles. Similar, smaller horns protruded from his shoulders, elbows, knees, outer wrists, and neck. His skin looked like a series of small thorns which broke only to accommodate the horns and the inward-spiraling pattern of wavy blades that served as its face. The face-blades moved continuously in and out and around, as if the head was shuffling them. A series of horns rose from the top of the head, twisting and weaving in and out of each other.

"Try the door," Kathy said. "We need to get out of here."

Jose crawled to the door and reached up for the handle. It turned into a snake-like thing with multiple heads and tails. Jose jumped, tossing it away from himself with a little shout of surprise, and then kicked it off the edge of the platform. Claire ran over to join Jose, sat before the door, and began pounding against it with the strength of her legs. Jose watched her a moment, then started kicking at the door as well.

A whirlwind of red smoke, acrid enough to burn Kathy's throat from several yards away, had formed between the two greater gods. It began to take shape as something womanish from the waist up, and something beastly from the waist down. As the smoke cleared, Kathy saw long, dark, matted hair in which leaves and twigs were embedded. She recognized the form from cult writings about the primary avatar of Imnamoun the She-Beast Mother of the Spheres.

The creature tossed her hair back and Kathy could see the head, a narrow, inverted pyramid, the blackish roots of the hair growing from the flattened, topmost plane. The downward-pointing surface where a face should have been was smooth and featureless, a pale pearl-white, like the rest of the creature's skin from the waist up. The head nodded on a longish neck-stalk that ended in two sets of shoulders, one front pair and one back pair. From them, extended long, graceful arms, perhaps the only true resemblance to a human woman. There was something motherly about those arms, something that drew her prey in for comfort before she crushed them to death and fed them to her young. Beneath two massive breasts leaking a thick white fluid from smaller, nipple-less mounds, was an overlong trunk. Two lips, more like labia than anything facial, ran vertically where the stomach should have been, and three pair of eyes surrounded them, opening and closing along the rib cage.

Nothing about the bottom half of the goddess was remotely human. To Kathy, it looked like the bodies of four hooved, horse-like things had been bound together, each pair facing the other, so that a massive, fur-covered, muscled body and set of four legs extended down and to the right of her waist, another to the left, the third behind, and the fourth in front. How the goddess moved was beyond Kathy. The outermost ends of those beast-portions of her body ended in puckered openings surrounded by tiny waving tendrils. These, Kathy had read, were the exposed canals from which she was said to give birth to monstrosities that tainted worlds and time itself. When Imnamoun screeched, the Void replied with a roar of its own.

There were three of them now, three malevolent gods.

"Gonna try the spell again. Can't promise it'll do anything to any of them," Kathy called over her shoulder. Behind her, she thought she heard the wood of the door groan and crack beneath the barrage of kicks.

"Let me help," Hornsby said, and another round of thumps sounded against the door.

"If you can just buy us a little time," Jose began.

"I'll try." Kathy began the words over again. Before her, whole sections of the ramp fell away. Staircases and splintering wood went tumbling down. She repeated the words.

The fourth god descended from a cloud that blocked out much of the space above them. Engulfed in a beam of bright blue light, Okatik'Nehr the Watcher sank slowly to the stage. In the files the Network had on ancient gods and monsters, there was a single illustration, painted by a madman who claimed the god watched him in his dreams, but it didn't do the god justice. The entity manifested on that stage was easily the height of and vaguely resembled an oak tree, with a massive trunk of a body above long multiple roots on which it could move, and countless branches rising upward. Instead of leaves, though, each branch ended in an eye. Some were small, a few even blinded, but many were fully the size of a human head, lightly veined, with a shining black pupil and an iris whose colors stormed and clashed and changed as the god gazed around. The trunk, sheathed in rough gray skin not unlike tree bark, had a ring of thick tentacles around the middle, and each of those ended in an eye, as well.

If those gods haven't seen us yet, they will now, Kathy thought, and stifled the mad laughter which threatened to escape her.

Kathy concentrated and mouthed the words again, this time with a little volume. They were still audibly lost in the howling wind and the noises of the assembly on the stage, but she could feel them moving through her, the runes of disabling and deconstruction, the binds that held the gods prisoner in a dimension no one understood. When she was finished, she started over.

Kathy heard Claire say, "We need to hurry," and Jose respond with "Working on it." Hornsby added his encouragement. "We've almost got it." There was more pounding on the door. Kathy didn't dare turn around, didn't dare take her eyes off the gods. She kept mouthing the words, each time a little louder.

The last god to appear was one that, to Kathy's knowledge, no one had ever seen before. It was said he took a thousand forms, went under many names no longer spoken out loud. He had allegedly been to every world in the universe of his own dimension, and had at least seen every dimension that ever was and ever would be. He was the god of the race known as the Travelers, the ones who sought to emulate the great lesson their god had taught them—to move, to see, to experience. There were no statues of this god, no descriptions other than the disguises he wore when visiting a world. He was the fifth, though, to be banished, and perhaps the one angriest about it. Thniaxom the Traveler could travel no more.

This last god was the shortest—taller than a human man, but shorter than the group on the stage. At a little over seven feet, Thniaxom had taken the form of a robed and hooded figure, standing upright. She couldn't see its hands, if it had any, beneath the folds of the robe, and its hood covered the head and left the face in shadow.

"You," its deep male voice bellowed across the space between them. "We know you, Kathy Ryan."

The thumping behind Kathy stopped. She, too, had been startled out of her incantation. In fact, all sound stopped. The passing of the stars, the turning of the galaxies—all of it stopped. For several seconds, there was no sound.

"And I know you," she said. It was bad, bad news to engage any of those entities in conversation. She knew that. She shouldn't have even been looking at them—who knew what kind of damage that was doing?

She couldn't help it, though. Jose was right. There was a crazy streak in her that would probably be the last thing to go when she finally fell apart.

"Why are you here?" Thniaxom asked. His voice, she was sure, was the sound planets made when they collided.

"We came to recover some of our own, left behind here. We look only to return to our dimension."

Imnamoun uttered something in her harpy voice, and with a glance in her direction, Thniaxom ostensibly translated. "No one leaves this world, Kathy Ryan."

"We intend to."

"Are you gods?"

It was a strange question to hear, but suddenly Kathy understood; they hadn't attacked Kathy and the others yet because they thought she and her companions were also banished gods.

"We are gatekeepers," she said. "We know the language of the beginning and end, the making and unmaking, and other languages, and we guard the gateways to and from our world."

"You were banished here?"

Kathy hesitated. "In a manner of speaking. But those who sent us did nothing to prevent us from returning."

"The gateway in the forest has closed," Thniaxom said. "It was not of our doing."

Kathy heard the gasps and groans from behind her. Calmly, she said, "There is another way."

"You lie. There is no other way."

"There is, for those of us not bound by the Thibzarvimus Lustaganul."

The gods conferred a moment, and while they did, Kathy whispered over her shoulder, "Get the door open."

Behind her, the thumping resumed, but it was muted, their kicks hesitant.

Finally, Thniaxom turned back to Kathy and said, "You will give us passage through your gateway."

Kathy steeled herself. If the gods meant to attack, her answer would be the thing to provoke it.

"No," she replied. "That is impossible."

"How is it that you deny us?" Thniaxom said.

"I will not undo the binds on you, and you cannot cross through."

"Why will you not release us?"

"You will destroy our world," Kathy said.

There was a pause, and Thniaxom said, "We will destroy you."

"No," Kathy said. "You won't." She spoke the words of binding in the First Language aloud, and her voice, clear and sharp, was the only sound. Then, silently, she uttered another spell, one she had never tried before, and wasn't at all sure would work.

"Is that all you have? A binding spell and a doorway spell? Is that all you know of the First Language?" Thniaxom's laughter rolled like thunder. "Now, you will die, Gatekeeper."

Kathy backed away from the edge of the platform as the god threw off his robe. What was underneath was much bigger than the other gods, a mass of writhing, silently screaming bodies from worlds in other universes contained in an enormous liquid cloud, the substance of which reminded Kathy very much of the gateway in the Paragon lab. It was a nightmare amalgam of half-digested, half-living souls—Kathy knew in every fiber of her being that those things were trapped souls, buoying and swelling the black substance that was the essence of the traveling god.

The cloud unleashed a bolt of green lightning that split the platform where Kathy had been standing.

"Guys," she said, and turned to face the door.

The others had managed to split the wood from the base to about where the doorknob had been. Kathy thought one more concentrated battering would knock the door inward.

"All of us, on three," she said.

Another bolt of lightning busted up a bigger chunk of the platform, leaving them with less than five feet of wood to stand on.

"One, two, three," she counted off quickly, and the four of them threw their weight into the door.

With a loud crack, the wood broke outward, and the four of them tumbled through just as a purple bolt of lightning took out what remained of the platform, falling forward into—

Dirt. Kathy caught her breath, listened for sounds of the gods, and looked around. They were someplace else, beneath a blue, cloudless sky and a sun. They were lying on a dirt path surrounded by irregular orange rocks.

Kathy pulled her aching body toward one of the rocks and saw that they were very high up. Off to her left she saw an indigo ocean that stretched beyond the horizon line. Beneath the cliff stretched the field of strange wildflowers, and beyond that, the forest through which they had all entered this world. To the right, she could see the high walls of the city.

"We're out," she said. "We're on the cliffs by the city."

She turned and saw the others dusting themselves off, Jose attending to Claire and Hornsby limping toward the cliff's edge to see for himself.

"Geez," he said with a small smile, "I never thought I'd be glad to see that damned city wall."

"Tell me about it," Kathy said. "Jose, didn't you say you found your way out while on a mountain pass?"

Jose, having made sure Claire was okay, looked around him. "To tell you the truth, this looks kind of familiar."

"Do you...do you think they let us go?" Claire still looked shaken, but she was holding it together. It seemed that having Jose around bolstered her strength, and that made Kathy smile to herself. "The gods, I mean."

"I think it was Kathy," Hornsby said. "The big cloud said she did a binding spell and a door spell in the First Language. The door spell—you made that little wooden door an escape route, didn't you?"

"I tried something new," she said, looking away. "I didn't know if it would work, but I figured we didn't have much to lose in trying."

"Well it seems to have worked, knock on wood." Hornsby grinned. "No pun intended."

"So far, so good," she said, "but we're not done yet. We still have to find a way out of this hellhole."

Chapter 14

Jose led the others along the dirt path. It snaked between the orange rocks, descending slowly under stone arches and around giant boulders, winding down without really seeming to go anywhere. They were all tired. The pelts and fabrics they had wrapped around themselves were dirty and torn, and their feet hurt. They were hungry, dehydrated, bruised, and bleeding. Kathy thought the only thing keeping them going was the vague promise that they might rediscover the gate Jose had happened upon once before.

The sun hung high in the sky the whole time, despite the hours on the path. The faces moved from stone to stone, watching, but this time, they kept silent. It occurred to Kathy that maybe contact with the gods and the Wraiths carried its own kind of infection, one even the faces wanted no part of. It was an unsettling thought, but one she didn't have the strength to deal with just then. If Xíonathymia had anything else to throw at them, they weren't in much of a condition to fight it off.

Just as the sun finally resumed its progress across the sky, clouds moved across it, casting shadows on the path. If not for that, they might not have seen the object, ebbing and flowing within its rectangular confines fifty feet ahead of them.

"Holy shit," Jose said. "The other gate! I think we found it. Look!"

The object was the size and measurements of a normal door. It hung a few feet in the air, its swirling substance neither thick nor thin, liquid nor vapor. It looked a lot like the gateway in the lab, the only fundamental difference being the color of the gate itself, a rippling pearlescent white.

They ran to the gate, their energy renewed by the hope of return. Jose dragged a nearby rock over to step up on, but Claire grabbed his arm.

"Wait," she said. "What if…what if that's a gateway to someplace else, and not home?"

From the expressions on the faces of the others, that hadn't occurred to any of them. After a moment, Kathy spoke.

"Claire has a point, but I don't see how we have a choice. For whatever reason, your people at Paragon closed the gate from their side. If we leave this one, we might lose it. There might not be any other gates."

As if to underscore Kathy's point, the whiteness in the gate rippled, and the whole thing contracted. The shrinkage only amounted to an inch or so from all five sides, but it was enough to decide the others.

"Let's take the chance," Hornsby said.

"Yeah, I agree."

Claire considered it a moment, then acquiesced. "Yeah, me too. Let's go."

Jose, from atop the rock, looked over the heads of the others to Kathy. "Ready?"

"Go ahead and leap, crazy man," she said with a small smile. "We're right behind you."

Jose grinned, and then stepped up and through the gateway.

Claire followed right behind him, and then Hornsby climbed up. The gate contracted again. With a glance at Kathy, who gave him a nod of encouragement, Hornsby climbed through as well.

Kathy jogged over to the rock Jose had placed as a step and climbed up. The gate was shuddering now, its rectangular edges growing irregular. Kathy took one last look at the world of Xíonathymia, then hoisted herself up and through the gate.

* * * *

The wet-not-wetness engulfed her and everything went white. Kathy's senses were saturated with the gate, and she couldn't feel anything except the sensation of falling, falling…she thought of the platform over the edge of an alien universe and closed her eyes. A moment later, she landed hard on asphalt.

"Where are we?" she heard Claire's voice ask, and looked up to see the other woman, Jose, and Hornsby, shaken but unharmed.

"I think we're home," Jose said.

Kathy looked around. They were in a small suburban neighborhood. Everything—the air, the structures, the feel and smell of the air, all of it—felt normal and familiar. There was no whispering, no faces in the inanimate matter. There were conventional cars in the street, houses on grass lawns, wooden fences, children's bikes. It sure looked like home to Kathy.

Claire began to cry and laugh at the same time. She managed through both to choke out, "I never—I thought I'd never see—any of this again!"

Jose put his arm around her shoulder, and she kissed him on the mouth. His eyes looked surprised and then pleased, and he leaned in to return the kiss. Hornsby looked on, grinning.

Kathy glanced back at where the gate had been. It was gone. It, too, had closed. She wondered if that was the work of Paragon's Blue Team, or if such gateways could only remain stable for a limited period of time. Ultimately, it didn't matter. The gates were closed. But Kathy couldn't rest until she knew Paragon would not be able to reopen them.

"I have unfinished business," Kathy said. Jose and Claire parted lips and turned to her. Hornsby was already nodding.

"Greenwood," he said. "We need to make sure that lab doesn't let anything more from that place get out into the world."

"You all aren't obligated to see it through with me," Kathy said. "It's my job to make sure Paragon's gate is closed for good and that the face creatures…and Greenwood…are dealt with."

"Where you leap," Jose said softly, "we follow. Lead the way."

* * * *

The few hours leading up to Kathy's confrontation with Paragon were a bit of a blur. It turned out, after walking for a bit, that they were on the outskirts of Haversham, a mile or two away from the lab. They had no clothes, no money, no wallets or purses or backpacks. Those things were rotting unevenly away on a stone-paved city center at the edge of a universe in another dimension. They walked to Darryl Lefine's house. Markham's men had moved Hornsby's car, but Lefine's was still there, and Hornsby knew where his partner kept the keys.

They drove to Hornsby's house and gathered clothes and shoes, Kathy and Claire borrowing from his wife Alison's closet. Then they ate and drank. Kathy called Reece, who tried to pretend he hadn't been worried. His voice, though, was flooded with relief, and despite the guilt she felt, Kathy was glad to hear it. She felt relief herself, not just for being lucky enough to have made it back to hear his voice again, but also because he didn't tell her that her job was more than he could take, that he couldn't live like that, that he was leaving her. He simply told her he loved her, and wanted her to come home soon. She promised him she would. She told herself she'd have to take some time off, do something fun and relaxing with Reece. Hornsby called his wife at work, and Kathy could tell he felt the same flood of relief in talking to Alison.

They slept for two more hours. When they awoke, it was about six thirty in the afternoon.

It was time.

The four loaded into Darryl Lefine's car and drove to Facility 18. They said very little in all that time, but they had come to understand each other's facial expressions and body language. She supposed they were probably in shock, traumatized by the experience, but they were an impressive group of people. They were holding it together better than most would have. It could have been anger or that same desire for revenge and for closure that Kathy felt; whatever it was, they needed it and it was keeping them going, and she was glad for it.

* * * *

They arrived at the gate at about seven in the evening. The guard, recognizing both Jose and Claire and offering the latter a warm welcome back, buzzed them in. He didn't know where Claire had been and didn't ask, and they didn't volunteer any information. The four of them didn't want to draw any more attention to their arrival than was necessary.

Since Jose's and Claire's employee IDs had been lost, the four of them waited by the front door for employees on their way home. Jose kept Doug Kehoe from subfloor 29 distracted enough with jokes to let them in without questioning where their IDs had gone.

Once inside, they collectively tensed, unsure what to expect.

"We're in," Jose said, "but we're going to need someone's ID to get anywhere."

Kathy pulled out Doug's ID from the pocket of her jeans and dangled it in front of the astonished eyes of the others. "Not everything I learned from my brother was bad," she said.

Jose laughed. "All right then, let's go."

They made their way along the same route Markham had taken Kathy and Jose and found the elevator. Another employee, Amelia Elwood, was getting off as they were getting on. She waved good night to them and told them she'd see them the next morning, and they nodded and smiled, then piled into the elevator. Doug's ID gave them access to the subfloors, and Jose pushed the button for 31.

When the doors opened, at first Kathy thought they were on the wrong floor. The sight stretching out before them was one of deconstruction. They wandered out of the elevator, looking around at the pale gray walls of the long hallway. The lighting had been removed and exposed wires hung from the ceiling. The drop ceiling was missing tiles, parts of the floor carpeting had been ripped up, and the door and wall signs had been scrubbed clean of names and numbers.

Jose found Suite 40, the research lab, by rote, and eased open the door.

"Jesus Christ," he said. Kathy and the others came into the lab and joined him, taking in the scene before them.

There were wires sparking from the ceiling. Puddles of blood coagulated or elongated in long smears across the formerly tidy floor. The Plexiglas enclosure around the observation control room had been partially shattered, its remnant slivers on the floor below it. The jagged hole was rimmed with blood, and next to it was a streaking crimson handprint. Stunned, Jose and Claire led the others into the room. The computers and monitors had been smashed; plastic and electronic fragments were strewn about the counter like confetti. Bodies in blood-splattered lab coats lay face down on the floor, many in pools of their own fluids. Kathy thought she recognized Abigail's ponytail. George's ID tag lay next to a body whose upturned head no longer had a face.

"What happened here?" Claire asked.

"The gate, maybe," Kathy said. "It looks like it wasn't Paragon after all that closed it."

"What do you mean?" Hornsby checked the neck pulse of a man with bluish lips, shook his head, and stood up.

"Those gods probably discovered the gate in the woods and tried to use it to escape. The spells binding them…they might have set off a reaction that blasted through the lab. I saw something like that happen once before, although this…this is far more devastation."

Sadly, they filed out of the observation control room and toward where the gate had been.

The quarantine chamber that had surrounded the gateway looked as if it had been blown outward from some explosion, possibly from the final closing of the gate. There were more bodies lying there, although most of these were only in pieces. A torso with half a head lay propped against the base of the chamber. A woman missing the bottom half of her jaw and most of the left side of her body had been swept against a side wall. Kathy saw a nose pointing upward, a charred hand, an orthopedic shoe with part of a foot in it. She also saw some fingers, and thought of her brother.

The gateway was gone. There was nothing left of it. For that, and that alone, Kathy was glad.

The group made their way around the carnage and back to the elevator. Jose pushed the button for Subfloor 24.

"There's a quarantine chamber there for neutralizing the parasites from that place," he told Claire. She looked confused, but nodded anyway.

The elevator doors opened and they made their way to the chamber and got inside. There was an electric hum which lasted for a good five minutes or so, and then the door opened on its own.

"Let's hope that does the trick," Hornsby said. He didn't look entirely convinced. In truth, Kathy wasn't, either, but she thought of the faces in the rocks of the mountain, and how they had seemed finished with the broken humans, the ones who had pissed off ancient gods. If Kathy and the others had been carriers of any of those parasites, she was pretty sure the faces had jumped off before she and her companions had gone through the gate. Further, whatever had torn through the lab and killed the researchers had likely killed any lingering face-creatures as well. The floor had felt empty, as this floor did. They were alone.

As they exited the quarantine chamber, they heard the gunshot.

They ducked, alarmed, until they heard a thump.

"What fresh hell is this now?" Jose said, exasperated.

"This way," Hornsby called, jogging in the direction of the sound.

They found Greenwood slumped against a blood-spattered wall outside an empty office. Amazingly, he was still alive, but there was a blooming red stain on his shirt and lab coat. The gun lay a few feet away, just out of his reach.

He looked up at them, pale and sweating. He might have looked worried to see them if he'd had the energy, but he didn't.

"What happened in the lab, Greenwood?" Kathy asked, crouching beside him.

"I noticed you didn't offer to call an ambulance," he replied.

"Because I intend to let you die," she said. "What happened in the lab?"

"I thought...ahh, I thought maybe...you could tell me," he said. "All our work, all our research...it's all gone."

"Your humanitarian soul is refreshing," Kathy said sarcastically.

"It worked," he said to them.

"What worked?"

"The quarantine over there. It worked, if you want to know. You're free of the parasites, all of you. The little ones and the big ones. I told you it would…but you killed all the samples before we could extract them. Now we really have nothing left."

"Good," Kathy said. "Then my work here is done."

"You think…we're the only ones…who will open a gate?" Greenwood's free hand clutched the wound in his gut. "There will be others…and we have nothing…nothing to show. Nothing to protect us."

"Let it go, Greenwood," Kathy said. "You're dying. Think happy thoughts." She turned away, disgusted. On the faces of her companions, she saw a range of emotions—pity, indignation, weariness. None of them moved to help Greenwood, though.

"Give me the gun, before you go?"

Kathy turned back to him, watching his shaking hand reach unsuccessfully for the gun.

"Please…I tried…to shoot myself in the head. I don't know how…I missed so wildly. This is agony. Let me die quickly."

Kathy regarded him with a cold look, then moved toward the gun. With the toe of her borrowed shoe, she sent the gun skittering off into darkness. Then she turned and walked back to the elevator. When she looked back, she saw Jose, Hornsby, and finally Claire turn as well, leaving the gun where it was despite the man's pleas.

The four got onto the elevator and the doors shut as the pleas became curses.

No one spoke on the elevator ride up to the main floor, or through the building to the front lobby. Kathy dropped Doug's ID on the front counter on their way out the door.

"What do we do now?" Claire said.

"Go home. Take a shower. Get some sleep."

"But what about all that?" Claire gestured back at the facility.

"Paragon will have it cleaned up by morning, I'm sure," Kathy said. "There's nothing more we can do."

"I—I can't go home. I can't be alone," Claire said.

"Then don't," Jose said. He regarded Claire nervously. "Come back to my place. You can have the bed, I'll sleep on the couch…and then neither of us has to be alone."

She smiled at him. "I'd like that."

"I'll drop you off," Hornsby said. "I'm looking forward to getting home myself. Alison's shift is over in a few hours. I want to be there when she gets home."

The three of them started for Lefine's car, but paused when they noticed Kathy hanging back.

"What is it? You okay?" Jose asked.

Kathy had been thinking of Greenwood dying alone on an unfinished floor of a corporate facility. There had been so many times—too many times—that Kathy had imagined her own life ending in a similar way. She figured eventually her work would catch up to her, and if some slimy, tentacled thing that was all eyes and mouths and fury didn't kill her, then her own guilt and exhaustion would. The people before her had seen more than any human ever should, and while maybe they were still in shock, their only thoughts were of the people they had to go home to. And all she could wrap her brain around just then was how close she'd been all of her life to dying alone.

She forced a smile for the sake of the others. She wasn't alone; she had Reece, and God help him, no matter how crazy her job made their lives, he was still there for her. She wasn't going to be alone; there were people she could trust, people she could safely love. This job wasn't going to get the better of her.

Kathy told herself those things even as she glanced back at the facility and the carnage she was leaving behind. The carnage she always left behind.

She pushed those thoughts away, and as she jogged to catch up to the others, she thought of Reece once more. She was going home.

If you enjoyed *Beyond The Gate*, be sure not to miss all the books in the Kathy Ryan series by Mary SanGiovanni, including

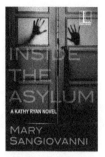

Kathy has been hired to assess the threat of patient Henry Banks, an inmate at the

Connecticut-Newlyn Hospital for the Criminally Insane, the same hospital where her brother is housed. Her employers believe that Henry has the ability to open doors to other dimensions with his mind—making him one of the most dangerous men in modern history. Because unbeknownst to Kathy, her clients are affiliated with certain government organizations that investigate people like Henry—and the potential to weaponize such abilities.

What Kathy comes to understand in interviewing Henry, and in her unavoidable run-ins with her brother, is that Henry can indeed use his mind to create "Tulpas"—worlds, people, and creatures so vivid they come to actual life. But now they want life outside of Henry. And they'll stop at nothing to complete their emancipation. It's up to Kathy—with her brother's help—to stop them, and if possible, to save Henry before the Tulpas take him over—and everything else around him.

A Lyrical Underground e-book on sale now.

Read on for a special excerpt!

Chapter 1

March 27 marked three years since Henry Banks had woken up from the coma. He kept track in a day planner, with new calendar refills for subsequent years, by drawing a symbol he had been taught by his friends in the upper right hand corner of each day's page. Other than therapy sessions, he had no real appointments anymore, but Henry jotted down notes about the day's events, things he learned or discovered, and each night before bed, he drew that symbol of his far-reaching goals. Journaling, even Henry's odd version of it, was encouraged and allowed to continue as a means of reconnecting with one's self and feelings. His was more of an odd, disjointed grimoire of his mind, but that seemed to be okay, too. He never forgot, not even during the trial when his mind was...elsewhere. On days he couldn't get to the planner, Maisie made sure that at least the days were marked. It was important to him. He never forgot, so neither did she.

Every day that passed reminded him that he was drifting farther and farther from the rest of humanity, so Henry didn't think the three-year anniversary was cause for celebration. Dr. Pam Ulster did, though, or at least convincingly pretended to. Every year prior, she had suggested Henry do something nice for himself to commemorate his "return to the world." The irony was not lost on him. He didn't see how he was supposed to do much of anything since the orderlies, who were not big on celebrations, watched him like hawks. Even if he wanted to, what could he really give himself in his current situation? A walk in the sunshine around the hospital grounds? An extra muffin with breakfast? Anything else—anything worthwhile—would be noticed and probably taken away.

Besides, it wasn't like he'd come back from the dead. He'd just come back from...somewhere else.

Henry figured other people would have had reason to celebrate March 27 if he'd died instead of coming out of that coma. Maybe that should have happened, but it didn't. Maisie, Orrin, Edgar, and the Others made sure of that. They'd come out of Ayteilu and saved him. Or maybe they were right, and he had saved them.

The police and the lawyers and the doctors told him he'd done something bad to the teenagers in his basement right before the coma. He couldn't remember much about that. He was pretty sure he hadn't been the one who'd done it, but it was his fault all the same. He'd seen those teenagers before; they hung around outside the Dollar Tree and said mean things to him from behind the safety of their cigarette smoke clouds when he went to shop there. The girl was pretty, but she was sharp where she should have been soft, like something made of glass or porcelain, something whose temper could shatter her into a thousand jagged, deadly pieces. The three guys were mostly messy mops of hair, black trench coats, and jeans. Their faces didn't matter to him. Their fists did, and their words; they often threatened the former with the latter. Henry wasn't even sure if they'd had eyes, but he imagined that if they did, those eyes were cold.

They made fun of the holes in his t-shirts and the way he walked and the scar on his shaved head. They made fun of the burn marks on the back of his shoulder and neck and the way he growled at them instead of using words. Still, they had always been an away-problem, an outside-the-house problem, like savage dogs on leashes. They were tethered to the Dollar Tree, and if he could make it past them to his car and then to his home, he would be safe.

Then it turned out that they weren't on leashes. They could move anywhere they wanted. And they had chosen to break into *his* house, *his* safe space. They'd brought baseball bats and knives. The Viper and the Others had come simply to protect him.

Sometimes, Henry thought he should have started keeping count in his planner on *that* night.

Dr. Ulster had asked him once during a session why he bothered to maintain such meticulous records of the past three years if he honestly believed everything in his life had fallen apart since the coma. Why approach the planner as a constant reminder of his deterioration, then? Why not just put the past behind him and focus on getting better?

Henry had told her then the truth about the Others, just like he had told the police when they found what was left of the four teenagers in his basement. He told them about Ayteilu and its tendency to swallow up reality. He'd told them about Maisie and Orrin and Edgar and all the Others. He'd even told them about the Viper. Maisie said that was okay. The problem was, he couldn't *show* the police or Dr. Ulster, so they hadn't believed. He couldn't make it all happen on command, not back then. But he was learning, and over the last 1,095 days, he was steadily growing better at it. What he didn't tell anyone was that in three days' time, as set forth by Edgar's prediction, he'd have complete control in summoning the Others at will and opening the way to Ayteilu. The Others hadn't wanted him to share that part with anyone else.

Henry peered through the gloom of his bedroom. His cot was against the wall across from the door, which of course was locked now that it was lights out. On the far side of the room was the door to his simple bathroom—one sink, one toilet, both gleaming white—and next to that door was a small closet in which hung his hospital-issued clothes, soft and harmless. No zipper teeth or sharp metal claws there, not even buttons or laces. Beneath the clothes, like obedient lapdogs curled up on the closet floor for the night, were a pair of loafers and a pair of slippers. Against the back wall near where the head of his cot lay was a small, barred window. The orderlies could open it sometimes to air the room out but they had keys to do that and were allowed to reach through the bars. That night, his window was closed but Henry didn't mind. He just liked having one, and from his, he could see the parking lot. Some people liked seeing the neat, tight little lawns that constituted the hospital grounds, but he preferred the parking lot. It reminded him that there was still a real world out there, with normal people who had jobs and houses and pets, and that those people could actually leave hospitals and move freely through it.

He got up from the cot and shuffled over to the window. The moon was mostly hidden behind clouds, but in the lot below, the arc-sodium lights illuminated patches of asphalt in a soft melon color. Shadows skirted those halos of glow, darting quickly from one spot to another in the dark. It wasn't their shape so much as their movement that Henry caught, but it was soothing all the same to see they were down there. Probably it was Maisie who had sent them. She was thoughtful like that. Maisie always knew when he was sad or angry or just feeling drained.

That night, Henry was exhausted. The geliophobia had been particularly bad all day. He had shouldered the burden of many crippling mental conditions since early childhood, but the one that garnered the least sympathy and understanding was his fear of people laughing at him. Decades of laughter, pressed between the pages of his memories, always found a way to resurface, to grow fat and loud again in his thoughts and even in his ears. When he was stressed or tired, he could hear a chorus of guffaws and giggles, tittering and peals from people who should have kept their damn mouths shut.

The laughter echoed in the back of his thoughts, jarring and ugly like the squawking of angry hawks, and he tried to put it out. Bad things happened in the dark when he couldn't, and he didn't have the strength to make the bad things go away. Not tonight. His limbs felt heavy and his eyes were dry and burning. He shuffled back to the cot and climbed beneath the blanket.

Henry forced each of his muscles to relax, starting with his toes and working his way up to the top of his head, just like Dr. Ulster had taught him. Then he worked on clearing his mind. He imagined the inside of his head as debris on a darkened stage, and with a big broom, he swept away all of them like they were piles of dust.

Sleep came on like a slow tide, lapping at him in waves and eroding his conscious thought. Just before he drifted off, he heard Maisie moving gently through the dark.

"Good night," he mumbled.

A butterfly flutter of lips brushed his forehead, and a soft, cultured voice replied, "Good night, Henry."

* * * *

Ever since Martha's death the weekend before, Ben Hadley had been on edge. He was a nervous man by nature; his nerves had, in part, put him in Connecticut-Newlyn Hospital to begin with. That damned clumsy woman, with her barking, thumping dog in the apartment upstairs from his, had finally compelled him to take action.

This was different, though. He was on meds now; he wasn't supposed to get nervous, not like this. Of course, it was hard not to be a little out of sorts when all around him, people were dropping like flies. There had been the suicides last month—the twins, Belle and Barney McGuinness, who had jumped off the roof of Parker Hall and made a terrible mess on the front steps. How they had gotten up there was anyone's guess; apparently security protocols were "still being looked into," for all the good that would do. And then there was Sherman Jones, who had supposedly died in his sleep. Sure, he was ninety-eight, but he'd been fine all day, alert and active as ever. Ridley Comstock had come as less of a surprise. They'd found him hanging all blue-lipped and bloated in his own closet. Autoerotic asphyxia was the culprit there, according to Toby Ryan, and given Ridley's proclivities on the outside, that was probably true—an accident, but an ugly one, if the orderlies' gossip was to be believed.

But then there was Martha, and hers was one death too many, and with far too many strange circumstances surrounding it.

At first Ben thought Toby had done it. Toby killed women; it was his thing. Of course, he'd sworn he hadn't killed Martha, that he couldn't have. He said he'd been locked in his room overnight, the same as everyone else. Ben didn't argue. Toby scared him.

As it turned out, though, a new and more likely suspect had emerged over the course of the week: Henry Banks.

Of all the inmates at Connecticut-Newlyn, Henry had always seemed the most harmless. Soft-spoken with an occasional stutter, he'd never seemed dangerous before. In fact, he'd seemed so *un*dangerous that Ben had even harbored doubts as to whether Henry had actually killed those teenagers.

That was, of course, before Ben learned about Henry's friends.

The thing about them, Ben had discovered, was that *they* weren't mild-mannered, and they certainly weren't locked down at night. Henry's friends came and went as they pleased, and they mostly answered to Henry. Martha had threatened to tell the doctors about them; she'd said so the day before in the common room. She was going to tell, and Henry had been worried. His friends, after all, were only there to protect him.

Toby had said it was a silly fight; Henry's friends were imaginary and Martha was getting all worked up over nothing. Still, someone didn't think it was too silly a fight to silence her. If Henry didn't kill her, then one of those allegedly imaginary friends must have.

Ben wasn't crazy, despite his lawyer's convincing case to the court. Ben was just nervous. Sometimes, he got very nervous, and he understood that if Henry's friends had gotten nervous, too, about Martha telling on them, they might have felt compelled to take action.

That didn't make Ben any less sad or nervous. There was probably a whole town out there that was glad Martha was dead—Martha, who had drowned her own four children in a bathtub on the advice of an angel—but she had been one of Ben's only friends. He didn't believe she would have told the doctors or orderlies anything.

The doctors claimed Martha choked in her sleep, but Ben had seen the blood all over her room—the walls, the sheets of her cot, her neck. He'd seen her eyes, wide and scared and glazed over. Her mouth had hung open like a small, crooked cave. Her tongue, torn out by the roots, had been on the pillow beside her, close to her ear. He'd seen it all…before two of the orderlies realized he was standing there and roughly led him away.

No, Henry's friends were not mild-mannered at all. And Ben didn't think Henry knew everything they got up to in the night.

He thought all these things as he lay on his cot, waiting for the sun to come up. He'd resigned himself to the fact that he'd be getting no sleep that night. He was too wired for that. Plus, he wanted to watch the door. Henry's room was right next to his, and if these friends, imaginary or not, were moving around the halls out there, he wanted to know about it. They could obviously move through doors and maybe walls. If they could get into Martha's room, they could get into his as well.

The doors to each room had small windows made of Plexiglas, and from his position on the cot, Ben could just see the top of the far hallway wall and a bit of the ceiling through his. It was quiet out there; the dark remained still and the ceiling tiles—twelve in his line of sight—were all accounted for. He'd learned not to try to look outside at night. Shadows had shape out there and moved in deliberate and predatory ways that shadows shouldn't. It was better for his peace of mind just to look out the little window in his door.

Ben might have dozed for a moment but he didn't think so; in the next, however, he saw a hazy, wavering face peer in, followed by an equally insubstantial palm on the Plexiglas. Ben froze, and a moment later, the palm was gone. His heart pounded. Who were they looking for? Would the morning bring another dead inmate?

There was no sound of footsteps. Henry's friends were quiet; he'd give them that. But they were also clearly on the move.

* * * *

Orrin and Edgar sat in the dark, waiting for Maisie. She watched over Henry at night, at least until he fell asleep, and while they waited for her to come out of the hospital, Orrin and Edgar watched over the Others.

Tonight, Maisie would be late. She had taken an interest in some of the other inmates there, who she claimed had special knowledge locked up in their heads that she was certain would prove useful to them. Of course, she made Orrin and Edgar swear never to mention this to Henry, because it would only upset him and Maisie didn't like to see him upset. They had, so far, held to that promise. Edgar didn't like to cross anyone, and as for Orrin...well, he had other reasons for wanting to keep Maisie happy. He couldn't understand what she thought she'd gain by getting to know these other guys, but Maisie was a thinker, and she probably saw a way to protect them and the Others somehow. Most of her plans involved protecting them or making them stronger, and Orrin could get behind that. He didn't trust damn near anybody, not even Edgar and they were brothers, but he trusted Maisie.

So they sat and waited while the Others ran and tore at things in the darkness, a silent show of mad, dancing, light-changing silhouettes. Two of them had set upon an owl and were pulling off its wings while a third extended the fingers of its tendrils into the meat of the bird to explore its insides.

"D-d-do you think she'll b-be out soon?" Edgar asked in that stop-start, jerking way he had. His good eye glowed like an ember in the dark.

"Soon," Orrin said, and gave his brother a reassuring nod.

"They're not easy t-to wrangle when they're this r-riled up," Edgar said, gesturing at the Others. "Henry's g-gonna b-be pissed if he looks out the window tomorrow and sees d-dead b-b-birds all over the parking lot."

"You worry too much," Orrin told him.

"D-do I?"

Orrin didn't reply just then. Edgar's worries weren't without substance. Henry could be pacified, but the longer Maisie spent in that hospital, the greater the chance that someone else would discover him and Edgar and the Others and cause them to make an unpleasant scene. That wouldn't be good for Henry or anyone else.

Finally, he said, "She'll be out soon."

"Then what?"

"Then we find the Viper and see what comes next."

* * * *

As Henry dreamed, the darkness spread in silence. Inside the utility shed about two and a half acres behind the hospital, the darkness pooled in the corners and seeped through the cracks in the floor. Waves of inkiness washed over the detritus of hospital maintenance. Tendrils snaked around and inside the lawn care equipment and tools. Bottles of chemicals were probed and poked until they spilled, and their smoking, acidic contents were drunk and assimilated. The darkness lapped up the shadows and the night itself and made them its own.

As it took the shed's contents, it changed them. It brought the imps through from Ayteilu to claim and reshape them. Orrin had called it "giving land to a country." Maisie and Edgar just called it "breaking through."

But the Viper knew it for what it was. He sat on a length of old fence just outside the shed and watched through the open door as a riding lawn mower became a silverbacked beast whose underside contained rows of mouths and bladed teeth. Leathery wings broke through the creature's back and folded themselves neatly against it. Its legs, shaped like a bulldog's only longer and more powerful, grew from its sides, hoisting its bulk a good two feet off the ground. It had no eyes and no discernible nose, but it seemed interested in sniffing around the doorframe of the shed, adjusting to its new surroundings.

The Viper hopped off the fence and strolled over to the shed. Inside, a new shape was forming from a puddle of darkness and industrial cleaner. He watched as the substance traveled upward, dipping in and out of feminine curves as it formed legs and hips, a waist, breasts, arms and shoulders, a neck, a head. The last things to appear were the eyes, which, when opened, focused a cold, bright green gaze on him. Black swirls lifted off her body like steam. This new being, an ebony mist condensed in human form, took a step forward and waited. She and the Others coming through and developing behind her would follow the Viper's orders. Maisie couldn't control them; the mist Wraiths only ever listened to the Viper, even in Ayteilu.

What had once been a rake wiggled off its hook on the wall and slithered by the Viper's feet. The rake head had formed a bottom jaw, and those rust-colored tines grew sharp. The creature's jaws were immense. What passed for the Viper's smile found his face as he watched that snaking tail, muscled though it was, just manage to push forward the large skull in front of it.

The Viper looked up at the sky. It was a clear night; the stars of this universe twinkled overhead like tiny eyes. He supposed that one night, he'd look up and see Ayteilu's familiar constellations...but not tonight.

He took a step back as the shed itself began to change. The wood creaked a little and then stretched, and the dimensions of the building increased. In minutes, it was the size of a large barn. The substance of the wood had taken on the faint red tint and rough grain of the trees in Ayteilu. From within, the newly formed were beginning to find ways to make sounds— little sounds, but new and exciting to them all the same. Soon, they would growl and roar, and find the strength to devour this world. Soon...when the constellations of Ayteilu remapped the sky.

Gently, he closed the barn door. The darkness and its changes would spread soon enough, but there was no sense in letting the creatures inside roam free just yet. Maisie and Orrin and Edgar had to do their parts first to make Henry stronger.

The Viper glanced up at the sky once more, then walked off into the darkness. The shed-turned-barn shuddered with the new life inside it, and the darkness began to spill out from under the door.

About the Author

Mary SanGiovanni is the Bram Stoker-nominated author of the Kathy Ryan novels, *Savage Woods*, *Chills*, and numerous other novels, novellas and short stories. She also contributed to DC Comics' *House of Horror* anthology, alongside comic book legends Howard Chaykin and Keith Giffen. She has been writing fiction for over a decade, has a master's in writing popular fiction from Seton Hill University, and is a member of The Authors Guild, Penn Writers, and International Thriller Writers. Her website is marysangiovanni.com.

Beyond the Door

Occult specialist Kathy Ryan returns in this thrilling novel of paranormal horror from Mary SanGiovanni, the author of *Chills* . . .

Some doors should never be opened . . .

In the rural town of Zarepath, deep in the woods on the border of New Jersey and Pennsylvania, stands the Door. No one knows where it came from, and no one knows where it leads. For generations, folks have come to the Door seeking solace or forgiveness. They deliver a handwritten letter asking for some emotional burden to be lifted, sealed with a mixture of wax and their own blood, and slide it beneath the Door. Three days later, their wish is answered—for better or worse.

Kari is a single mother, grieving over the suicide of her teenage daughter. She made a terrible mistake, asking the powers beyond the Door to erase the memories of her lost child. And when she opened the Door to retrieve her letter, she unleashed every sin, secret, and spirit ever trapped on the other side.

Now, it falls to occultist Kathy Ryan to seal the door before Zarepath becomes hell on earth . . .

Chills

"True Detective" meets H.P. Lovecraft in this chilling novel of murder, mystery, and slow-mounting dread from acclaimed author Mary SanGiovanni . . .

It begins with a freak snowstorm in May. Hit hardest is the rural town of Colby, Connecticut. Schools and businesses are closed, power lines are down, and police detective Jack Glazier has found a body in the snow. It appears to be the victim of a bizarre ritual murder. It won't be the last. As the snow piles up, so do the sacrifices. Cut off from the rest of the world, Glazier teams up with an occult crime specialist to uncover a secret society hiding in their midst.

The gods they worship are unthinkable. The powers they summon are unstoppable. And the things they will do to the good people of Colby are utterly, horribly unspeakable . . .

Savage Woods

Bram Stoker award-nominated author Mary SanGiovanni returns with a terrifying tale of madness, murder, and mind-shattering evil . . .

Nilhollow—six-hundred-plus acres of haunted woods in New Jersey's Pine Barrens—is the stuff of urban legend. Amid tales of tree spirits and all-powerful forest gods are frightening accounts of hikers who went insane right before taking their own lives. It is here that Julia Russo flees when her violent ex-boyfriend runs her off the road . . . here that she vanishes without a trace.

State Trooper Peter Grainger has witnessed unspeakable things that have broken other men.

But he has to find Julia and can't turn back now. Every step takes him closer to an ugliness that won't be appeased—a centuries-old, devouring hatred rising up to eviscerate humankind. Waiting, feeding, surviving. It's unstoppable. And its time has come.